Jaden's First Thirty Days in Heaven

A novel of orientation to heaven through the eyes of a child

Ruth Robbins

Spiritual Artist Ministries
Greendale, Wisconsin

All the main characters in this novel are fictional characters. Well-known people—Bible people, a scientist, and two musicians, are placed in the novel in a manner consistent with what the author knows of their earthly life. Other known historical people are at best in the periphery in the novel. Any resemblance to others even with full names given, living or dead, is purely coincidental. For permissions or questions, contact the author through either of the following methods.

Ruth Robbins
Spiritual Artist Ministries
P.O. Box 272
Greendale, WI 53129
Psalmist3ruth@netscape.net
©2015 Ruth Robbins
ISBN-13: 978-0692522097

Dedication

To the Father who gave us life and His Son. To Jesus without whom we would have no hope. To the Holy Spirit who causes us to walk in newness of life.

To my mother June Drews, who is the first of many mentors to guide me in this adventure of life and to the memory of my father Hilbert Drews, and the others who have gone before.

And finally to you my readers. May you find the journey of your walk in the Lord filled with love and a desire to be like the One Who gave His life for all. My desire is for you to find this book comforting and able to give you a small foretaste of Heaven and what God has in store for all of us as His children.

2

Table of Contents

Introduction

Many people wonder what will happen after they die. They have thought about Heaven, at least a little, but have not gotten as far as what they would do once they got there. As for the other place, well, the Bible does have a lot to say about it, and reassures those who believe in and follow Jesus that a place has been prepared for them with Him, better than anything they could imagine.

When I reflected on the subject at various times, reading from books, listening to CD's, and praying, it seemed like if we all were supposed to play harps and sing when we got there, then we would know how to play harps and sing now or at least have some interest in doing it. Actually, only one group of people in Heaven is named as the ones who play harps. The redeemed will sing a new song that the angels cannot sing.

Then there were a number of people who had experiences that taught them something about Heaven. I checked most of those against the Bible accounts. Those that didn't seem to match up went on a back burner, so to speak, but not in this book.

That being said, we are going to a prepared place for a prepared people. A child looks at life with great wonder, and he would do the same with Heaven. So I have chosen to view the experience through a child's perspective. Whether this is about an actual child named Jaden who is now there, eternity will show us. Meanwhile, sit back and reflect as you read this view of Heaven.

Chapter One Homecoming

Jaden was a little boy about nine years old. He lived with his mother, Joanna, and his dad, Tony, in a small town with lots of people in it. He had an older brother, Jamal, and an older sister Susan. Susan had got married two years ago and had asked Jaden to be the ring bearer for her wedding, but he had refused. Today he was thinking maybe he should have been.

Even so, her wedding had been fun. They had eaten lamb, moussaka, dolmada, and lots of other fun foods. After they ate, the men danced fast dances, and then the women danced. Finally, Susan and her husband, Joe danced by themselves in the center of all the other dancers. She and Joe moved to a bigger town, but they visited every weekend, sometimes bringing presents for Jaden.

His brother Jamal was also married. Thinking about him always brought a big smile to his face. He was fun-loving, playing jokes, and always bringing things for a game to play. Just last week they had played catch in the backyard of their home. He didn't bring a bat with him, but had said he had a special treat lined up for Jaden for the next weekend.

Rosetta, Jamal's wife, always brought something fun to eat. Last week it was baklava, a very sweet dessert taking a lot of time to make.

This was the week after Easter. School was out for the week, so he immediately thought of his best friend, Pascal. He had a number of friends, from school and from church, but Pascal was his favorite. He lived near the park close to his home, a half mile after the first left turn past the park. In fact, he often went there after going to the park on his bicycle.

Today was Wednesday. After he woke up, he got dressed and sat down to a breakfast of cereal, fruit, cheese, and milk. Joanna asked him, "What do you want to do today?" She was preparing eggplant for moussaka as she asked the question. Just looking at it made his mouth water, even though he was still eating.

He replied, "I'd like to go to the park, feed the ducks a little, and go to Pascal's house to visit with him."

She said, "That sounds like a good idea. Maybe some time this afternoon? I'd like to send some lamb and moussaka with you. If we wait until after lunch, I could have it all baked and hot for you to take with you when you leave. Then you could come home again and have supper with us."

"Sure, Mom. Sounds great. You know how much I like it, and I know Pascal does, too."

After lunch, she took the dinner out of the oven and, slicing the lamb into smaller chunks, put enough for Pascal's family in one dish, and put the baking dishes aside for that night's supper. That being done, she wrapped the dish for Pascal's family so it would keep hot and not spill.

While he watched his mother fix the food, he thought about his grandma Orpie. It was about this time last year that she had died; but his parents had told him she was in heaven. He thought about heaven often, and not just because she was there.

Just before she died, he remembered, she had told him how to ask Jesus into his heart, and he prayed with her so he could have Jesus live in his heart. That's where Jesus was now. He knew this, because all his sins were forgiven and he felt better inside.

She gave him a special Bible that she had bought just for him, and he read it every day. She had even marked in it the date he prayed with her. That anniversary was coming up fast. He remembered

Jesus said He was going to prepare a place for His people and that in His Father's house were many mansions. He often tried to picture his mansion.

"Go get your bike," his mother said, "and we'll tie this dish into the basket." He brought it, picking up his helmet also, and helped her tie the dish securely.

On his way to Pascal's home, he stopped to watch the ducks at his favorite pond. He threw some crumbs to some of them, while others stayed swimming. They just came last week from their migration, and he almost ran to meet them.

He talked to the ducks as he fed them, telling them about Bill, the man who sold him his bike. It was solidly built, but older than the ones most of the boys rode. "Wonder how he knew my favorite colors, he told them. It must have been hard to find one in green, gold, and white. And he charged me only two dollars! Wonder if he painted it." It seemed as if one of the ducks understood him.

After a few minutes he stopped feeding them and started riding again. At the next corner he put out his hand to the left like he was taught, and made a left turn. Just as he turned, a car from the left swerved to avoid another car and ran right into him, throwing him almost onto the sidewalk.

He didn't feel this, because at that moment he was looking at a shining white bicycle riding up to him, going faster than he had ever seen one go. The man riding it had on a uniform just like some people he had seen in books, in the brightest yellow he had ever seen. And he stopped right in front of him.

The man said, "Jaden, hop on the back seat. We're going for a ride. I'm here to take you to your new home."

He said, "Who are you? My new home? What about Pascal? I have a meal for him right. How's he going to get it?"

The man said, "Someone is taking care of it right now. I'm Jeb, and we're going to meet Jesus. I can't explain everything right now, but Jesus is waiting for you. Look at your bicycle."

When he looked, he saw that it was just a few feet away. He saw a shining man in gold taking the dish out of the basket, then flying towards Pascal's home.

Looking again, he saw himself on the ground next to it. Some men in uniform were leaning over him. One of them shook his head. "Now I see myself, and I'm bleeding. How can this be? What am I doing here?" He heard singing, and the men in uniform faded away.

Jeb said, "Jaden, you died, and I'm here to take you to your new home. We'll see Jesus shortly. Can you get on the bike right behind me? I could help you. You may have seen something like this in books, but today you're riding it."

He got on the back seat. Looking down at his feet, he saw that his shoes had changed. There were no holes. Seeing his clothes, he noticed that they almost shone.

"It's really made for two? And we don't have to pedal? If Pascal could see this...but he can't, can he?" Jaden asked as they rode. They were turning left onto the street Pascal's home was on. The man in gold rang the doorbell at Pascal's home, leaving the meal. He saw, but didn't hear.

Pascal's mom opened the door, saw no one, and opened the package. He could see Pascal right next to her, but already he was in the air. Trying to tell him about the bike, he noticed that mother and son were back in the house. They were flying faster now.

As they passed the moon and the sun, he saw many, many lights of many colors. It seemed to take a long time, but in earth time less than a second, to get to a beautiful planet looking so much like earth. He blinked his eyes.

As they got closer to the planet, the colors began to get clearer to him. He saw many colors that he had never seen before, and wondered what their names were. Jeb said, "Some people have named the colors. Maybe you would like to do that? We humans really like to name things."

He said, "You're really a man? I thought I'd get picked up by angel. I'm so glad you came for me. My new home is going to be so much fun. Elijah got a chariot and I got a bicycle that goes faster than light. Where's Jesus? Who are you, really? Who are all these people?"

He said, "I'm your great-great-great grandfather. Jeb is my nickname. Your great-great-great-great grandparents gave me that nickname when I was young, almost your age when you got here.

"I was sent on this to bring you home because I was a messenger and my sweetheart and I rode a bicycle built for two in our spare time." All this took less than a second in earth time, for they were traveling faster than light.

When they landed, Orpie and Jesus were at the front of a group of people. "Hi, Jaden," they said together. "Welcome to heaven." Many other voices also said, "Hi, Jaden, and welcome to heaven." But the loudest voice belonged to Jesus.

Jesus held His arms open wide, and he ran to Him. Jesus again said, "Welcome home. I'm so glad you came." Orpie came up to him with a big smile and hugged him. She walked without a cane and looked so young.

After others hugged him, Jesus scooped him up in His arms, laughing and swirling him and dancing with him.

He was even more beautiful than the pictures he had seen of Him. Artists' pictures were all wrong. He had hair like Jaden's, but curly and shiny with light, and He lit up the whole place where they were just by being there. It was like he was the moon, stars, and sun in one bright light, but to him, the glow around Jesus was easy to see, for his eyes did not hurt him in the brightness. He set him down again.

Children who were with the others ran up to Jesus also. He hugged them all. "Welcome to heaven, all my children, young and old," He said. As he took all the children to a quiet place, he reminded them how much He loved them and how welcome they were in their new home.

Orpie came up to him after Jesus was through talking to the children. "Jaden," she said, "It's time to go for a swim. As we go there, we will introduce you to some of the other people."

Very soon, they came to a river. Leading the way, they showed him how easy it was to get into the water. Some of the people with them—the children who went with him to Jesus, and others—joined them in it. Even though it looked deep, no matter how far into the water they went, everyone could float, swim, and play water games. He and the other children splashed each other as they swam or floated in the river.

He got up out of the water and found he was dry right away. "Jesus, I can see so well now! And look, my foot is all straight, and I can walk and run and everything! Thank you! Thank you! Thank you!" And he ran almost in a circle several times. All clapped their hands at the goodness of God.

He said, "If you gave me a cob of corn right now I could eat it and I wouldn't break out. And if I got some milk, it wouldn't hurt anymore." Many other people told Jesus how much better they felt, as well.

Jesus said, "That's right. You just swam in a part of the River of Life that comes from the throne room of God."

After the swim, Jesus led the way, holding the smallest child, as they went through a huge gold gate with pearls on it. They went into a huge building with the words "Welcome Home Center" on the door. After they entered a large ballroom, each person was brought to a big man in the center. "Father Abraham, these are your children who came home today," Jesus said.

One by one, the big man danced with each of the new children and new adults, and all the people, more than he could count, danced with each of them. The song that they danced to seemed familiar to him, with the words, "Thank you, Jesus, for bringing your children to us. We love you Lord for you are worthy."

His eyes lit up and he looked into the face of Jesus. "I'm really in heaven, now? It feels so much like home already."

"Yes, Jaden. You are now in heaven. This is your home now for all eternity, and very soon this city will come down to earth to stay."

He said to Jesus, "I never met most of these people. How do they know so much about me?"

Jesus replied, "Some watched you from here. Because you love me, many saw how you helped change their lives. Many saw angels come to their families because you prayed. You will meet many more as they come to heaven."

Orpie and Jeb were also dancing at the party for newcomers. They took turns dancing with him, as did many others. All the people who danced with him introduced themselves. He recognized some from his Bible, and some whom he'd told about Jesus. Some people came to him and thanked him for what he'd done for them, but he didn't recognize them. He asked a man named James Peterson, "I remember you. But how did I help you?"

Mr. Peterson said, "When I sat on the sidewalk one day, you gave me an ice cream cone and talked about Jesus. Everyone else that day walked by me, and some spat on me. I went to a church after that and heard more about Jesus. Jesus became a real friend to me, and it started with you."

A boy smaller than he gave him a big hug. "I'm here because you gave a missionary some money to go to my country. When I got here, Jesus told me that your money helped me hear about His love for me."

By the time everyone had hugged him and welcomed him, he met hundreds of people who wanted him to go to their mansions and visit with them, twenty people wanted to share more about what he had done for them to get them to know Jesus, and many teachers told him they had asked Jesus to allow them to teach him some of what they had learned. Some teachers were people he had only read about, others knew things about subjects he was interested in, but his school never covered, and a few people were some he had met in his home town.

Orpie and Jeb took him to another huge building called the Portal Building after the dancing stopped for a while. He asked, "What does that mean. Is this something new?"

Orpie said, "Jesus asked us to show you what's happening on earth right now. This is where we go to see it. The sign calls it the Portal Building. You could also call it "door", but it's more like a window. There have been many portals to Earth and this building for a long time."

When they got into the building, she led the way to a room with a number of people and angels in it. As they came in, she told the angel at the door, "We want to look at what happened to Jaden on earth and look at his town."

As the angel led the way to a viewing area, he said, "You will see the past as well as the present."

First they saw the paramedics put his body on a stretcher and take it in an ambulance to a hospital. After viewing what happened in the hospital, they saw his parents at Pascal's home telling his family about Jaden's accident. Then they saw both families eat together. While the families were eating they talked about Jaden and his love for the Lord, how much they missed him already and how they knew that they would see him soon in his new home.

As they watched, Jesus came up behind them. He wrapped his arms around Jaden. As Jesus held him, he cried for a little time (about a second), and Jesus wiped away his tears. He reached up and hugged his neck.

When he saw his parents, he thought about asking the Holy Spirit to do something special for them. Then he realized that he'd already talked about it the last time he prayed. He'd also asked God to make Pascal an evangelist. Now that he was with Jesus, he realized that those prayers were already being answered. He also saw angels comforting them.

Some went with him to another building, called "Bible Knowledge." When they got there, they saw a video of part of earth. It was unlike anything he had seen on earth, but what he saw looked like it was from Revelation, including the Battle of Armageddon. He saw his father Tony, Jamal, and Joe fighting in the battle. He also saw his mother, Susan, Rosetta, and his friends watching the battle. Jesus was their leader, riding a big white horse. He saw some of the enemy, but the main thing was that the enemy was defeated in less than a minute.

Among the people watching the battle action were Grandma Orpie, Jeb, and others who looked like people from pictures in his Mom's photo albums. After the Battle of Armageddon was finished playing, the others came and introduced themselves. Some were aunts and uncles, some were second and third cousins. He had no trouble remembering their names now, but on earth he had found that a difficult task.

In heaven they do not tell time like they do on Earth, but there it was the same day when they left the Bible Knowledge building. As they left, Grandpa Jeb said, "We want to take you to your new home."

As he spoke, a path seemed to open up for them, showing them the gate to leave the city by. They were on their way to what seemed like a village outside the city. Several of the relatives he had just met came with them. People were walking on the grass, and the aroma of cooking greeted them. He said that he was hungry.

"Jaden," said Grandma Orpie, "here's a piece of bread and some fish to eat while we're walking. When you finish that, I have a cob of corn for you to eat on your way to your new home. Knowing you would want to eat when you got here, I got these at the party. We were all so busy dancing, I thought I might as well take some with us for when you got hungry, knowing you're a growing boy."

He smiled at her and mumbled his thanks around the piece of bread with fish on it. Before he realized where they were, he saw a shining big home near a quiet pond. It had a gold door and a sparkly brick exterior that looked more like his mother's jewelry than any place he had ever seen. Big windows sparkled in the light, and it felt good to be here.

He saw a gold swing on a huge porch, and got up on it and ate the cob of corn. Somehow he knew nobody would mind. Nearby was his favorite kind of car and a new bicycle like one he saw down the street from his parents' house, but with sparkly stones around the wheels. He even heard a horse in the distance.

"Come inside," Orpie said. "This is where you'll be living until your parents come. We arranged for you to have a room built in my mansion, just like you had a room to stay in when you were at my house on earth. We all thought very carefully about what you'd like."

When he looked around, he saw a table just the right size for all the people with him. It was set, with a dish of lamb and moussaka in front of each gold chair.

In a living room there was a throne in the center. All around him were all his favorite videos about the Bible, and some videos he had never seen before. One was labeled "Jaden's family life," another "Jaden at school," yet another "Jaden at church." Others were about his family and his ancestors, including Jeb.

Orpie asked everyone with them to come in and sit down to eat. She asked Jeb to bless the food. Even though he had just had food, he felt hungry again, and the lamb tasted better than any meal he had ever had. Remembering the meal he had on his bicycle for Pascal, he knew that he was eating the same meal that Pascal, his family, and his own parents were eating.

After supper, he started singing some of the music that was in the air around them. Some of the songs were hymns he had sung in church, others were older songs that his mother had hummed. But so many were new to him.

All of them were fun and he started singing the one he liked the most, "Glory to God and to the Lamb who sits on the throne. He is worthy to be praised. Bow before Him, all His people. Make His praise known to all you know." Before he knew it, all the others with him were singing as well.

On Earth, it was near the end of the day. Jaden's parents visited Pascal and his family, telling them about the food for them, the accident and his death.

But Pascal's mother said, "Some lamb and moussaka was dropped on our doorstep today. We heard the doorbell ring, went outside and found a package. In it, there was the food in a hot dish. We kept it in the oven for company because there was so much. We have plenty. Come in and eat."

She showed them a plate much bigger than the one tied to the bicycle that afternoon. It had lamb pieces piled high on one side of the dish. And on the other side of the dish moussaka was piled just as high.

Jaden's mother said, "That's the dish I wrapped on the bicycle for Jaden to take here, but so much bigger, only he never got here. The dish had to have been broken in the accident. It's a miracle! And I'll tell you the other miracle. We put in just enough for your family to have a meal. But this is more than three times as much as I put in there."

Pascal's mother said, "Yes, that's a miracle! I know you're sad that he can no longer be with you. Didn't you say he knew Jesus? If I know him, he's asked Jesus for this very meal today, his first day in heaven."

He learned many things that first day. Already it was after supper, and he knew that on Earth it was getting dark out. But here it was still light. He could not see the sun, moon, or stars, so it did not seem like the day would end. "Grandma Orpie," he said, "why is it still light out? I'm so tired that it must be almost night."

Orpie sat down with him on a couch and talked to him for a while. First she explained that the sun and the moon and the stars still shone, but the glory of God and of Jesus were so bright that he couldn't see them.

She also said that in heaven time sometimes

seemed to be different from time on earth. There were going to be heaven days when much was done and someone who decided they would have a watch in heaven found out that it only took a second to do something. Later, Orpie got out one of the videos, labeled Jaden's Family Life, and they watched it. He said goodbye to the rest of the family as they went to their own mansions.

After they watched the video, Orpie took him upstairs and showed him his room in her mansion. It was decorated in green, gold and white. On the bed was a quilt like the one she gave him on Earth, but so much more beautiful. The colors were intense, and included ones he had never seen before.

In a beautiful bookcase made from a rare wood he saw many books. "Orpie," he said, "you got me some of the books I loaned to Susan, Tommy, and Jacob, and so many more. They're hardcover, too."

"I can't take all the credit. People who know you and heard about what you did on Earth helped make your room a home for you. All I did was make the quilt. You won't need it for warmth, but I know how much you liked the one you had in your own room on Earth."

"Wow! I'm so glad that you wanted to have me live with you. Jesus let me stay with my family in heaven! That's so great."

"That's right. As you know, your Grandpa Jeb has been a real help, and he's not the grandpa I was married to on earth. He came to heaven long before I was born. Your grandfather that I was married to lives in another mansion. You'll meet him later.

"We went through a bad time called the Holocaust. Because of that time, he came here much earlier than I did and got a little used to being by himself. So we have different mansions. God has healed my hurt from the Holocaust, but it made me want to make sure that every person I met came to trust in Jesus. People were taken away and some came here very young because of it. All of our family mansions are very near each other, so you'll see us all as often as you want."

While he thought about that, she opened a closet in the bedroom and showed him his clothes. "All of these clothes are part of your robes of righteousness. Each is for a particular assignment or task, just like when you changed clothes on earth. God created us to enjoy variety.

"I know what your favorite colors are, so when I was allowed to put in some clothes for you to wear for fun, I made it a point to get your favorite colors. But most of the time you'll forget you have them on."

There was an ornate rocking chair with carved curlicues on it next to the bed in his room. Sitting on the rocker and rocking as she spoke, she told him, "It might take you a little time to get used to the light here, but the reason it's so bright all the time is that the glory of God outshines the sun, moon, and stars, and the glory of God is what makes this place so bright." She stayed with him until he fell asleep and then went to her own room in the mansion.

Before she rested, she made some notes of things she wanted to look at in the Bible Knowledge building and read verses from the Psalms before going to bed.

Chapter Two Gardens

Jaden woke up smelling pancakes. He quickly got out of bed, put on some green and white clothes, and went into the kitchen. Both Orpie and Jeb were there. Jeb was flipping the pancakes and Orpie was cutting up some peaches. He poured three cups of milk and set the table with some dishes he saw in the cupboard.

"Grandma Orpie," he asked, "is this for real? This is my new home?"

"Yes," she answered. "Did you notice it did not get dark out last night, just like I said?"

"Sure did. I can tell that things are different here. Are you going to show me the rest of your mansion? Jeb too?"

"Of course we are, child, and we have all eternity to visit back and forth, and you can visit whoever you want. You can go to the city and visit the throne room at any time, just like you did on earth when you prayed. Did you notice something different about yourself?"

"You mean something like wings?"

"Yes. That means if you don't use your bike, you can fly or walk or go whichever way you want. The car is for later, when you're ready to drive, not that you really need it with all the other ways you can go."

He blessed the food and they all sat down to eat. Afterwards, he learned how to do the dishes. As soon as they had finished all the food on their plates, and as soon as the pancakes were done, the dishes were clean.

He found that even when he dropped one dish, it did not break. He was glad, because he had broken a few of his Mom's dishes. All he had to do was put the dishes away. He noticed when he spilled some of the syrup there was no stain. His clothes stayed clean.

"I want to look outside, Grandma. I saw such beautiful plants, flowers, fruit trees, and so many other things I haven't seen before. I heard the sound of a horse. Where'd it come from? Where'd you get the stuff to make the quilt?"

"First of all, Jaden, it's okay for you to call me Orpie. I like it, so it's what people call me. You saw how young I look, right? When you're grown up, I'll still look this age.

"The horse stays with a neighbor who likes to ride.

"About that quilt, as you can tell, it's different from the one I made for you while I was on earth. I have needles, thread, and all the fabric I want in my sewing room. When I got to heaven, I found that some of our relatives and my friends knew how much I liked to sew. They found many kinds of fabric at a store in the great city, then brought fabric and other things needed for quilts so it would be waiting for me when I came."

"That's like people did for me before I got here, when they brought the books and you put the clothes in my closet."

"Yep. Every once in a while someone comes to me or I go to them to make a quilt or something else. Do you think you might like to learn to do something like quilt making? Or maybe some other type of art?"

"I hadn't thought about it. I know I like making things once in a while. Maybe later."

"Anyway, making a quilt goes so much faster now because I don't wear glasses any more. My eyesight is perfect, my hands are just fine and I don't hurt any more. Jesus gave me a new body and had me swim in the River of Life, too.

"The embroidered cloths you see on some of the furniture were made by Aunt Rose. She likes to be called Rosie here, so be sure to call her that. Jeb and I want to show you our gardens, and Jesus said He will join us for a little bit so He can show you another."

They walked for what seemed a short time, but in Earth time was more than half an hour, to a garden with a brook running through it, some deer, some corn, two apple trees, grapes, and some olive trees. A cool mist watered parts of the garden, but it did not feel cool to him. In fact, it felt like he was visiting a woods near his home, except for the olive trees and the large garden around it.

Jaden asked, "Whose garden is this? It's beautiful."

"I'm the gardener," Jeb answered. "When I first got to heaven, I had a small garden with lots of woods around it, but some gardeners who did gardening on earth helped me get it tilled. This isn't what I rule, but Jesus put me in charge of this land near my mansion for my own special place to invite others to come and rest, and maybe pick some fresh grapes once in a while. I'm really fond of corn, and it grows all the time here. People showed me how to fix the soil so it would grow really well, and the same with the grapes.

"As for the deer, Jesus knew I love looking at them, so he asked these deer to come live here so I could learn to talk with them." He called one of the deer to him with a sound that Jaden had never heard. It came up to Jeb and rubbed his shoulder. He gave it some leaves and petted it.

Afterward, they walked back to the pond near her mansion. Around it were plots of some vegetables he recognized and quite a few he did not recognize. Around the vegetables were a number of fruit trees. Orpie reached up to one of them and handed him a piece of fruit and took one for herself. He laughed as he bit into it. "This tastes like the baklava Rosetta brought for Easter dinner last week. What fun!"

"Later on we'll get to taste some of the vegetables, both fresh and cooked. And when you do taste some of the vegetables, you'll get to taste where our lamb last night really came from. As for the moussaka, that really was from eggplant. By the way, did you notice what happened to that cob from the corn yesterday?"

"Yes. It just disappeared, like the food from our plates this morning when we were done."

"Nothing dead or corrupt is allowed in heaven. When food is finished, the seed or the peel, the pits, and so on, are caught up.

"When we first are given our garden, we are allowed to choose the seeds for the plants we like. You know I liked to garden on earth. Well, around here I do some gardening, but mostly I just speak to the earth after I plant the seeds so I get the size fruit and vegetables I want. And those plants more or less just stay around after being planted. As for the watering, well God knows what He's doing here in heaven as on Earth.

"You see the pond? Well, there are some plants that grow in there and are food for some creatures that I love to talk to. They're not here right now, though. I think they went on an errand for the King. When they come back, you'll have some ducks to feed."

"That'll be great."

While Orpie was talking, Jesus came up with four children. He ran up to Jesus and hugged Him. He said hi to the other children, too. One of the children was the little boy who had told him about the missionary.

"Jaden, it's Bible story time, and then you and these children and some others are going to school," Jesus said. They went past her mansion. Some other children ran out from their homes to meet Jesus. Parents and other relatives waved goodbye from doorways of mansions as the children went with Jesus.

Soon they got to a shaded park with a playground and lots of trees. Jesus sat down, holding the smallest child. Jaden snuggled up against Him, two other boys sat next to Him on one side, and three girls snuggled up to Him on the other side. Five others sat in front of Him while he held the baby in his arm.

While they all listened, Jesus told them about a boy called Samuel and how he first learned to hear God's voice. As He told the story, he asked questions so they could really feel like they were there. Then Jesus asked him, "Jaden, how do you think Samuel could have known sooner that it was God calling him?"

He answered, "Spend a lot of time reading the Bible and praying and listening for God's voice."

Jesus answered, "Samuel was born before I was and before the whole Bible was written. Jaden, that's a good idea. Samuel could learn from the books of Moses about God and could find out some of God's ways by reading about Moses. The books of Moses were the Bible Samuel could read."

Other children answered some other questions. One girl said, "I think his mommy thought he might be lonely with no children to play with."

Jesus answered, "Hannah, how right you are. But Samuel's mother, also Hannah, knew that Samuel loved God and would not be lonely all the time, just sometimes. She came to visit him when she could." After the Bible time, Jesus told the children to go play. He also said their teachers would come later.

When Jesus had been gone maybe about fifteen minutes in earth time, three people and some angels came to the children. Two of the people and all the angels stayed with the younger children in the park. One person came up to Jaden and the older children.

"Jeb," he said, "You're a teacher? I'm so glad that you'll help teach me things. Somehow it seems so good to learn from people you know."

He answered, "I always did want to teach, but never got enough education on Earth to teach. Instead, I got to be a messenger. After I got here, Jesus showed me all the schools here and I figured out which classes I wanted to take to go to school. So here I am to take you and these other boys and girls to school today."

"How fun," Jaden said. "At least, since I have to go back to school, someone I know will be the teacher."

"There will be no tests, because you'll remember everything. You're going to get to try a lot of different things. You'll learn games, run and play, and find out lots of things about a lot of different people and things. And I won't be your only teacher. Along the way you'll find out what you like to do and what you're best at. And you won't have to wait till you're all grown up to help people."

The other boys and girls were nodding while Jeb was telling him this. They'd been to school before going to heaven, also.

While they were talking, Jeb was leading them toward a huge building, with many doors and windows, and large doors around it. They could hear people talking inside it, but they did not go in. "What's that building?" Jaden asked.

"It's your school," Jeb answered. "Children come here just like on earth to learn some of the things they need to learn to do the work they want to do here. We call this place the Orientation School.

"The people in there now are some of the teachers Just like schools where we came from, there are days when the teachers do some work to get ready for the children. At first, to get you and others used to the idea of school here, they are off the same times you were on earth. What were you doing when you came here?"

"It was a vacation day after Easter and I was riding my bicycle. School doesn't start till next week, I guess. It's like day all the time here, so I don't know what day it is." Others answered with activities they were doing on Monday (Earth time), or whatever the day was before they got to heaven. While they were talking like this, they walked around the school itself.

"Well, today's Thursday, same as Earth days for time. Since where you all came from we're still in Easter week, we're sticking with vacation days until Monday. So school is going to be different for all of you today. We're going to look at some gardens, right here at school."

All the children got excited, especially Jaden, and jumped up and down. Some of them started to run toward a garden. Jeb said, "Wait a minute. I know you know where your garden is, but Jaden needs to see where his is. Do you remember the garden we were looking at yesterday?"

"Yes, and we helped fix the ground for him, too," the boy he had met earlier said.

"That's right, Chong, and now we're going to show him his garden." They all came back to Jeb and started leading the way down one of the paths. They walked about ten minutes Earth time, and came to an area that had some young plants in it, a pond, some fruit and nut trees, and some vegetables ready to pick. On the pond were five ducks swimming among some grasses and other plants in the water. While they were looking at the ducks swimming, Jesus came and joined them.

Jaden ran to the pond, forgetting he did not have bread to give the ducks. The ducks did not fly away when he reached them. "Jesus," he asked, "what should I give the ducks to eat?"

Smiling, Jesus answered, "Let's ask the ducks." While they were talking, one of the ducks left the water and waddled up to him. He picked the duck up and held her.

Wondering how to ask, Jaden said the first thing that came to mind, "Mama Duck, what do you like to eat?" Anyway, that's what he wanted to say, but it came out like a series of quacks, not all the same. Hearing himself quack, he shook his head in amazement.

Jesus set the duck down, and they watched as it went to a pile of bread, picked up some with her beak, and gave it to Jaden. Then she went to the pond, and swam to a small section of weeds (or so they seemed to be), pulled off a few leaves, and gave them to him also. The other ducks kept on swimming and quacking while she did that.

When she quacked, he looked in wonder at the duck and then at Jesus. "You know what I think she was telling me? It seemed like she was saying she ate the bread because she liked me a lot when I was at the pond so many times, but the weed leaves were her favorite. Bread was like her dessert, a special treat because of me. But how'd she know what I was saying? And how did I know what she was saying? And how did she get to heaven?"

Jesus answered, "When animals, birds, other creatures, and plants were created, they were made to understand people. I gave you a language to talk to her with, her language. She heard you speaking her language, and you heard her speaking your language. This was my gift to both of you.

"You will teach her and other ducks how to worship me. This mama duck is one you fed in your pond on earth. She asked to be your duck in this pond in heaven. She and her ducklings will be the ones you begin to teach how to worship, and later you will teach more ducks the wonders of worship. Later I will show you more of your inheritance, but for right now I have to leave. Jeb and these others will be with you."

While they were doing this, Jeb let the others go to their gardens. After Jesus left, Jaden stayed with the ducks for a long time, or so it seemed in Earth time.

When he finally turned around, Jeb came up to him and asked, "What do you think you'd like to grow in your garden? We planted some of your favorite fruits and vegetables, but maybe you'd like to plant some more. Tell me about your mother's garden."

"She planted corn, tomatoes, beans, carrots, and potatoes. But some of that didn't grow too well. Last year some of the leaves came off the tomato plants early," he answered.

"Here things grow a lot easier than where we came from. Nothing eats the leaves off of plants unless you tell them they may, like I do with my deer. There are no thorns, weeds, or thistles growing in your garden where they're not supposed to. It doesn't get so hot that you have to mop sweat from your face. And the plants act a little differently from what you're used to."

Jaden asked, "What do you mean, Jeb? I thought all plants just grew and made fruit, seed, nuts, whatever they were supposed to."

"Well, they do that, yes, but what you want from each plant here is going to decide what you get. Let's use tomatoes as an example. When they grow, before the tomatoes come out, the deer like to eat the leaves. Now you can tell them to grow extra leaves just for deer, and they will do it. You can also tell the deer how many leaves it can eat and it will obey you. But you also have to make sure that there are other leaves the deer like in your garden. That's if you have deer.

"Let's say that your favorites are the kind that grow really big, and your plant is the kind that grows really big tomatoes. You can tell the plant how big you want them, and that's how big they'll grow."

"Wow!" he said. "I can tell plants what size vegetables or fruit to grow?"

"Yes. And it gets even better. Even people on Earth were picturing things in their minds, which is like visions, and they got those things. We do that with plants here, too. We get an idea of the tomatoes we want, we see it, and that's what we get. When we go to pick them, we just think about picking them, and they're in our hands."

"I really hadn't thought I could do things like that here."

"It gets really exciting, the longer you're here, especially when you realize you'll never run out of time to do things. You get tired and rest, but you wake up and find out that you can still do what you were working on before you slept. And it gets done faster.

"Aren't you getting a little hungry? Let's see if we can pick some food and eat it." The other children came to join them. They began by walking through a garden which had peanuts, grapes, and other good things to eat. "Now we're going to pick only what we can eat," Jeb said. So they each picked a few peanuts and some grapes, some picking oranges or berries as well.

Soon they were met by other people holding baskets, offering them plates, showing them a small table to sit at, and giving them some of what was in their baskets, and joining them at other tables nearby.

"What happened?" Jaden asked.

"The garden we were in is managed by someone who used to own a restaurant on earth. He wanted to have a garden that people could walk in, pick food, and sit down with other people, and fellowship like at a sidewalk café. That's what these tables are like, and that's why we're here. I found out about this garden not too long after I got to heaven."

While they were at their table, a messenger came with an envelope addressed to Jaden. He tore it open and read the few words. "I want to talk to you in the throne room, [signed] Jesus."

"Jeb, Jesus wants to talk with me in the throne room. How do I get there?" he asked. But even as he asked the question, it seemed like his wings were taking him there. When he said the words "throne room" he could see the throne room in a vision and soon he landed right in front of the throne.

He was so excited to see the Father on His throne that he bowed down before the throne and worshipped Him. While he was worshipping the Father, Jesus came and held his hands, then stood him on his feet. He whispered in Jaden's ears a new name that he had never heard before, and told him that was His special name for him. No one would know that name, just Jesus and Jaden.

Then the Father took a crown from in front of the throne. When He placed it on Jaden's head, He said, "This is the victor's crown, for you came through great adversity and overcame it. Along with this I place on your head the Crown of Life, for you were faithful to me even unto death. I am rejoicing with you this day for your victory and faithfulness."

The Holy Spirit rubbed his forehead a little.

When he went back from the throne room, he came the same way he had left. He just thought, "School," pictured it, and the way seemed to be shown to him before he left the city. While he experienced this, he thought, "I could get used to this. It's so much fun."

Jeb greeted him with, "When you were in the throne room, we were there also, watching you receive your reward. Jesus gave me a new name after I got here.

"On Earth you spent a lot of time in school, sometimes learning things that you didn't like, but you still learned them. Teachers made sure you learned how to work and about the world around you.

"Here what we learn is based on what God wants us to do and on what He made us to enjoy doing. The assignments we get are not hard. He trained us for them when we were still on Earth and trains us even more here. History was really fun for me. I got to watch everything happen as though I were there all the time."

While they were talking, they joined the other children setting out the food on tables. People with baskets set out some of their food as well. "Wow," Jaden said. "I wonder what tomorrow will bring. Right now I'm really hungry again. Is there anything like yogurt or cheese around here too?"

They found a pantry nearby, with a number of food containers clearly marked. The building seemed cooler than the outside, and they found that the food was cool. Besides the yogurt and cheese, they found some nuts, more fresh vegetables, greens, and other good things. So they had a regular feast out there at the table.

Parents and relatives came to the tables and picked up their children to bring them home. Orpie met Jaden and asked him, "How about going for a ride on a carousel or a merry go round? Or would you prefer a roller coaster instead?" she asked.

"There's something like that near here? I mean like Four Wheels at the Zoo or some other ride?"

"Sure is. I want to show you how to get there so you can try these rides. Any time someone wants to go there, they start up the ride. There's no waiting to get on, either."

27

"Sure. I always wanted to go to amusement parks, but there wasn't much money for them."

"You don't need money here, though."

As soon as Jaden said "Sure" they found themselves at the entrance to an amusement park. The sign in front of the entrance said "Heaven West Amusements. Try your hand at something new every time you come. Experience travel without leaving the park."

As they came through the gate, they saw a man giving out ten tickets to each person that came in. Orpie gave one set to Jaden, keeping another set for herself.

Looking at one of the tickets, he saw that it was for a ride called "Mechanic's Dream." When he looked up, he saw that the ride was to the left and about a half block away.

When he got onto the ride, he noticed he was in a car with controls like Orpie's had. One control was flashing yellow and had a label "Start Button. Wait for instructions." As a sign lit in front of the car, it showed "Start your engines." He started it. Then it showed "Check your brakes." The brake light button was flashing. He pressed it. It turned steady green. Then it showed, "Steer your car around all obstacles and stop when you have passed the last obstacle. That is when your brake light will flash."

When Jaden started steering around obstacles, he saw that the scenery in front of the car changed. Soon he saw that he was up in the air, still steering around obstacles. The sign in front of the car showed, "Push on the top of your steering wheel." When he did that, the car started going forward and down.

The sign then showed, "Pull the top of your steering wheel back to start position." As he followed that instruction, he steered around the last obstacle, the car gently nosed up and the engine began to slow down. Before long he was on the ground again. Looking around, he saw that he was still at the amusement park and back at his start position.

"That was fun," he said. "How about the carousel next?"

"Sure." Looking at his tickets, he saw that the carousel was named "Ornery Horses." Seeing the sign straight ahead, they went to it and got in line. All the people in line got onto the carousel as soon as Orpie and Jaden arrived.

The horses appeared to be real as they walked up to them, so he reached out to one of them just to make sure. As they rode, it seemed like the one he rode was trying to get away from the carousel. As he pulled on the reins it seemed to settle down. Yet when he touched the mane, it felt like wood.

When they got off the ride, he said, "I had a really great time. I know we haven't tried all the rides yet but I'm getting hungry."

Looking around, they saw a stand with caramel apples, nut cakes, and ice cream, and another stand with burgers. They settled on nutty burgers and chocolate ice cream.

After that, they noticed an airplane ride. Getting out their tickets, they hopped on. The ride took them around the village and the outlying areas, over Crete, and back to the amusement park in less than an hour, Earth time. While on the plane they drank tea and slept. When they got back to the park, they went back to the mansion.

Jaden picked up a book he had loaned to Susan. It was about the work Jesus had done on the cross, and he started reading where he had stopped when he loaned it.

After he started reading, the music in the air seemed louder and he joined in the music, sometimes making up his own melody for the words that he heard.

When she heard what he was singing, Orpie jotted down some ideas for instruments he could try out. In her quiet time with the Lord, she asked Him to consider some things for Jaden to try his hand at over the next few weeks. Her time with Him was sweet, and it seemed to be such a short time before it was over.

Before she rested, she slipped out quietly and picked some fruit for the next day after taking a swim in a small river that was part of the River of Life. While she was there, she saw Rosie.

"Rosie," she said. "What would you think of taking up the recorder again and teaching it to Jaden? He seems to be so talented in music that he would enjoy it."

"Sure," Rosie answered. "It's been a long time, Earth time, since I played, though." With that, they each went to their own mansions.

Chapter Three Neighbors

When Jaden woke up again, he saw that he was already dressed for the day. Orpie came into his bedroom with a tray of fruit and milk, and some odd vegetables he had not seen before.

This morning he had not noticed any food cooking, and now he saw why. Nothing she had on the tray was cooked. Yet it had a fragrance unlike fruit he remembered, and unlike vegetables he remembered, as if everything he had tasted on Earth were a shadow compared to what she brought in.

He asked, "Orpie, would you tell me something about this food? It really seems different from what I've smelled before, but also seems familiar."

She laughed. "We're in heaven, remember? Yesterday when we looked at gardens, I mentioned that you'd get to try some different vegetables and you'd get to try how the lamb was cooked the other day. Dig in and tell me what you think."

Obediently, he took a knife, peeled the fruit, eating the skin first, then chopping up the rest and eating it. Then he had a vegetable. "Hmmm," he said. "The fruit tastes a little like granola with cinnamon and sugar, and this vegetable tastes a little like sausage, only better."

Again, she chuckled. "Yes. Isn't that great? The Father knew that we had gotten to like some things that weren't really the best, so he arranged to create some things that matched the taste but are better because they're fresher. Remember when we ate the 'pumpkin pie' over at Rosie's mansion? Most things just don't taste the same."

They finished the breakfast together, with Jaden laughing at eating the "dessert" before the "meat" and having a good time together. Just as she was putting the tray back in the kitchen, there was a knock at the door. "Go ahead and answer it," she said.

So he answered the door. It was Jesus, carrying a young boy and leading three others. "Come in, Jesus," he said, "and sit on the throne with your friends."

"I'd be glad to," He said, "but first I want to bring in something your Grandma asked me to bring. Would you come with me to the porch? We would like you to help us bring it in for you."

When he went out to the porch, he saw not one musical instrument, but three, two stands, and some sheet music. Before he asked about the instruments, he helped bring them in and the other children set up the stands. "What's this about?" he asked.

"Orpie asked the Father to let you try playing some music after she heard you singing with the angels last night. I asked some people to leave the instruments and music at her door. When I knocked on the door, the instruments waiting for her. I came to ask you to share one of your Bible videos with these friends and then we can talk about it."

He picked out the one about Noah's ark. They sat and watched it, some of the children giggling when they saw the giraffes and the hippopotamuses and the aardvark going into the ark. They asked questions about how Noah got all those animals to come to the ark and they could all fit in it.

Jesus answered, "Noah saw plans for an ark from my Father. He was told what to make it out of. The Bible has a record of some of the directions he used to make it. When it was time for the animals to come into the ark, my Father told two of most kinds, and seven of other kinds, called clean kinds, to come into the ark.

"Your parents and relatives can read the story from Genesis to you. Also, you can make a visit to the

city and go to the Bible building. My Father made
pictures of it as it was happening so people can
remember His judgment and mercy, as well as the
wonders of what He's done. While you're there you
might want to watch Jonah's adventures, too. Ask
your relatives to help you." Jaden remembered
watching the Armageddon battle and thought about
what else he'd like to see in that building.

After they were done talking about the video,
Jesus said He had to leave, but Orpie would take him
to his school for the day. So He left with the four
children, and she came back into the room.

She asked him, "So what do you think of my
surprise? Last night I was telling the Father that I
thought you had musical talents. You sang so well it
seemed that maybe you could learn music and play an
instrument.

"On Earth in many schools in fourth grade they
had children learn the recorder first to get used to
playing an instrument and later play other
instruments if they like any others. Here we can learn
any time, having specially made instruments for
ourselves to entertain others, or borrow an instrument
from an orchestra or get one at the store in the city."

"I'm really excited about this. But what about
teachers?" he asked.

"We'll talk about that later. Part of today's
school is meeting our neighbors. Many of our
neighbors want you to visit, so we'll see some today.
The Father told me the neighbor to visit last. Please
take the smallest instrument with you. You'll need it
later."

They walked out the kitchen door of her
mansion. Birds sang as they walked, and some flew
around her, and she sang back to them. It was sweet
pleasure for both of them. They walked past some
fruit trees and trees that were blossoming.

Soon they came to a mansion that had some columns in white and a gold door, with brick of rich brown and gold colors. The windows were huge, and a blond haired woman was looking out the window. She ran to the door, and opened it wide. After looking at her, Jaden thought she seemed familiar, like maybe from a picture he had seen at home on Earth.

"Welcome Orpie," she said. "And this is my nephew so soon brought from below to stay with us. Jaden, welcome to my home. I have seen what you did to win so many to righteousness during the short time you knew Jesus. Welcome. Hallelujah, Lord, for you have brought greater sunshine this day to see my nephew again."

"Aunt Rosie!" Jaden shouted, when a picture from on top of his mom's piano flashed through his memory. "I'm so glad I get to see you again. I hope I get to come again often!" He said this as he was wrapped in a bear hug by his aunt, who also lifted him up and swung him around in a little dance.

"You remember me from our welcoming committee, and I wanted Orpie to bring you here first after you got to see your home, your school, and your garden. But I knew our Lord comes first, blessed be His Name. And now you're here."

"I was talking with our Father last night because he was singing so beautifully. I thought he might want to learn to play a musical instrument or even sing. This morning when Jesus brought some children to watch a video with him, He saw some instruments on the porch. I remember how beautifully you played the recorder when we were in school. And we got one. Could you play something for us?"

He gave her the recorder. Rosie listened for a while to the music in the air all around them. She started playing the recorder with one of the tunes she heard, played some variations on that tune, played along with another tune she heard being sung and played variations on that tune, finally playing a new melody that somehow seemed to blend in with all the others.

"Now, let's hear you sing along with this hymn." And she played one of his favorite hymns, "All Hail the Power of Jesus' Name." He sang the first verse in unison with the recorder. Then he sang the second verse with the recorder playing harmony, and finally the third verse with Orpie singing harmony, the recorder on harmony, and Jaden on melody by himself.

Afterwards, Rosie said, "Orpie, you're right. He has a beautiful voice. He can hold a tune when someone else is doing something different, and when two people are each doing something different. He definitely has musical talent.

"We should do something about this with him during his school days, and have him join our little group after he learns some more about singing and about reading music. I can use some manuscript paper to write down some music for him to learn on this instrument and get back with you when I have it ready. God has a timing for this."

"We will leave the recorder with you so you can see how the music sounds on the instrument, and we'll talk more about it. Now how about one of your famous pumpkin pies?"

"Pumpkin pie?" Jaden asked. "I haven't had any since Christmas on Earth."

"And it's not the same pie as then either." With that, Rosie went to one of the trees next to her mansion. She plucked two fruits, shaped a little like apples and colored like pumpkin, from the tree, sliced them up and mashed them. Orpie rolled out slices of something that looked like a thin bread and put it on three plates. Rosie put the mashed fruit on the bread.

As there were both spoons and forks on the table, they all sat down to eat. Rosie blessed the food and they dug in.

"Why that does taste like pumpkin pie!" Jaden exclaimed as he finished the last bite. "God made this fruit taste like pumpkin pie? Really?"

"Yes," Rosie said. "He loves to surprise us all the time. Once as I was walking through my garden looking at the trees, I thought that pumpkin pie would be really good. Not long after that this fruit tree just started growing. In about six months earth time it started having flowers, and fruit started ripening just about the time I thought about pumpkin pie again. It's been doing that ever since then. I've given a lot of people slices of pumpkin 'pie' since then."

"It's been great visiting, Rosie, but the Master wants us to visit some more friends for Jaden's school today." With that, they both hugged Rosie and went on their way. They waved at Rosie as she went back into her mansion. As they walked away, they could hear strains of recorder music floating through the air back to them.

"Jaden, it sounds like the Lord wanted Rosie to start playing recorder to bring praise to Him as well as to teach you. Maybe he wants you to have another recorder, too? We'll see."

After visiting several other friends and family members in their mansions, they went to a great big mansion with many windows and doors. When the door was opened, they saw a man who was very small. He seemed to be about three feet tall.

He exclaimed, "Why he's like General Tom Thumb, except maybe a little taller!"

"Well, wait a minute, young man! Tom Thumb I'm not. What I am is Sam Clayburn from right in America. God made me small and I asked Him just to let me stay small even though he could have let me grow big here in heaven. So here I am, no bigger than I was on Earth and loving it.

"He made me small so I could reach many people for Jesus, and I'm so glad He did, that I wanted to let everyone here know that it's not looking good or being tall that's how people got to know God. I've got some videos to show you about what God did while I was in America in my own little town and then some other places as well."

So they spent the rest of their time away from her mansion looking at videos and eating supper with him. After they left his mansion, they went back to theirs and talked about some of the people they had visited, and then they went to their own rooms.

Jaden got out his Bible and looked at the passages about heaven, especially about being welcomed into heavenly mansions. As he thought about how he could start to serve others here in heaven, he started writing them down and asking God about these ideas.

Orpie spent some time in her sewing room. A friend had asked her to put together some drapes for someone who was coming home soon. She made happy plans to go to the store for the cloth to make the draperies with and thought of a welcome gift she could give as well.

Chapter Four Funeral Service

On earth, Jaden's parents woke up smelling eggs, sausages, pancakes, and coffee. When they got down to the kitchen for breakfast, they found their two older children, Susan and Jamal, at the stove. Their spouses, Joe and Rosetta, were sitting next to each other at the table. Susan and Jamal were busy filling serving dishes for the food. "Mom and Dad," Susan said, "we knew you wouldn't be thinking of food with the funeral today, so we fixed a meal for all of us. We wanted you to be strong for it."

Their mother Joanna answered, "Thank you. We weren't thinking about food. We were thinking how great it was that Jaden knew the Lord before he died, and what a great chance to tell others about Jesus. Even though we miss him, we know he's with Jesus now. When we were praying, the Lord told us that he wanted to stay in heaven and that he would be working with Jesus in many ways while he waits for us to come to him."

Jamal said, "How can you say that, Mom? Aren't you angry with the driver who hit him?"

"It's not easy, but we have forgiven the driver. Your father and I agree that it was right to forgive him. Along with that we gave up our right to be angry. We gave that to God. He will see us through. This next month without Jaden will seem hard but God will see us through."

In heaven, he woke up in the arms of Jesus. He had fallen asleep in his bed in Orpie's mansion. But now he saw that Jesus had him in a room much like his bedroom, with a rocking chair, and Jesus was rocking him in it, singing songs about heaven and about the Father's love.

He looked up right into eyes with such great love and the broadest smile on Jesus' face. He smelled a fragrance like rain and flowers and food all mixed together. It was the best fragrance Jaden had ever smelled. He didn't want it to stop, but he was hungry.

"I'm glad you woke up, Jaden," Jesus said. He reached to his left, and put a tray table with fruit, cheese, bread, and cups of milk on it in front of them. "We're going to eat right here, with you sitting on my lap. We have lots to do, and I want you to eat before we get started. Thank you, Father, for this food that you have so richly blessed us with. Cause us to rejoice in this provision you have given us. Amen."

While they ate, Jesus told him about His plans for Orpie, Jed, and others to watch his family at his funeral, so they could see how the Holy Spirit answered his prayers for the people at church. When he was finished eating, Jesus set him down.

Jaden put one hand into Jesus' hand and he flew while Jesus floated to the Portal building. Some of Jaden's heaven family met them at a window where they could watch the service. As they turned toward the window, they saw the church begin to fill. A few sat down, but more came and talked with his family as they stood near the casket.

"I have to leave now," Jesus said, "but you'll be with your family." As He was saying this, Jaden saw his brother and sister wiping their eyes a little but smiling a lot. His parents were holding hands and smiling at people, but also wiping their eyes a little.

Because he was able to see angels now that he was in heaven, and he saw them around his parents and the rest of his family, just holding them and wiping their tears, whispering verses from the Bible about God's love for them. In heaven, Orpie and Jeb held his hands.

Pascal and his family, Jaden's teachers from

school, and some children Jaden knew and some he did not know were all at the service. There were some people in park uniforms, some policemen, and some men and women Jaden remembered from stores and passing by on the streets.

The preacher used many of the verses that he had talked with God about in his prayers on earth. All of the people at the service were listening to the Bible verses. Some wiped tears from their eyes as they heard Psalm 23, Revelation 21:1-8 and John 3:16 for the first time. He also reminded them that they needed to repent and get to know Jesus if they did not know Him already, for that was the only way to get to heaven, where Jaden was. He also said that Jesus is the Truth and the Life, and the only way to come to the Father.

After the sermon, the preacher did something that the town talked about for a long time. He stood in front of the casket, and asked people to bow their heads. He told them that they did not know when Jesus was coming, but for every person there was an appointed time to die, and after that the judgment. Some may live until Jesus comes in person for His children, but the people in front of him could not guarantee that they would be one of those that lived until Jesus came for His children. They needed to make sure they were right with God.

Then he led them in a prayer very much like this one: "Father, I'm a sinner, I have disobeyed your law. I thank you that you sent Jesus to die for me. Thank you, Jesus, for dying for me. Forgive me for my sin. Come into my heart. Make me a new person. Live inside me. Lead me through Your Word to be like you. I thank you for doing this."

Many of the people who were there prayed along with the preacher. So many people's lives began to be changed that some bars were closed down and some became restaurants. Some stores got rid of x rated movies. Many other things became different in that town. This did not take place all at once, but newspapers reported the funeral, including the text of the sermon.

Later, some people came to Jaden's parents to ask them to help them get started reading the Bible. They began to be leaders in their church. Others went to the preacher to ask for help. Still others went to their own church for the first time in years and began to be leaders in that church.

In heaven, a party began. All of Jaden's relatives and all of the relatives of the other people at the funeral who were in heaven, and all the other people shouted and sang before the throne. The praise in heaven in front of the angels was like the sound of a huge football game, with so many people shouting and praising God for those who repented that day. Jaden was one of the leaders of the party, for many of Pascal's family came to Jesus that day, as did several of his own relatives.

The party lasted more than a day in Earth time, but seemed a short time in heaven when it was over. Because Jaden knew how the Holy Spirit works, he was again reminded that the Holy Spirit would call some of the people there to be pastors, evangelists, teachers, apostles, and prophets, and would heal some of the people who were there, because they were hurting and also looked sick.

Later, Jaden went to Jesus and asked him why he was not tired after the party. Jesus answered, "Jaden, this is why you were created, to be someone who is around the throne a lot in worship, in this kind of party. There are many other things you will do in heaven, but this is what will feel the best. This is what gives you strength."

He had not eaten, but he had not felt hungry all

that day. Orpie took him to a place in the building where many kinds of food were set out. He filled a plate and sat down at a nearby table, not noticing what he was eating because he was so excited about what had happened at the service on earth. The whole time he was eating, he got to talk with Jeb and Orpie about plans for the next day.

In Earth time, it was the next day when Jaden fell asleep, right there in the building, and was carried by Jeb to his own room in Orpie's mansion.

Chapter Five Rest Day

On Earth the next day, it was Sunday, and Jaden was used to having Sunday as a day of rest. Even though when God created the earth Sunday was the first day of the week and Saturday was the day of rest, for Jaden Sunday (Earth time) was a rest day.

He had had a celebration the previous day, and slept a long time. But there, where the glory of God surpasses the light of the sun and the moon and the stars, it is hard to tell when a new day begins.

We do know that our new bodies will need rest, and it seems that it would be a twenty-four hour cycle, but the Bible is not clear on this. So for now, I have chosen to use Jaden's sleeping times to determine the cycle of days for him. In heaven time it is difficult to tell exactly when Jaden woke up. But on Earth it was some time on Sunday.

Again, when he woke up, he smelled a breakfast. Someone was making toast and tea, chopping fruit, and getting something from outside. He got up, found and put on a new outfit laid out for him, stretched, yawned, and went toward the kitchen.

When he got into the kitchen, he saw Peter and John in the kitchen. He knew them because he met them at the welcome-to-heaven party. John had a string of fish in his hands, and Peter had a bag of nuts and some cheese. Orpie was standing next to them smiling broadly, and saying, "We're having a fish fry for breakfast. I asked Peter and John to bring some fish, but they said only if they did the cooking."

Jaden clapped his hands. "I've always wanted to ask you guys some questions, but when I was on earth I knew I couldn't. I'm so glad I can now."

"Hold on," Peter replied. "We'll have plenty of time for that later. First we'll eat and then talk. Orpie, please bless the food."

And that is just what she did. As they were eating, they talked about the big mansions that Peter and John had. Then Peter talked about waiting for John to come up to heaven, and having a party each time one of his friends came to heaven, and the parties they threw for sinners who came to repentance. And John talked about some of the big fish they caught while they fished before they became disciples.

Then Peter said something that surprised Jaden. "No matter how long I lived on earth, it was very short compared to how long I've been here, and how long I'm going to be here. Your time on Earth was very short as Earth lives go, but it's also very short compared to eternity.

"We watched you sometimes when you were on Earth. We also got to watch your funeral, as you did. You affected more people during your short time since getting to know Jesus and at your funeral than you'll ever know."

"That's right," John added. "While you were sleeping the Father threw five more parties because five more people heard about Jesus and repented because they had read newspapers about your funeral. And there's ten more parties planned for this afternoon for those who repented. We are all praising God for what He's doing to get people to come to Him."

"But I didn't do anything. All I did was follow Jesus and do what He wanted me to do."

"That's right, and now we're going to look at some things we wanted you to see. But first, there are going to be some other people joining us."

There was a knock on the door. Orpie let in some of the children that Jesus had brought with him when they talked about Bible stories. Peter and John both held out their arms to the children. Some of the children came up to Peter and some to John. Jaden decided to go with Peter. After the children were all settled and comfortable, Peter continued, "These pictures will help answer some questions you may have about what we did during our lives on earth. We borrowed them from one of the libraries in the city, but they were made a long time ago."

The first film (it looked like it was done by a movie camera, but there weren't any cameras when Peter and John were walking with Jesus on earth) showed a small building in a little town of Galilee. The inside of it looked like a small church, but with no pews or benches. It also seemed to have a dirt floor.

Boys came into it, and sat on the floor. A man held a book called a scroll and read to them from it. The boys repeated the words back to the man. He read it to them again, and they repeated it back to him again. When they said it the same way the man did, he read another part of the scroll. This continued a while.

Then one of the boys got up and said, "Rabbi, what does this mean?" And the man took another scroll and read from it.

After he read from the second scroll, he said, "That is what the rabbis in the Talmud said and think it means. As you heard, some rabbis say one thing, some another. Now what we have been reading is about the Messiah. Some say the Messiah will suffer. Others say that He will come in glory and every one will see Him. Some say these are two Messiahs, others say there is only one, the one who suffers and then comes back in glory."

The same boy said, "But Rabbi, what do you believe?"

After a little time, the rabbi answered, "Son, it seems to me that it's one Messiah, and the first time He comes not everyone will recognize Him as the Messiah. Then when he comes later everyone will see

Him when he comes down to Israel, splitting the mountain."

One boy said, "I want to know the first Messiah. The second sounds scary."

Others said, "I want to be here when the conquering Messiah comes. Our parents say that the Romans are so bad. We see so many people on crosses because of the Romans. I thought the Messiah would conquer our enemies, like the Romans."

Peter said, "That's how it was when Jesus came to earth. Few people recognized Him as their Messiah. They were looking for the conqueror."

"I was the one who wanted to know the first Messiah," John said.

"And I was the boy who asked what the rabbi believed," Peter put in.

"So was that how you learned the Bible?" Jaden asked.

"That was our Sabbath school," was John's reply. "Our fathers also taught us what they had learned, but we did not learn Hebrew all at once. When the rabbi taught us, we learned well. Even so, Jesus was better than our village rabbi."

The next movie showed two fishing boats and Jesus on the shore. Jaden watched as the disciples heard Jesus tell them to let down their nets for a big catch. The boats struggled to get ashore. "Peter, that's you swimming to shore. I never saw anyone swim so fast. And all those fish. You must have sold all of them."

"Actually, that's what our partners did. You saw that we left them in the boats while we followed Jesus."

"Jesus taught a lot about catching men by showing us His way of catching fish. It was so much better than our way," John said.

"You see, he was up all night asking his Father to show him who should be his disciples. The Father showed Him John and me and ten others, as you know. The Father also showed Him where the fish were gathering together that day. When He looked in the water, there they were. So he told us where he saw the fish. He only did what he saw the Father doing. The Father loves to give His children gifts and to provide for them."

They also saw some of the miracles Jesus did, people He healed, and the teaching He did every day. Many times in this film there were blind people healed, deaf hearing, and lame people walking, and dead people raised. John shouted, "And there were so many more miracles and things Jesus did, that I did not have enough scrolls to write them all down. For all eternity, we are going to be able to look on His wonders and His mighty acts and praise Him. And we still will not know everything Jesus has done."

Afterward, they said, "It's party time. Let's go to the throne room and hear the reports. We'll eat again, and you'll be able to praise God and decide what you would like to see next."

When they got to the throne room, less than a second later in earth time, they saw groups of people and angels in every section of the room. They were shouting and praising God. The voices were loud, but no one seemed to notice, for they joined the praises as they came in.

Everywhere there were people telling the angels about people they knew who just came to Jesus. Messenger angels went to special rooms with the name of each person. In those rooms and in the throne room every time a name was mentioned, a bell was rung. This particular time, it seemed like the bell ringing was constant.

Angels were going to and coming back from the

rooms, reporting how many new names were in the book of life, and how many had their sins washed away.

Every time the Father shouted to His new child, whether young or old, "Welcome, my child, to your new family. I will watch over you and protect you so that you can know how good Jesus is and how welcome you are. Even when you have trials and problems, you will know that I am there. Welcome, welcome." The Father was saying this constantly during the party.

People ran up to Jesus, thanking Him for His work in bringing their friends, family, neighbors, and coworkers to Himself. Prayers of the saints on earth were coming up with a beautiful fragrance, as they praised God for what He was doing to bring people to Himself. Some were also asking God to make changes in the nations, in the churches, in the states, in the cities, in the workplaces, in social outlets, and in their families.

All during this time of praise, Jaden could see people going to the outer courts. It seemed that they were gone for just an instant, but they were stronger when they came back.

When he looked around, he saw Jeb and Orpie also heading to the back of the throne room. He followed them and found that there was some food available to eat there. He filled a plate, sat down with them and ate. "Orpie," he said, "This is great. Tastes lots better than the pineapple Mom bought. And the vegetables taste like really great hamburger."

"Child, that's the way it is here. God really loves to surprise all of us with our favorite foods." With that she let him taste some of her apple and gave him a part of her vegetable. "Take some of this apple. Doesn't that taste a lot like apple pie? Doesn't the vegetable taste like meat loaf?"

"Sure does, but better."

After they ate, Jeb and Orpie said they were going to the Portal building. Jaden decided to go with them. They went to the same room from which they had seen Jaden's funeral, but this time they were looking at Jaden's church. It was crowded, with more people than there were on the day of his funeral. (Was it only yesterday? Yes, it was, but so much had gone on in heaven that day, he wasn't sure.)

The pastor was telling about the people who had come to Jesus the day before. He told the congregation to pray for these new babies in Christ and to welcome them this morning. He also said that there was a special class in Sunday school starting that morning for people who wanted to know what the church believed about Jesus. There was also another class he called "Getting to Know Your Bible", and a third one called "Getting Close to Jesus".

Jaden asked Jesus, "Why is the pastor starting so many classes all at once?"

Soon after Jaden asked the question, the pastor mentioned seeing in a dream many people will be coming to the Lord in a very short time. "Some of these people have never heard about the Lord," the pastor said, "and some only know a very little. I want them to get to know the Lord so he can heal them and show them how to get others to know Him also."

While Jaden was remembering the parties that were thrown for the people who repented the day before, the pastor was starting his sermon. Jaden looked again when he heard his own name.

"Yesterday Jaden, a boy from this congregation, was buried. But only Jaden's body was buried. He himself went to heaven, because he knew Jesus. Jesus said in John 11:25, 'I am the Resurrection, and the Life: he that believeth in me, though he were dead, yet shall he live.' Jaden told many others of his faith in Christ. Today we want to thank his parents for bringing Jaden to this church and teaching him how to witness. We also want to pray for them as they begin a time of transition without their youngest child.

"Before we pray for them, I want to tell you a little about how Jesus loved the little children." Then the pastor read from the accounts of how mothers brought their children to Jesus that he might bless them. He told about Jesus raising Jairus' daughter from the dead, and healing so many people.

He then said, "We don't know why Jaden was done with his work on Earth so early, but we do know he was, for his parents told me they felt Jaden wanted to stay in heaven. They said they'll see them again.

"Today we continue the celebration of life in Jesus with Communion, celebrating the death and resurrection of Jesus Christ that we might live in Him. I want you to know that even though you may not be a member of this church, you may take Communion with us.

"But before we celebrate Communion, we want to ask if you have a personal relationship with Jesus Christ. Have you ever asked Jesus to take charge of your life? God does not guaranteed tomorrow on Earth. He does guarantee that if we know Jesus and have surrendered our lives to Him, we will have peace in our hearts and we will be able to fellowship with Him now and for all eternity.

"Those who don't know Jesus when they die will hear the words, 'Depart from me. I never knew you.' And God will weep as He sees part of His own creation leave His presence forever. He does not rejoice when people go to a hell made for the devil and his angels. He rejoices when one sinner repents, when one sinner leaves his evil ways and turns to God. Won't you pray with me and make sure that you are on the path of following God?" And he led the congregation in prayer.

Many angels were in the church, urging people to pray and mean it from their hearts. Ten people prayed with the pastor before Communion. They had big smiles on their faces as they took Communion. Others just sat there staring, some crying, as they listened to other voices that told them lies about having much time. Some were healed as they took bread. Some were set free as they took the cup.

Jeb, Orpie and Jaden went back to the throne room and gave the angels in heaven the names of the people who came and repented. Ten bells were rung for these people. All across the throne room more bells were rung and people were shouting praises to God for what He was doing to bring sinners to repentance.

Angels went with the names of the people and recorded them in books. They took big erasers, wiping away the dark marks of sin in the people's books. Not even a smudge was left and the pages looked new.

Jaden went to thank the Holy Spirit for His work in bringing the people to salvation. He went to Jesus to thank Him for what He did for these people. He talked with the Father about what the Father wanted him to do. The Father sent him to get some food outside the throne room and to talk with the people there.

When he left the throne room, he saw his friend Chong at a table with some other boys and girls. Before he joined him, he filled a plate with strawberries, blueberries, carrots, and many other familiar foods, plus some others that smelled so good he just felt he had to have them. He asked Chong how his day had been since he woke up.

His friend giggled and said, "Why, it feels like just yesterday I was in a hospital, but I've already been to school, eaten a lot of meals, seen my garden, eaten more meals, and met lots of people. Sometimes it seems like one long day, since it's so light out all the time. I guess I've been here a few days.

"How's today been? I watched a pastor talk to some friends of mine back home. They weren't too sure about Jesus. My grandpa and I threw a party for one friend who came to Jesus, and thanked the Holy Spirit for what He did to bring that person to repentance. That was some party the Father threw for my friend. Everyone shouted and whooped and hollered. Think they did that for me when I turned to Jesus?"

Jaden answered, "Sure. I read in the Bible that there is rejoicing in front of the angels over every sinner that repents. I guess that means that people and God Himself are throwing a party just like we've been seeing here."

Soon Jesus joined them and gave each one of them a hug. When He hugged Jaden, he whispered to him, calling him his new name, and reminding him to tell no one else his special name, which was just between the two of them. Then He told Jaden it was time to go outside near the river and play. He also told Jaden to pick some of the fruit from the ground underneath one of the trees and take it to his home after they were done playing.

When Jaden looked around, he saw that all the other children were going to the same place. So they started a game of tag, went from that to hide-and-seek (giving up on that because it didn't get dark), and then played on some equipment they found nearby.

In between games, they each went to one of the trees and picked up some fruit, putting it in baskets which they saw nearby. Jaden also saw some nuts that he liked and picked up some of them as well.

Jesus came by as they were going by their homes. He invited them to bring their fruit and nuts to a birthday celebration. Jaden asked, "Whose birthday are we celebrating?"

"We're celebrating your birthday. One year ago today you decided to be my child. So all your friends and relatives here in heaven are celebrating your 'born-again' birthday."

"Wow," he said. "I didn't know they had birthday parties like that in heaven."

"Anytime someone is born again, they are taken out of Satan's kingdom and into my Father's kingdom. We want to celebrate the fact that my Father made you His child and you stayed His child until death brought you to Him. You are still my Father's child, and we love you very much."

As Jesus was talking, they came to a park with many picnic tables. Each table was spread with tablecloths, napkins, and many plates of food. At each of the tables there were people Jaden knew. Suddenly they all said, "Happy Birthday, Jaden! Surprise!"

Orpie was at the center of the group. "This party was my idea. I talked to some of these people about having a picnic right here near your playground. So many helped put this together. We want you to know how much the Father loves you. This is why he sent you to talk to your friends." As she was speaking, Jesus waved goodbye.

"Wow! This is so great. I'm so glad that I got to bring this fruit and nuts for the party." The other children told her the same thing. At each of the tables there were some nutcrackers and empty bowls. There were just enough bowls for all the children to put some fruit and nuts at each table. No one was left out.

"Some of you had fruit that the children picked from today. If you are having this for the first time, this fruit is from the Tree of Life. Each of the trees by the river where the children were playing is part of the Tree of Life. The fruit of the tree is different each month, but there is always fruit for you to pick. Enjoy your food." And she blessed the food for them. It was truly a feast that day in heaven.

After they ate, they had a group hug before going home. Parents and relatives put their children to bed, for many were yawning. Because Jaden was the birthday child, Jesus left a gemstone for Jaden right before leaving the picnic. He put it on his dresser in his room.

Jeb told Jaden that he would see him when he woke up, for the next day would be a school day. He was so excited over his birthday celebration that he did not notice that he still had fruit and nuts in his basket. Orpie put the fruit and nuts on the kitchen counter, cracking the nuts first before putting them in a bowl. She put a new shirt on the chair next to his bed, and left to go to her own room.

Chapter Six School

On Earth it was a school day. Pascal went to school crying, missing Jaden. Some of his friends went to him and hugged him. They told him how sad they were for him, because they knew he and Jaden were best friends.

In gym class they played soccer, in math class they did fractions, in history they looked at the history of their state during World War I. In social studies they looked at how people lived during that time. And in science they planted some seeds to grow in their classroom.

Often Pascal got up to look at Hortense, the class guinea pig. When it was first brought into the room, their teacher had read a book with the name Hortense in it. She had asked the class to give her names to choose from. They voted, and it won by four votes among three other names. Jaden had said he voted for it. Pascal had said he voted for another name. So the guinea pig reminded Pascal of his friend.

At the end of the school day, the principal said that there were counselors to talk with them about Jaden if they wanted to.

In heaven, Jaden woke up smelling fish, eggs, and bread. "Orpie, what a good breakfast! You know I never had fish for breakfast before being here.

"What's so special about today? And breakfast in bed, too?" She was sitting by his side with a tray with this food on it. With the fish and eggs, there was fresh fruit and juice.

She laughed and said, "In heaven every day is special. Sometimes I just feel like doing something different."

Afterward, Orpie and Jaden left her mansion

and flew to a huge building, with many windows, and the children's gardens nearby. Jaden remembered the school because he had seen it before his funeral. Orpie said, "You'll have many teachers, including some of the teachers you saw earlier. It'll be fun. Jesus will still be with you all the time, and you know you can talk to Him any time you want."

Jeb joined them at the school. They told Jaden about some of the work they did while on earth, about the hard times and how Jesus gave them special things to take care of their family so they could live and declare the work that God had done in their lives. They told of the years before they got to know Jesus really well, but they were happy they did know Him all those years. Some of the relatives Jaden saw in his family video met them near the building also.

It was like a family gathering as they all walked into the building. Inside, it did not look like any school he had ever seen. There were no chalkboards, no desks, and no storage cabinets.

Instead, he saw angels, one next to each of the twenty people in part of a huge room. There were as many children as there were grownups.

There were four other people in the room, looking up from where they were sitting, talking together, in another part of the room. Four angels were behind them. As he looked around the room, he saw yet another angel, looking straight at him, arms held out to Jaden. He ran up to the angel and asked, "Were you my angel on earth too?" He nodded and smiled. When Jaden turned around again, he saw that the others had angels with them, too.

Jeb asked, "Jaden, are you ready to get started?"

He answered, "What are we doing? I don't see books, cubbies, cabinets, nothing that looks like a school. This looks like fun."

Jeb answered, "Well, you are going to get to work. Instead of tests, you'll explore how to apply what you learn. Your memory has been made perfect, and you are going to learn the right way for you. You will learn some science, some math and algebra, and some history. But most of all, you're going to learn the things you're best at doing.

"Some of these things you've been doing already on earth. But many of these things will take some time to discover. Remember, though, we have all eternity (and that's longer than anyone can count), to find out what these things are that you can do. Orpie and I are still learning the things we can do. We've already looked at your garden. Later we can practice what you learn on your garden.

"Remember when you talked with the mother duck in your garden? You could say that was a biology lesson. In the city the libraries you visit operate a little differently from libraries on Earth. In time you'll get to know them. One thing we do during the first few days here is teach you how to get around here."

While Jeb was talking, the four people by themselves came out to the center of the room. Each of the four people called three children and three adults by name to meet with them.

Although many names were called out, everyone heard his or her name clearly. Jaden found himself with Chong, Hannah, Orpie, Jeb, and someone he had not met yet. There were some adults who were not paired up with children, because they had come in with Jaden.

He turned to Chong. "Hi," he said. "I'm so glad we're in the same school here. I remember you from when Jesus told us some stories. You told me about the missionary, too."

Chong said, "I'm glad we're here together too.

By the way, my whole name is Chong Choi Bou. I was born in China, but came to Taiwan. I didn't get to grow up on earth because I got very sick and the doctors could not help me. Jesus healed me here. Now I can run and play and learn many things. People call me Chong. We'll be friends for a long time, perhaps forever." He was laughing as he said that.

The leader of their group, a man, led them to one corner. "My name not important, because on earth I was big sinner. Jesus saved me, put me here to be with you.

"You will learn much. Some of your teachers are in this group. My job is to show you where some things in city are. Today we go visit temple. You see the Father. Visits with you. Shows things He wants you to do. We go now."

With that statement, a pathway opened up through one of the doors. He stepped onto the pathway, and Jaden's group and all his relatives with him followed.

When he heard the word temple, an excitement, but even more an awe came over him. He remembered a verse that said, "But the Lord is in his holy temple; let all the earth keep silence before him."

He remembered hearing that when Jesus died the veil in the temple was torn from top to bottom. So he knew he could now go into the Holy of holies, where only the priests went before. The closer they got to the temple, and it seemed to take a long time, but in Earth time only seconds, the more he wanted to just kneel down in worship.

When they did get into the temple, the leader and all who were with him did just that. They sang songs for a while, then lifted up their hands, and watched in awe as God began to smile on them in a way that Jaden had never experienced.

Soon Jaden was not watching. He felt a search light testing his innermost being. He was shown all the thoughts of his heart at all times in his life. He was shown God's presence at all times. He was shown how much he was loved even when his thoughts were not right. His tears were wiped away as he realized that he had been wondrously and truly forgiven.

Then he was shown his heart when he became God's child. He saw that his heart was clean and that what he did for God was done with a pure heart out of God's love. He was shown his love for certain birds. He was shown many possibilities for learning.

He was also shown many different paths he could choose from. But one path seemed lit up for him, a path that led straight to the heart of God. The path would take much training and much help from many, but led to great warmth and great light, also to great responsibility. He saw how what he had done on Earth started him on that path and was shown some of the steps he would take along the way to the heart of God.

Jaden wept many tears of wonder, joy, and awe during that time. Even as he cried, he felt the tears being wiped away as a deep joy began to flow through his being.

All became silent around him. He became silent also. A voice resonated through the room, speaking to all, each one hearing it for himself or herself. "You are my child and I am pleased with you. Go your way and know my peace. I am indeed with you this day."

They walked in silence from the temple, each deep in thought. As they left the temple, they found themselves in front of a small cabin at the foot of a mountain, with fruit trees outside it, the fruit nearly ripe. Going in, they found a table set with refreshments: cheese, fruit, bread and water. The fragrance of flowers filled the room. They sat down and ate, talking quietly.

A knock was heard at the door. Quickly the teacher went to the door and let in the visitor. "Welcome, and join our repast," he said. "Although, I think you have brought much to share with us."

Indeed, he was right, for it was Jesus. All went to Him to receive His hug. Jaden wanted to ask about his vision. As he looked into Jesus' eyes, it was as though he saw the answers even before he asked. So he remained silent, thinking about the answers and the vision.

"Children," Jesus said, "I have much to show you and all eternity to share with you, as you know. When you are in heaven, as on Earth, you have duties and tasks to do.

"Today some of you were shown what your goal is in school. Others were shown how you are to teach some people here, as well as others you see. Those who are mostly learning at this time will have some homework. It will seem like fun and I or your teachers will direct you in this work. Welcome to the city. All of you will find many things to see."

Jaden thought about his path. He knew he had to start with the Hall of Martyrs today and then go back to the school to meet with others. As he thought Hall of Martyrs, he found himself speeding down the path to it.

The names Wycliffe, Hus, and Stephen were clear to him. Also, he was to look at the role of the Holocaust martyrs of World War II. When he got there, he saw he was in front of a screen that showed one of the men he had thought of, followed by scenes of people in Europe.

He saw Grandma Orpie standing next to him, wiping tears from her eyes. Looking more closely, he saw her in the World War II screen, helping people who were martyred for their faith. She had lived, for he saw a bright light around her the whole time. Hugging her he said, "I didn't know you were there. I'm so glad you lived so you could be my grandma. Those people you helped really hurt a lot."

Together they went down a street that seemed brighter than the rest, went out the gate, and soon found themselves back at the school.

All the other adults and children were setting tables with plates of food and many beverages. Looking at all the food, he was surprised he was hungry again. Some coming in were wiping tears of joy from their eyes.

They all helped themselves to foods that they knew. Jaden found a table to sit at with Chong. He ate what tasted like meat loaf and baked potato with carrots. Chong had rice with bean sprouts, beef, and snow peas. For a beverage Chong had tea and Jaden had coconut milk. They each tried some of the other's food, for there were many kinds of food at that school lunch.

"Chong, this is the first time I've tried chopsticks! When we had Chinese food at home, we just used forks and spoons!" Jaden said laughing as he dropped some food on the table

"And this is my first time with a fork and spoon," he said as he picked up a carrot.

"Aren't you glad we don't have to pick up spilled food? Did you see what happened to the food on the floor?" Jaden asked.

"Yes, it's gone already." Both laughed again as they saw each other drop the food a few more times before they got it to stay on the fork or the chopsticks. It seemed like a long time, but on Earth, this was still morning of their day.

They did not know it, but the many foods they were trying were there so they could learn how others in their room ate, for most in the room were from different countries and did not know the foods of the others. And so the first social studies class in Jaden's school in heaven concluded with gales of laughter and songs of worship in twenty languages.

After their meal, Jaden, all the children went out to play in the nearest garden. Their angels, Jeb and Orpie were with them. They played catch, tag, and some other games. They were laughing as they followed Jeb and Orpie back into the building.

On earth, two days after the funeral, Jamal and his wife and Susan and her husband were still visiting Jaden's parents. It seemed that their refrigerator was filled almost to overflowing. So many people brought so much food into the house that Jaden's parents had many different foods to choose from. Many different cuisines were represented, for their friends loved to experiment. Some was put into the freezer, and they did not tell anyone what they ate. Pascal and his family came to visit and shared their concern for them.

Jaden and Orpie went back to her mansion. Many people came to visit them, asking him about his visit to the temple. All the visitors brought food. She set out plates and silverware, chopsticks, glasses and cups for those who stayed. Jeb stayed to eat as well. Even though they had much to eat, nobody was uncomfortable with how much they ate, and the leftover food on their plates was taken care of without washing plates or spoiling, for there is nothing impure in heaven.

The video Jaden watched after the people left was about how people came into Orpie's life so they could come to know Jesus. By the time it was over, he saw how she had prayed for him and more than thirty others who got to know Jesus by the time Jaden got to heaven. It also showed her praying for many other people who did not yet know Jesus.

She told him that every time she watched the video, she saw that more people she had prayed for had come to Jesus. Each time that happened, the video itself changed. After the video, Jaden talked to Jesus quietly and fell asleep.

Meanwhile, Orpie got out some drapery fabric she had picked up in the city. After checking the length and cutting it to the pattern in her kit, she began stitching the first panel together. When she was done with that, she too had her quiet time talking with the Father.

On Earth, Jaden's parents were going back to work. His father had worked at the machine shop as a foreman the day of Jaden's accident, and his employer had given him a number of days off so they could do so many things because of Jaden's death, but it was time to go back to work. He also wanted to share everything with his friends and coworkers.

Going back to work was harder for his mother. Her drive to work took her past Pascal's house every day. She thought about going another route, even looking at maps to see if it was possible, but she could not find a different way. She had to go that way to get to work. She too felt that it was time to start back to work.

Before they left for work, they prayed together, asking the Lord for strength as they faced these new challenges that day.

After work, when they got home, they shared with each other how many people had asked questions about the Lord. It turned out that everyone at the machine shop had read the sermon in the newspaper, and everyone in her hospital janitorial service had heard about it on the news or had seen one of the patients watching the news about it. They too had asked her questions.

It seemed that they hardly had a chance to get

their work done, but somehow everything that was needed to get done was done. They spent time in quiet prayer before eating their supper of turkey from the funeral reception, beets, Jello salad, potatoes, and chocolate cake.

Afterward, the pastor and some friends came to visit and share plans for training new believers, with Joanna and Tony leading a home Bible study group for some of them. Afterward, they were so excited that they spent at least an hour after the visit talking about how to set up the Bible study and who they could invite from their own neighborhood to share in the Bible study.

Before they went to sleep, they had a list that included Pascal and his mother, the people next door, and friends from work. Looking at the list, they realized they might even host two Bible studies instead of just one.

Chapter Seven Exploration Studies

When Jaden woke up, he saw Orpie sitting in the chair by his bed. She had a book in hand, and the cover showed a big breakfast on it. He asked her, "What are we doing today? Yesterday at school was so different from school on Earth.

"Going to the temple was the best part. There was so much I learned there that I know I have to do, especially learning more about history of the Bible and people, and so much more.

"I also know you and the rest of our family will teach me a lot of stuff. This part about homework has me puzzled, but I know you'll show me."

She nodded and smiled, then led him into the kitchen. Bread, fruit, nuts, and milk were in the kitchen, and a small knife on the counter. Three plates, glasses, and cups were on the table, along with silverware. Nothing was cooking on the stove, and it looked like nothing was ready to eat.

Orpie said to Jaden, "This morning you can cut up some fruit and put it on the plates at the table. Last night I chopped up some of the nuts you picked, and we're going to eat that with the fruit. Have you ever made toast?" Jaden shook his head. "Well, it's really simple, and today we'll have you do that. First the fruit."

First Orpie showed Jaden how she cut a piece of fruit. Then she held his hands and guided him while he cut a piece of fruit. Then she watched Jaden as he cut a piece of fruit.

"Very good. As I knew you would, you learned very quickly how best to cut fruit. Now it's time to toast some bread. I already sliced it. We have three people eating here today and we want to toast six slices. We have room in the oven, so all we do is put the slices in on the rack, shut the door, and turn the oven on to toast." He put in the bread, turned the oven on, and the timer.

"So how is the mansion set up for toasting, and so on? I didn't ask you that when I got here. Is there electricity in heaven?"

"Well, God hasn't told me how he did it. Because we were used to electricity when we were on Earth, he made sure our mansions had electricity in some form for cooking our food. You'd have to ask God how He arranged that. All I know is I can make supper the way I'm used to doing it, if I want. There are also other ways, as you'll find out later."

While the bread was toasting, she got out another piece of fruit, chopped it, and mashed it. Soon it was smooth enough to spread. When the toast was ready, she asked him to bring it to the table on another plate. She mixed the mashed fruit with the chopped nuts, put it in a dish, and set it on the table. While she was doing this, Jeb and Rosie came to the door. Hearing their knock, Orpie got out two more sets of dishes and toasted two more slices of bread.

"Well, Jeb, breakfast is ready. Would you please bless it for us?" she asked.

Jeb blessed the food, and they all ate a good breakfast, adding milk and coffee as they wanted. As they talked, she suggested going back to the amusement park later. Jaden nodded over his food.

After the dishes were put away, they heard another knock at the door. When Jaden answered the door, he saw Jesus with a group of ten children.

"It's time for morning Bible time. We'll be getting one more friend, and then we start. After that, you'll go to school again." Jaden saw Chong and Hannah, as well as some of the other children from his last Bible story time.

They sat under a tall tree. Jaden cuddled up near Jesus, sitting next to Chong and some smaller boys. Hannah sat next to Jesus on the other side, with some other girls. He was holding two babies this time, and didn't seem to mind when one of them patted his hair while he talked.

He told them about the time when he was born, how the angels sang, the shepherds came to visit and later, when he could walk, some wise men brought gifts. When he shared with them, Jaden could see the sheep and the shepherds. He could see the wise men. When Jesus told about going to Egypt with just His mother and father because that was what God told Joseph to do, Jaden thought that was very brave.

When Bible time was over, he played tag, catch, and other games for a while with Chong and Hannah and some of the bigger children. Then he saw Rosie and Jeb coming to him. "Hi Rosie, hi Jeb. Are you taking me to school today?" he asked.

"You could say that," Rosie answered. "We want to take you to a concert and a music school today. We're going to the city for that. Afterwards, we're coming back to your school. There we'll get started on some other things."

When she said the words concert and music school, a path seemed to open up in front of them. As they got onto the path, Jaden found they were traveling very fast even as they walked.

So it seemed like they arrived in two minutes' time in front of a building with the sign, "Beethoven, Handel, and Asaph direct the seraphim today for your listening pleasure. All welcome to listen. Guest musicians more than welcome to play with us."

When they came into the building, the first thing they saw was a room with many different instruments of every description possible and more besides. Both Jeb and Rosie selected an instrument: Jeb a fife and

Rosie a piccolo. Rosie handed Jaden a drum and drumsticks. Jaden said, "But I've never played drums. A concert where I can try playing? With angels?"

Rosie said, laughing, "No time like the present to start. They did say guest musicians are welcome. We're actually backstage of this concert hall." Jeb and Rosie warmed up as Jaden listened. While they were doing this, he heard other music coming from another room.

Jeb then led the way to a big stage in front of an auditorium larger than any auditorium Jaden had ever seen. The main sections of the orchestra were filled with seraphim. Next to many of the seraphim were several chairs for people with instruments. Some were seated.

"You see the section near where we came in with all the drums?" Jeb asked. "That's where you'll go with your drum and drumsticks. The seraphim and other players will help you get started. You're just going to do rhythm today. You have a good feel for that."

"If you say so," Jaden said. "I never tried drums or any other instrument."

The conductor was gentle, and had a meek style. A mighty hymn of praise had just ended as they found their seats in the orchestra. Many in the audience were weeping for joy as they worshipped using the words of a psalm.

He did not have the same kind of robe as Jaden had seen on other people in heaven. He was wearing a crown, but it was almost as if he were not wearing it, for no one paid attention to it. He had an ornately carved baton, with leaves, pomegranates, and herbs. He said, "We will play and sing 'In Judah God is Known' and remember God's goodness to Israel."

The man next to Jaden said, "This is Asaph. You would not know by looking at him, but he led the first choir of Levites under King David. God has greatly rewarded him with a mansion and a home for children to whom he teaches Hebrew music. He has graciously allowed those who never knew the old melodies to learn to play his songs by ear. Many people come to sing when he conducts."

Asaph's conducting style was to lift his hands as the melody flowed upward and bring them down as it went down in pitch. He conducted the beats to the right or to the left in time with the words. Jaden saw he was looking at Psalm 76. He also recognized the melody as one of those he heard often in heaven. As he caught on to how the music went, he began to play his drum. While they played, he could hear audience members singing.

When they finished, the audience kept worshipping using new melodies and songs of praise and thanksgiving. They did not notice his departure from the platform.

After a time, the audience got quiet again, and Beethoven came to the podium, carrying a simple cane. He rapped with the cane on the floor for attention. "Seraphim and people, we will play 'Joyful, joyful we adore thee.' Those of you who know this are welcome to sing with us."

Jaden saw that he had music for this song on his stand, but not for drums. It was a voice part. Instead of using hands, like Asaph had done, Beethoven kept time with the cane. First he tapped the floor four times with the cane, and then raised one of his hands to cue the orchestra to start. As the music reached the crescendos of "Hearts unfold like flowers before Thee, God of mercy, God of love," some in the audience began to kneel.

When the music ended, again fresh melodies, songs and quiet worship filled the room. Mostly the seraphim in the orchestra noticed Handel as he stepped to the podium. He mouthed "Hallelujah Chorus" to those who were watching. Jaden watched nothing for he had his hands on his drumsticks. He knew in his heart he was to sing and play during this music. He had no music in front of him, but he felt the other drummers getting ready to play also.

Handel conducted the chorus, using a small baton for a time, then simply his hands showing the beat. The rest of the audience stood to their feet. Those in the orchestra whose instruments allowed them to do so also stood to their feet. The music went from crescendo to crescendo.

When they began singing and playing "The kingdom of this world is become the Kingdom of our Lord and of His Christ," Handel stopped conducting and knelt down as Jesus Himself stepped in front of the podium, wearing His crowns and regal garments, carrying His scepter, and received the adoration of all. As more and more realized Jesus was there, they stopped playing or singing and knelt in worship. Finally, there was silence.

"Children and angels," Jesus said, "it is good to be here with you. You angels were created for this. You people were redeemed for this. You are here from every kindred and every nation and I welcome you into the joy of heaven.

"For those of you who don't know what today's duty or homework is, I declare that you are to look into the joys of my creation. You may use any library you choose and write down anything you would like to learn more about. Near the end of the day I want you to share this with others.

"If you have not started making a gift for someone you know who is here or is coming here soon, go shopping first in the city for materials for your gift. After you have shared what you learned about creation today, you may start to make your gift for your friend or family member. I now welcome your joy as you go about your tasks today."

Jaden looked at Jesus. From where he had been playing, he was behind Him and to His right. As he looked, Jesus turned around and smiled. In that smile, he saw pools of love.

Jesus held out his scepter. He knelt and kissed Jesus' hand. He lifted him to his feet and again let Jaden touch the scepter. He felt the power of Jesus' authority flow through his entire being. Finally, when he felt like he could experience no more, he discovered he was alone. He took his drum and drumsticks to the room in back of the stage. Rosie and Jeb were there, putting their instruments away. The auditorium was silent, but felt full of the presence of God.

"Jaden," Rosie said, "it's time for us to go back to our mansions. But before we do that, you will meet another teacher here. He will show you what you are to study today and tell you which libraries to visit."

While she was talking, a group of children came to the building. Among them were Chong and Hannah, and all were carrying notebooks, lists of things to do or get, and pencils or pens. With them was one of the teachers from the big school, carrying a notebook with Jaden's name on it.

"Jaden," the teacher said, "We were all in the auditorium in a section for our school. It was our day to go to this concert that you were in. Before we went here, a messenger told us to come back stage so you could join us on the assignment that Jesus gave us.

"Here is your notebook and other things you need for your assignment. Rosie and Jeb asked me to remind you about the music school, also. We will meet back here for lunch as a group and then again after our afternoon research so we can carry on our assignment of sharing.

"Children," he continued, "you will not go by yourselves, because you don't know your way around the city yet. Each of you will have a guide for the city, someone you met since you got here or someone from your family. Some of you, because of your assignments, will have several other guides. All are specially chosen for you because of your purpose."

Jaden looked around for his guide. He saw someone coming down the street almost at a run, carrying one of the instruments he remembered from Grandma Orpie's mansion. He saw someone else driving the car he remembered seeing parked by the mansion. Finally, he saw a duck inside the car sitting next to the driver.

Almost at the same time, both people and the duck came up to him. The person with the instrument was Uncle Jake, whom he had met when he first got to heaven. Orpie had driven the car, and the duck was none other than the mother duck he had seen at his own pond.

Jake spoke first. "Rosie and Jeb told me that they wanted to show you the music school. They got called away to welcome someone else to heaven. As you remember, I'm one of your mother's uncles. Orpie wanted me to bring this instrument with me. It's an oboe, and is a challenging instrument to play. But Rosie also wants you to know that she'll be bringing your recorder back with some music for you to learn."

"That's right," Orpie said. "Your first stop on your list is the music school, isn't it?"

Checking his list from the teacher, Jaden found schools, libraries, stores, and special attractions in the City of New Jerusalem. Next to some of the names of places were handwritten starred numbers. The words Exploration Day were at the top, and Composers' School had number one and a big star next to it. "Do you mean Composers' School?" Jaden asked. "That's the one with number one next to it."

"Yes," she answered. "Composers, besides writing music, also teach music and play instruments. You will find teachers for every kind of instrument here. I think that would be where to go to find out what music you like to do the most."

Jaden replied, "I had a vision in the temple and found out that I'll be doing lots of things. I think one of the things I'm supposed to do is teach ducks new songs."

"Whether it's music for animals, birds, or people, that building is the place to go. It's on the other side of the auditorium, but a few miles away. I thought you might like to see some of the city on our way there."

So they all hopped into the car, including the duck. Orpie and the duck sat in front, and Uncle Jake and Jaden sat in back. The inside was more luxurious than the limousines he had seen on Earth. The quiet ride of the Rolls Royce he had seen once was no match for this car.

Before he knew the Lord, he had seen a few cartoons about the future. In them moving walkways and flying commuter vehicles docked in the air. This car did more. Orpie drove it like she was a pilot on an airplane. Takeoff from the roadway was achieved in about three feet.

They flew over some of the buildings, and around the taller ones. As they flew, she pointed out the Conservatory of the Masters, the Hall of Creation Knowledge, the Visions of Ezekiel Art building, among other landmarks.

Even so, they got to the Composers' School very quickly. The sign on the building also included "Music Lessons from Well-Known Teachers of Your Instrument," "Ever Wanted to Learn to Write Music? Ask Your Teacher," and "Daily Concerts of Music by New and Well-Known Composers in Your

Neighborhood. Inquire Within." Jaden said, "Wow! Sounds like they cover everything about music. No wonder it's such a huge building."

They were at the entrance of the building. The door opened and a man wearing a blue sash said, "That's because many people coming to heaven had musical talent or wanted to learn to play an instrument, but never had the opportunity because they didn't have the resources like we have here. We also have master craftsmen making our instruments."

"So we cover all levels of interest and ability at the Composers' School. We can help you find out the type of music you like most and help you grow that. In this building (and it's really a mile high and miles wide and long) people also learn how to make their favorite instrument from people who made them on Earth. I recognize your oboe as made by one of the masters after he got here."

Jaden looked at Orpie and saw that she was wearing a blue sash, which she had not worn before. He made a note to ask what the sashes meant.

"Now you're here," the man continued, "because Orpie thinks you have an ear for music. First we'll let you listen to the oboe and five other instruments. I understand you've already tried the drums."

"Yes, I have," Jaden replied. "I'm not so sure about always playing them, but they were fun because I did not have to learn to play them. Actually it was just one drum, though."

"That's okay. Now you can try other instruments. Listen to these and see which one is your favorite of what you hear. That's the one you can try along with the recorder. After you decide, every few days you take a lesson on one instrument besides the recorder and learn how to put notes on a staff. If you would like to try another instrument before settling on any one or two, that's okay. We have all eternity for you to discover and learn things, including music."

So Jaden listened to some music with the oboe, the trumpet, the flute, the clarinet, the violin, and the piano. As he was listening and watching people play, he thought about how he would have to make sounds on each instrument

The duck herself quacked along with the violin and the oboe, almost in rhythm with it, but he did not let that influence him. He wrote down all the instruments he had heard in his notebook, and thought some more about them. "I really don't know yet which one I would like to play all the time, except I liked it when Rosie played the recorder. Wouldn't the piano help me get started reading music too?"

"Sounds good. We'll put you down for lessons on the recorder. Your teacher for that is not here right now, but can get in touch with you soon. After some recorder lessons, we'll see if you still want to learn the piano or maybe something else. Who knows? Because you have all eternity to learn, you might learn many instruments.

"Now let's take the grand tour." So the guide led him through the building, Orpie, Jake and the duck following. He looked at practice sessions, a master class on violin, viola, and cello, teachers and students on violin, flute, and horn, a composition class taught by Beethoven, another by Berlioz, a Stradivarius original being made, and many other activities in the building. After bringing them back to the door where they came in, the guide said, "We'll see you many times. After all, there is so much available to you here in eternity."

"We need to get back to the auditorium," Orpie said, "so your teacher doesn't wonder where you are. As if he didn't know already, writing out your schedule as he did. There are still some things to do after we eat." Once again, all got into the car and she drove it by flying the shortest route to the auditorium.

Once there, after a lunch with all the others, Jaden asked to go to the temple before going anywhere else. A bright path opened up to it, and they all went there. When they got there, he showed the duck how to bow her head, spreading her wings out in worship. She quacked and the others sang in worship.

They noticed that they were not alone in their worship, but other people and even a few animals had entered, the animals with human beings who seemed to be showing them how to kneel or bow as they worshiped. After a while, feeling refreshed, they left quietly while others stayed in worship.

"Orpie, it wasn't really quiet in the temple, but it seemed that way," Jaden said.

"That's because we were all thinking about the Father," she replied.

"Jaden, we're going to take you to your next stop on your list, and then you will be on your own for a while. I think that you will find that you want to stay there." Orpie smiled as she said that. Sure enough, when he looked at number 2, he noticed auditorium and lunch.

Number 3 showed Creation Library. The thing he had mentioned most frequently after getting to know Jesus on Earth, was that he would have liked to have been there when God created the heavens, the stars, and the angels.

He had dreamed about exploring space, things outside the Earth, seeing if God had made life on other planets and if so, what life on those planets was like. He wasn't too sure if the films he'd heard about would have got it right. Now he had the chance to look into it, and it would be for real, whatever it was.

Orpie looked at him. "I remember you drawing pictures of some of the stars. I think you named stars you saw and some you drew. You could start there."

"Just what I was thinking," he answered. "I would think that's in the Creation building. Drop me off there, and I'll see you later after we go back to the school."

Jaden watched some type of three-dimensional film of God creating the heavens. He saw huge balls of fire going out of God's hands and getting hung in galaxies. Then he saw the angels begin to sing praises to God in heaven. His notes filled some of his pages, drawings other pages.

Looking up, he began to see the ceiling fill up with stars as if he were in a huge planetarium. As he looked at one galaxy, it was as if a portal opened up for him to look through into a hub in the galaxy, and he saw the stars of that galaxy whirling around him in their paths.

When he got nearer while looking, he seemed to get near to one sun and land on a planet in that sun's solar system. Looking more closely, he saw that the planet had some creatures on it.

Then he was taken back through the solar system, through the hub of the galaxy, and got a glimpse of the galaxy again as the portal seemed to close. He made a drawing of the galaxy and drew some of the creatures on that planet.

A guide touched his hand and said, "Son, what do you think of all this? Remember this is just the start of creation. What you saw took place before man was created. You didn't see some things being created, and then you saw creatures. You only saw what you were interested in."

He turned, and saw Moses. "I was thinking, did you actually get to see what I just saw, even before you wrote the books? I mean, it looks like God made this a long time ago for people to see."

"You got the idea, child, except that I was born a long time after Moses. People say I look like him, but

I'm a descendant of his. I was part of the Sanhedrin, which is all descendants of Moses, when I was on earth. After I got here I asked Moses about his experience.

"When you think about it, the Bible doesn't even mention half of what he saw when he visited with God. I still don't understand it all, and I've looked at all these videos and then some, read many of the books in this library, even writing some of them, and the more I learn the more questions I ask."

"Well, you've certainly helped answer some of my questions. I'd like to see some of the books and maybe check out a book or two."

As Jaden said this, a bright path opened up in the building, leading to a section marked stars and galaxies. One section stood out for him, with one of the books was facing out from the shelf. Its cover had a picture of the galaxy that Jaden drew. "Does this mean I should check this one out?" Jaden asked. "Let me show you my drawing."

The man answered, "Of course, son. That's the way this system works. You looked at the video of creation and stopped at creation of stars and angels. The path led you exactly to what you had looked at. That's how it's designed, so it's easier to find the information you need. Instead of having an index, it lights the way to the book or video you need."

Just then another path lit up. Jaden followed it and found another book on a shelf facing him. On the cover of the book was the name of a planet and inside were pictures of the creatures he had seen.

So Jaden checked out both books. The guide led him out of the building. As he was coming out, he thought that he would like to make something for Orpie as a thank you gift for letting him live with her. He looked at his list, and found the number 4 next to one of the stores. It was near the Creation Building.

He saw again that as he mentioned the store, the path lit up towards the place he wanted to visit. He looked at the instructions on his list for how to pay for the things from the store. The note said, "I have given you an unlimited account according to my riches in glory by Christ Jesus, [signed] Your Heavenly Father." He laughed when he saw the note, and hurried inside the store.

When he entered the store, he saw many people browsing, and others walking with a purpose to one section of the store. He thought of something he saw Orpie use a lot on Earth, and then saw that a part of the store seemed brighter than the rest, so he made his way there.

Sure enough. A section of the store had fabric and needles, thread, and other things, neatly packaged up. In fact, he saw a package labeled "for Orpie from Jaden." It had bright fabric in a very soft weave, and seemed ready to use. He picked up the package, wondering how it got wrapped up so fast when he had just thought of it.

Then he thought of something to make for Jeb and something else for Rosie. As soon as he thought of each, a path lit up for the things to make for each of them. Again he found a package with his name on it at each location, one labeled "for Jeb from Jaden", and the other labeled "for Rosie from Jaden". Both kits had instructions, a complete set of parts, and tools to make them. Feeling ready to check out, he went to the lanes. He handed the cashier his list with the note at the bottom.

The cashier took a look at the sheet and laughed. "Child," she said, "When you got here everything in this city that you need became available to you with that signature.

"We're all children of our heavenly Father. We all freely give as He has given us. Each time you come into a store like this, you will find that what you want packaged up for you as soon as you think of it, for our Father tells someone else of your need right away, and that person gets it ready for you. Your account will always be good here wherever you go."

Shaking his head in wonder, weeping tears of joy, Jaden went on his way. The next stop was the auditorium, as before. Again, when he pictured it, the path lit up for him. When he got there, he found Hannah and Chong waiting, some guides coming up with other children, and the teacher collecting lists, notebooks, pens, and pencils as the children came up.

"Children," he said, "our school day is almost over. Before we go back to school, get together with your friends and share some of what you found out. After all of you have been sharing for a little while, we will head back to the school, where your parents or relatives have brought some food to share for all of you. Some of you may find your animal friends there, and we will have food for your animal friends, also."

After sharing with Hannah and Chong, Jaden went with them to the teacher, where the other children were starting to gather again.

Some guides were with children who did not yet know any others and listened as their children shared what they saw and then led their children back to the teacher. Everyone had someone to share with, and everyone had a chance to listen to the discoveries others had made. As it happened, no two children went to exactly the same place. So, they had much to learn and share.

After all were together, a lit path led them out the gate toward the school. Again, the distance to their school seemed very short as they seemed to almost fly there.

Getting back to the school, they found the room was filled with the aroma of many kinds of food.

Vegetables smelling like roast beef or fish were on one table, next to other vegetables that he knew. Many kinds of fruit were on another table.

Many tables and chairs were scattered throughout the room. Parents and relatives helped the children put their projects near their chairs and then put food on their plates. Not sure which ones to take, Jaden helped himself to two vegetables and two pieces of fruit. He found himself seated at a table with Orpie, Chong, Hannah, Jeb, and one other adult and child.

After dinner, Orpie and Jaden went back to her mansion. Jaden carried all his packages, books, and notebook. Even though it seemed like much, he found he could handle them with little effort.

After he came into his own room, he sorted out the packages. He decided he'd give Orpie her gift right away. When he looked at the kits for Jeb's and Rosie's gifts, he decided he would start Rosie's first and later do Jeb's.

When Jaden found the door to Orpie's sewing room closed, he knocked on the door. When she let him, he held out the package. "Orpie," he said, "I wanted to give you this because I love you so much. You took me into your mansion so I would not live here by myself. Thank you so much for all you mean to me."

When she opened the package, Orpie discovered it was fabric for a delicate throw quilt. The pattern was so much like one she had seen as a child she burst into tears, which lasted such a short time that it was hard to tell she cried at all.

"Jaden, your package shows the Father's love for both of us so much. I had a quilt made from fabric like this when I was a little girl. I loved it so much that it wore out. When my mother threw it away, I was so upset. Thank you so much. I'll make it look like that old quilt when it was new. It'll remind us of our

Father's love for us."

"Could I help you? So I could learn to sew a little?"

"Sure," she said. "I love sharing my skills with you. I think there's even a place at the school where we could work with others who are sewing as well."

After that they talked some more until they both got tired. He found that even though he wanted to start the gift for Jeb right away, he was simply too sleepy to do so. Remembering the amusement park, he knew that would have to wait, too. Before he went to sleep, he prayed, thanking the Father for his goodness in letting him live with Orpie and make things for Jeb and Rosie. Before he could finish his thank you list, he was asleep.

On earth, Jamal and Susan and their spouses went back to their homes, taking with them one thing to remind them of Jaden. At first they did not want to do that, but their parents insisted that they do this.

After their children had left, his parents decided they would look at some of his school work. They found a notebook on his dresser, separate from the rest of his school books and papers. Joanna opened it up. In Jaden's third grade scrawl, she saw the date April 30, followed by a few lines of writing, big like his handwriting sheets were. She read it out loud to her husband Tony. Tears went down her cheeks when she read, "Today Jesus said to me, 'Jaden, you are going to do some good things for me. Some of the things I show you today are things that will happen soon. Some of the things you see are about you and some about your parents after you leave them. Be happy and trust me no matter what happens.'"

She remembered some things they had talked about with him after that day. He said some things to her about Orpie and other people that she knew, telling her that they would see them in heaven. He said Jesus was really a king and wanted people to love Him always.

One time before Christmas he said that it would be great to see Jesus at Easter when He rose from the grave. How he wished he had been there to see the empty tomb on that day!

When they saw him limping, struggling to keep up with the other children, they reminded Jaden that he could ride his bike and get along just fine. After they told him that, he had no trouble keeping up with the other bicycle riders as they rode along the bike trails.

After remembering this, they went to sleep smiling and thanking Jesus for him.

Chapter Eight Surprises

Orpie woke up Jaden with a breakfast tray in her hands. The aroma of the food filled the room so much he thought he was in heaven. When he opened his eyes, he realized he was in heaven.

During his sleep, he had dreams of things on earth that had been sad to him. While he slept, he felt God wiping tears from his eyes. So when he saw the tray filled with fruit smelling and tasting like crullers, a coconut with two straws stuck in it, his favorite nuts, and some cooked vegetable that looked and tasted like the best omelet he had ever had, he felt like God had really healed him of everything.

"After we eat," Orpie said, "it's time to go back to the River of Life. God wants to heal us of more of the things that were wrong on earth. Not only is it a good place to splash and play, but it's a place where some of these fruits and the vegetables that taste like meat come from. After we eat, others will join us. You're already dressed, as you've seen. We will have our Bible story time together today."

They read about how the blind man's sight was restored when he asked Jesus to heal him. Then they read Isaiah 61 and Luke 4 about the anointing on Jesus to heal the sick. After talking about it for a while, they heard a knock on the door. Jaden ran to the door. When he opened it, he saw a man he recognized from his time on Earth. "Benjamin," he said. "How good to see you. Didn't you carry one of those canes last time I saw you?"

He laughed. "Of course I did. I was blind from birth. Soon after you saw me, some friends took me to someone who prayed for blind people. My eyes were healed. I could see. They took me to him because he prayed in the name of Jesus and things happened. I could see for the first time ever. Now I'm one of the people who take others to special spots in the River of Life. I'll be your guide. You could call me one of your teachers."

Then he opened the door again, and Rosie, Jeb, Jake, Chong and Hannah came in. At first, it seemed as if all were talking at once as they again shared their stories of what they learned the day before.

While they talked, he remembered his gifts for Rosie and Jeb. Under cover of the talking, he said to Orpie, "I brought kits to make stuff for Rosie and Jeb, but I don't know how to use the tools. Do you know someone who can help me?" They went into his room, and he showed her the kits.

"Oh, that's easy," she said. "Two of the teachers at the school did things like that on Earth. When we get there, I can show you who they are."

From the front room, they heard Benjamin's voice. "It's time to go to the River of Life. Take everything you brought here with you." He led the way along a path that seemed brighter than the others.

Jaden noticed that he no longer had grey hair, but had rich brown hair that glowed even in the bright light. His shoes seemed to be almost sheer, made of something that appeared as soft as a moccasin.

As he led the way, Benjamin started to describe where they were going. "Off to your right, you can see mansions of those who threw themselves into evangelism. The largest is that of someone who won only one person to the Lord in his lifetime, but spent all that he had to give out tracts to people he saw. Many people, not all, accepted his tracts from him, and later came to know the Lord because of what this man did. On Earth people often passed him by because he was homeless. Once he gave me a tract. To my sorrow, I was not the one he led to the Lord."

They looked at it. It almost seemed to reach as

high as a six-story building on earth. The outside gleamed like jewels with the gold of the stones on the outside. Transparent windows made of one stone lit up the inside of the mansion.

The walls of the rooms they saw as they walked by glittered with reflected light from facets of single stones on the walls. Sheer draperies in all colors of the rainbow and many other colors besides framed the windows. The sounds of many instruments could be heard from inside the mansion. It seemed as if an entire orchestra were playing in the home as many played for those within.

After looking inside for a while, they followed Benjamin down a path with gold stones that led down a small bank to a shallow stream. "This is a part of the River of Life that you may wish to visit often." Jaden looked around, seeing fruit trees and small plants on both sides of the stream.

He thought about picking a piece of the fruit near him, and found he had it in his hand. Taking a bite, he found it to be the flavor of pumpkin pie, not quite pear-shaped, and juicy. Some of the juice dribbled down his chin and onto his garment, but when he felt his chin, it was not sticky, and saw nothing on his garment.

"Come into the stream," Benjamin said, "and taste of God's goodness. Let him open your eyes to more of what is here for you." One by one, all went into the stream. They found they could float, sit on the water in the middle of the stream while the water drifted by them, and even find a lower layer of water to rest on in the flow of water.

In this stream, farther from the Throne of God than the first branch Jaden swam in, fish came up to them, poking snouts at them. He reached out to one, petting it, and finding that it seemed to enjoy the touch of his hand. For a brief time he talked to it.

While he talked, they swam and jumped, making bubbles.

Again, as with the duck, he heard himself making sounds unlike the words that he was thinking. They made sounds back at him, and he understood them, too. Then he remembered what Jesus had said about giving him a new language for the duck and thought He had done it with the fish as well.

When he left the stream, he saw many more colors than he saw when he first got here. In turn, when he first came here, Jaden had seen many more colors than when he was on Earth. He began wondering if there was a way of mixing colors of paint to come close to the colors he was seeing. He heard better now also.

After they left the River of Life, Benjamin led his group back to the school. He had his kit for Rosie with him, but had left the kit for Jeb in the mansion when he saw Jeb was coming with them. When they got to the school, he saw workbenches set up in one area, sewing machines set up in another area, and supplies of colorful beads and tools in another.

Each area had at least two people in them already, an adult paired up with a child. He looked for the chair with his name on it, and found it in the section with tools and beads. When he opened up the kit, he found he had beads, small pliers, and several other tools he did not recognize. Across the table from him he saw a colorfully dressed person wearing many pieces of jewelry.

"Hi, Jaden," she said. "I'm Caroletta. On Earth I didn't wear jewelry, but I always wanted to. Instead I made a few things for rich people to wear. Now I get to help other people make jewelry and other fancy things. When I heard that you wanted to make something for Rosie, I knew I had to help you. Do you have any idea what she might like?"

"I'm not sure," Jaden said, "but I think that she might like something special for her mansion, something that might blend in with her walls." After they discussed it for a while, they looked through the kit Jaden had picked up, finding many colorful gems which seemed to go well together. She had him make some drawings, trying different colors, until Jaden thought he had a good design.

Soon they were getting hungry, and saw people bringing in plates of food. Some were people Benjamin had pointed out to them on the way back from the River of Life. He was asked to lead the prayer over the food. They helped themselves to what they wanted. Jaden saw that he was eating food like lamb and cheese with moussaka, and drinking cherry juice.

After lunch, they went through the drawings, selected one, and laid out the beads along the design. Before Jaden realized how fast they were working on it, they had put his design together, stringing and weaving it, and making a seam for it to be hung on her wall. They saw they had everything they needed in his kit.

Caroletta would demonstrate something, and his hands seemed to fly as he followed her instructions, it was so easy. Later he took the drawings to the mansion with him, planning how he would give the wall hanging to Rosie.

After his project was done, he went to his garden talking to and feeding the ducks, and sharing in prayer with Jesus how much he loved the day he had.

Coming back to the mansion and picking up some of his ride tickets, he asked Orpie if she would come with him to the amusement park. When she agreed, they both went there. The rides he tried this time were "Parallel Universe" and "Ocean Wave Roller Coaster."

In the Parallel Universe ride, Jaden traveled to a number of places on Earth. It did not seem like what he had known. People were doing good things to each other, but still left the planet after many years, coming to a welcome party in heaven. He got out of the vehicle and walked around. Finally he was taken back.

Ocean Wave Roller Coaster was better. He was on a seat with Orpie. Friends from school sat in front of and behind them. As they rode the roller coaster, they were taken all around the park and the nearby neighborhood. They saw brilliantly colored mansions and trees of every kind. But best of all, it went higher than any roller coaster he had been on or seen, having much deeper curves as well.

Later they went back to the mansion, and had a meal of vegetables that tasted like mulligatawny and fruit that tasted like baklava.

Before he got sleepy, there was a knock on the door. Opening it, he saw some of his friends from Orientation School, on scooters, with an extra one in tow. Chong said, "When we were asked to think of something special to make for someone we knew, I just knew I had to get someone to help me make the scooter for you, and here it is."

Jaden hugged Chong, and they all played on their scooters until they were tired.

Then he went back to Orpie. He told her about the times he worked with his dad on his workshop projects. He remembered handing him the tools while he repaired a chair.

"Your dad told me about the time you got up onto the work table. You were reaching for his toolbox to bring it to him. Remember that?"

"Now I do, but on Earth it was just something they told me I had done. I was about three years old, I think. I could barely climb on the table. Anyway, I was trying to help Dad."

"Yes. Now that reminds me about the kit for Jeb. I don't think you'll be able to do it right away, but the instructor for his kit should be in some time during Orientation School when they have another day like today. If not, when you are in your regular school later."

Before Jaden got sleepy, he spent some time in prayer and asked the Father about some of the things he wanted to learn.

Chapter Nine Bible Stories in Action

When Jaden got up the next day, he heard some children shouting, "Wake up, Jaden. Jesus is here. He brought some disciples and we're going for a boat ride."

"I'm coming," he said. "Orpie, how about a piece of fruit to take with me?"

"Check the tree, I think you'll find some in easy reach."

When he got out the door of the mansion, he found some ripe fruit on it, picked something that looked much like a pear, and ate it. "Mm," he said. "It tastes like bread with cheese and honey. I wonder what today will bring."

Jesus looked at him, smiling, and went up to hug him. He stopped at the mansion door and chatted with Orpie. She smiled and laughed with Him for a while, and then the children gathered around Jesus and the disciples.

Jesus said, "Today we're going to visit some places here that look much like where I lived on Earth. When we get there, you'll be in a drama with us."

"Yay!" they all shouted.

"This is so that people can see what children did when I walked on Earth. I did so many things with children, and not all were written in the Bible. There is no room anywhere for all the books that could have been written."

Soon they got to a big lake with some boats on it. There were some nets on the shore, and two of the disciples went to work on the nets.

Some people started gathering around Jesus, and He started to tell them some things. Very soon the shore got very crowded. The children tried to get into the boats, but Jesus told them to wait.

As many people gathered on the shore, He told them, "Today I am showing you what it looked like when I was teaching on the earth and healing people. I've asked the children to help me, and you see my disciples here also. Peter and John are at the nets, and the rest of them are among you. I have asked them to wear things a little like they wore some of those days.

"When I called Peter and John, they were at a lake much like this, but even bigger. They did not have fishing poles, but big nets. They were in the business of catching fish. They knew a lot about how to catch fish, but the fish were not coming into the nets.

"Fish are like people. You have to get their attention to get them to do something. The Father told me to call the fish to the side of one boat. I called out, 'Have you caught any fish?'"

Peter answered, "No, master, we have toiled all night, and caught nothing."

While Jesus had been talking, the boats were leaving shore, with nets showing on the sides of the boats. There were three people in each of the boats.

Jesus called out, "Let down your nets into the deep, and you will catch some fish."

Peter said, "We have toiled all night, but at your word we will let down our net."

They let down their net. Even as they were letting it down, Jaden could see the fish swimming into the net. As in the narrative they read in the Bible, Peter called out for help, saying their net was breaking.

The other boats came to their rescue, but Peter jumped into the water right after he said that, and swam to shore. He fell at Jesus' feet, worshiping Him. "Master," he said, "Every time you provided more fish than we needed to sell for our livelihood. You gave us more than enough for our families. Thank you for allowing me to fish for men for you."

Laughing, Jesus said, "My Father wanted you to come with me, and so did I. We had such a good time recruiting people for His kingdom. You are now in the joy of the Lord. Now help bring the fish to shore. We'll use them and the fruit these people have gladly brought for a feast."

After the feast, each person found that they had extra to bring back to their mansions or eat while they walked to the next place Jesus led them to. He brought them to a hillside. Orpie came to Jaden with some fish and bread. "Jaden, this is your lunch," she said. "You may be here all day and get hungry again." Jaden looked around, and saw some other children. He joined them.

Some parents went to their children and said, "Come with us. We want Jesus to bless you." Others simply brought their children to Jesus. He looked around for Orpie, but she was not there.

As those children went to Jesus with their parents, some of the disciples said, "Jesus, send these children away."

But Jesus said, "Let these children come to me, for people like children are part of the kingdom of God." Then he laid his hands on the children and blessed them. To some of them he said, "You are going to go to faraway places here in heaven, but I will be with you."

To others he said, "You will think great things and see them happen, for my Father needs many like you."

Seeing Jaden watching, he also called him and blessed him, saying, "It doesn't matter how long you were on Earth, whether you had a short or a long life. Your life matters, and you will yet touch many because you obeyed while you were on Earth. Enjoy the fruit of your obedience."

Then the disciples who tried to send the children away came to Jesus and worshiped him, saying, "Lord, we thank you for forgiving us when we wanted to send the children away. You gave us many children to teach during our lives and even now you allow us to watch what you do with children. You're so great and merciful to us. Thank you for your love."

To those disciples, Jesus said, "What you did, you thought was to protect me. My Father saw your love for Him, and that you would come to love these little ones even as you love yourselves. He also showed you that through children like these He would reach many for me.

"Rejoice in my Father's love. After my resurrection, you reached many children for me because of the Father's love for these, even those who were orphans or fatherless. He has rewarded you greatly for this."

Jaden asked, "Now may we ride in the boats?"

Jesus said, "Sure. The disciples will take a few of you in each boat." Jaden and three other children hopped in with Peter and John. The others went in the other boats. Jesus told the disciples to sail to the other side of the lake.

Many who had eaten lunch with them, when they saw the boats leaving shore and going to the other side of the lake, walked around to the other side of the lake. Those who had leftover food ate it on the way to the dock.

After the boats landed, people went up to Jesus, telling all how he had healed them in a place much like this one. Those who had been blind on Earth demonstrated their sight by describing something far away. Those who had been lame leaped and ran, showing how fast they could run. Those whose who had had hunched backs showed how far they could bend over and stretch with no pain. Jaden showed how straight his feet now were.

After several hundred had talked and Jesus had taught for a long time, He was beginning to get hungry, and others began to look for some nearby mansions or fruit trees or gardens. There were none.

Jesus called some of the disciples to him, and told them, "Find out how much food we have in the crowd." (They had been telling him to send away the people so they could look for food in a place where there were mansions, not near a lake with no homes.)

So four of the disciples went through the crowd, seeing if anyone had any food. Andrew came to Jaden, who told him, "I have some food," and gave him the fish and bread.

After thanking him, Andrew went to Jesus and said, "I found a boy with two fish and five loaves of bread, but what is that among so many here?"

Jesus replied, "Tell the people to sit down on the grass by fifties." And they sat down. He sat on the grass with Chong and Hannah.

After all were seated, Jesus took the loaves and the fish, thanked the Father for them, blessed them, and broke them up, giving the pieces to the disciples to give to the people.

He watched the disciples go out into the crowd, and handing groups of fifty pieces of fish and bread. As they gave food to the fifties, the men handed out the food to their groups, who also broke the fish and bread into pieces. It seemed that the bread they had stayed the same size, when they broke off the pieces, and all the fish stayed the same size, no matter how many times they broke off pieces from each. Jaden and all the others ate until they were full.

Jesus told the disciples to pick up the leftovers. They gathered twelve baskets. "Give the baskets to your families," he told the children, "as a reminder of how the Father provides for his children. There's enough in these baskets for your family to eat when you get back to your home. Now it's time for the school children to go to school."

One by one the children went up to Jesus and received their baskets, then found their family members. Jaden brought his basket to Jeb, who said that he and Rosie would join them for supper after school was over.

As Orpie and Jaden left the site, they saw a path that seemed brighter than the others. Following it, they quickly found themselves back at the school. Walking in, Jaden found two new teachers there.

One of the teachers came up to him and said, "Hello, Jaden. I'm Samuel and I'm here to get you started on math. I can see that you're not as excited about this as your other teachers have reported to me on other subjects, but we'll see how well you do.

"First tell me about your experience with multiplication today. You were in the feeding of the five thousand plus women and children, right? So, including women and children, how many groups of fifty were there? And how many people were fed with your lunch, not counting what people took home for their families?"

After Jaden answered those questions, they went on to other examples in the Bible of how God demonstrated basic math in telling about people's activities in the miracles and everyday life in the Bible. As they talked, Samuel discovered Jaden had a good grasp of addition, multiplication, division, and subtraction, measuring, and basic geometry.

"Well, Jaden," he said near the end of their time together, "I think we can start you on learning some more geometry, especially applying it to helping Orpie with her quilt.

"When you make a quilt, you have to know how big to make each piece, to allow for stitching it together into blocks, and how big to make the blocks for the quilt to be the right size. Orpie's a good teacher for this. So your homework for me is to start making a quilt with Orpie. Write down everything you do for it and show me how you two decided each step."

"Now you make arithmetic fun. In school on Earth I didn't learn arithmetic this way. If it keeps on being fun like this, I think I can learn it fast."

"Jaden, we're only just beginning. In music, you'll learn another way to make arithmetic fun. When you read music, you'll use arithmetic too. But after you've been doing it awhile, you'll not even think about the arithmetic in music because it will be so much a part of how you've grown that it will be just something that makes music fun."

"Sounds better than the arithmetic at my old school on Earth," Jaden replied. "That's part of what I was shown in my vision, too."

When they were done, it was time for Jaden to leave the school. He and Orpie left together and took the bright path, which this time led them to Rosie's mansion. When they got there, Rosie opened the door first, before they even knocked.

"Welcome. I have a special visitor. He just got here from Earth, but I think you might know of him." They looked behind Rosie and saw on her couch Jaden's favorite musician, a man who played violin and other instruments as well. On Earth, sometimes when Jaden went to concerts with his parents, he would see him playing with other violinists and sometimes playing solos. He remembered crying one time during a concert when the music was over, because he had wanted to keep on listening to him. Jeb and another woman were there also.

"I know who he is!" Jaden shouted. "It's the

man who played for Pascal when he was sick in the hospital that one time. Aren't you Yoshe Schlomo or something like that?"

"Well, I did play violin at a lot of hospitals, and I did not learn your friend's name, but as for my name, you're very close to correct. Yosef Schlomo would be correct. My name was often misspelled in concert programs. This is Katie, my wife on Earth. She's been here a while and was in the homecoming party also. Your aunt Rosie very kindly welcomed us both here after the party.

"I lived a long time on earth, and I heard that you came here just a little over a week ago, Earth time. I was in the hospital at the time, and I knew Jesus was coming for me soon. So I asked him to let me meet you soon after I got here. Rosie told me some things about you too."

"Well, you know how it is with us musicians," Rosie said. "It only takes two to get a worship service going. I told him about your instruments, Jaden, and showed him the recorder and your oboe. He said he wants to teach you the other instrument you chose to learn, piano. Would that be okay?"

"Sure. I know it will help me with the recorder, and the recorder with the piano. But I'd like you to teach me the recorder."

"Yes, that's what the folks at the Composer School asked me to teach you. I'm one of their teachers more than I'm a teacher anywhere else. I can't think of a better way to get to know you well than by helping you learn music," Rosie said.

He asked, "Did you enjoy your welcome party? Did Father Abraham dance with you? A lot of people danced with me at my welcome party. Did everyone dance with you at your welcome party? Did you know a lot of people there? Have you been to the River of Life yet?"

Yosef laughed. "That's a lot of questions. The welcome party was more than I dreamed of when I thought of being here. Rosie and Jeb took me to the River of Life first thing after I saw Jesus, and it seemed like I danced all day, I had so many people I saw and danced with. I think everyone danced with me. I don't know if I know a lot of people yet, but I saw a lot of them at the party. My body feels so good. I know I feel and look very young."

Orpie asked, "Have you been to your mansion yet? Jeb worked a little on it, but other friends of yours really put it together for you. I put a little in because of the help you were to me during the war, but the others were given so many materials for it because of all the ways you served the Father during your life."

"Not yet, Liebschen. Katie is taking me, though. To me you were my little girl during some of those years, and I still think of you that way. I've heard it's not that far from yours. I am getting tired and would like to go there and rest after a busy first day here."

"Of course," Rosie said. "We'll walk with you there and then leave you two. We'll see you whenever we want or you want. We have all eternity to visit back and forth, after all."

Orpie and Jaden walked with them as far as her mansion. Rosie walked with them to their mansion. She was later seen coming back, wiping tears of joy from her eyes. Jesus later came and visited with them. Then they had a long reunion after their many years of separation.

Meanwhile, Jeb brought the basket of fish and bread leftovers to Orpie's mansion. He heated up the fish, and set the table for four. When he heard everyone talking, he went out to greet them and the four of them had a feast.

After dinner, Jaden took out a game, Heaven's

Borders, from his room. After reading the directions, they played two rounds of the game before calling it quits. In the first round, Orpie was the winner, and in the second round Jeb won.

Then Rosie and Jeb went their separate ways for rest, agreeing to come back in the morning.

Chapter Ten Planning

Jaden woke up the next day thinking it was time to get organized. School seemed a little disorganized, with no set times for activities and things that he felt he needed to learn.

So he got out the notebook he received on the day he went to the Creation library. In it he wrote down the title Things I Want to Learn First in Heaven (Besides School Stuff Like on Earth). As he was writing things down, if he did not spell a word correctly, he was shown the correct way to spell it, and changed it with his eraser.

This is what his list looked like:

1. How often do I get to go to the throne room? I'd like to go every day.

2. How can I get to visit people from places like where Chong used to live, other than school?

3. What do the sashes mean when people wear them?

4. Who can I talk to about ways to get around in heaven?

5. What classes, if any, do I need to start taking at the University of Leadership now?

6. Schedule recorder and piano lessons.

7. Schedule practice times for piano, and find out where.

8. What was it like to live before things I used?

9. How can I visit with Noah and other people I want to meet?

10. Where can I listen to sermons by good preachers and then hear Jesus right after the sermon?

11. Where are the special auditoriums for speakers I hear about?

12. Where's a place for ball games?

13. Where can I meet people who did special

things, like maybe build the temple or churches?

14. I'd like to learn different games and maybe find out other things I'm good at.

While Jaden was working on his list, Orpie came in. She asked him, "What are you doing? Is it something I can help you with?"

"Oh, Grandma, hi. I was working on a list of things I want to find out, like what I can learn and where I can go. They didn't mention this at school yet. I really want to visit the throne room a lot. I just don't know how to do it. I want to go there every day, if I can.

"Then there's all the people I'd like to visit or hear sermons from or ask about things they made. I want to know how to arrange for that stuff. Then there's the recorder and piano lessons and stuff. Here, take a look."

Orpie looked at his list and said, "That's quite a big list. It sounds like you feel you've been on vacation and want to get to work, except for the throne room. Is that right?"

"Yes, it does feel that way. Even the things we've done at school have been so fun, it doesn't feel like school."

"We can talk about some of those things right now. Some of the colors of the sashes have to do with the fruit of the Spirit people were known for during the life. Each fruit has a different color. The man you met who wore a blue sash was known for patience and grace during his time on Earth. You'd have to ask other people what I was known for on Earth to understand the meaning of my sash. Other sashes mean something else.

"As to going to the throne room, one way to get there is to picture it and a path lights up for you. As for how often you can go there, that really is something God delights in for you, and longs to hear from you. It may be that this longing you put on your paper has something to do with your assignment. Go with it."

"Great," Jaden said. "I do want to go every day, and I'll ask God when I can go each day."

"Now about all these questions about how to meet people and visiting people who lived in other parts of the world, there are a number of ways. Heaven is a big place, and you can visit many parts of heaven without going to New Jerusalem. You think about where you'd like to visit, and a path opens up or maybe you fly or take a boat. It depends on where you're going and what the Father's pleasure is for you."

"How often can I visit with Jesus?"

"As often as you want and in whatever way you choose. Remember, Jesus lives in your heart here in heaven, just as He did when you were on earth. But to see Him as King, you may want to visit Him in the throne room, and to see Him as teacher of little children like you are, you can still be part of the group that Jesus teaches every day here.

"You really have a lot of questions on this sheet of paper. Sounds like you want to visit Rosie and your piano teacher and get some practice time in on the piano at the Composer's School rather often. Why don't we go see Rosie and maybe get to school a little later?"

"Can we do that? I thought that schools should have regular times to meet and set times for classes and all that."

"They do and they don't. Your school is like an orientation school here in heaven. You're still getting used to heaven. Every once in a while we do have a regular class there for crafts and things like that, like you did with making Rosie's gift, and you will for Jeb's gift.

"However, you're still choosing what you will do for a time here in heaven, and discovering what you will do. My Orientation School lasted at least a month Earth time, and I think that's how long yours will last."

"Great. Sounds like I need some help planning where to go for learning what I need to know."

"Right. Remember the person who talked to you about arithmetic? He's a visiting teacher from a school that's even bigger than the one you've been going to. The classes there are for those who are interested in learning science as it really is, not as science was taught on Earth.

"You see, what people learned before they got here was based on what they could see with microscopes and telescopes, things like that. It was also based on what people can hear.

"What we saw and heard on Earth is just a fraction of what we see and hear in heaven. It was all we had without knowing God. When we got to know Jesus we added the spiritual realm to how we learned.

"When you went to school on Earth, you didn't get as far as fractions and atoms and electrons or microscopes. But if you want to learn that kind of science, there is a school here in heaven for it. In fact, there are many schools for it here in heaven, because the truth about what God made and how he made it is so vast it will take all of eternity for those of us who are interested in finding out about this to get to know even a small portion of it."

"You're right, Grandma Orpie. There are a lot of things I can learn, and so many things to explore. I already have ideas about what I need to learn. Where do I go for sermons to listen to?"

"Instead of talking, let's get breakfast from the tree and leave for one right now. This is one of the ways, and we'll talk about others on the way there. Now who would you like to hear?"

"The youth pastor of the church I went to who died before I was born."

"I've seen him speak in a park near here. Get some fruit and let's ask God to show us the path to hear him." Before Orpie was done speaking, a path lit up and they were on their way. In a second Earth time, but seeming longer there, they were outside an auditorium.

A sign on the outside showed, "Explore the lives of Jesus and Old Testament and New Testament people. James Stettler, Owen Master, and others lead you through play and other media so you can get to know what their lives were like.

Opening the door, they found that many children were there, playing with puppets and other things. As they entered, they saw a man at the center of the auditorium, standing on a platform. While they watched, he rapped for attention. "Children, it's time to get started now. Each one of you take a puppet. If you're new here, the puppets are off to my left. We'll talk about them in a little while."

They each picked up a puppet. Jaden a donkey, and Orpie's a rooster. Some children had people, but most had animals. In the center of the stage, next to the man, was a boat.

"Can anyone guess who we're talking about today?" the man asked.

"Jesus!" "Adam!" "Moses!" "Noah!" All the children were answering at once, but somehow the man sorted out the answers.

"It's not Jesus. It's not Adam. It's not Moses. Those of you who said, 'Noah,' you are right," the man answered. "Today we're going to talk about how Noah preached repentance and how the animals got on the ark. You will get to put your animals and people on the ark. Are you ready?"

"Yes!" they all said.

"Here's how it all started. God created the heavens and earth, animals, fish, plants, birds, stars, and everything in the heavens and on earth. Then he created Adam and Eve, and they disobeyed God. But they still had children. Some of their children listened to God, but most did not. One of their children, Seth, was a great-great-great something grandfather of Noah. Noah learned to listen to God and pray to Him. But most people on earth did not like God. They knew they should listen to God, but they did their own thing and sinned.

"Earth got so bad because of people sinning that God was sorry that he made them. But Noah found favor with God. So God made a way to save Noah and his family. What was that way?"

"Jesus!" many said.

"Not Jesus. He had not been born yet. What was it?"

"A boat!" others said.

"Yes, it was a boat, a special big one called an ark. It looked like this boat, but it was much bigger, and could hold many animals but just eight people. Noah worked on the ark for a long time, one hundred twenty years, in fact. During that time he talked to many people about repenting and getting right with God, for the time was short.

"Most laughed. Many came from around the world, but still laughed. Noah's wife, his three sons, and their wives were the only people who listened. Even the people who were not his sons or their wives who worked on the ark did not listen.

"Finally the one hundred twenty years was up. The last board was in and the ark was watertight. Noah lived in a country that had never known rain, but God said there would be rain.

"He told Noah to put food for each animal and all the people in the ark. He said to put in enough food for a whole year for all the animals and people. When the ark was finished, God spoke to two animals of each kind and seven of the clean kinds, telling them to go to Noah.

"Look at the name of your animal or the name of your person. When I say the name of your animal, bring it up and put it in the ark. When I say the name of your person, bring your person to the ark."

The children and Orpie looked at the name of their puppets and waited expectantly.

"Noah, Shem, Ham, and Japheth, and their wives waited at the ark for all the animals to start coming." Eight children brought their puppets and placed them in the ark.

"Aardvarks, chickens and roosters, ants, buffalo, deer, elephants, giraffes, and bees of every kind came to the ark. Noah and his sons and their wives led them to the cage where they were to stay. Doves, ravens, robins, llamas, hippopotamuses, dinosaurs, pelicans, iguanas, lizards, snakes, cats, and lions of every kind came to the ark. Dodo birds, grasshoppers, locusts, termites, spiders, emus, kangaroos, and worms of every kind came on board.

"Somehow Noah found he had room for all of these and many more. If I didn't mention your person, your person didn't make it. If I didn't mention your animal, bring your animal to the ark, because your animal came on board.

"Even though your person in this Bible true story did not make it onto the ark, remember that you are here because you trusted in Jesus. The people of Noah's day who did believe in God made it onto the ark. You are here because Jesus came to die for you and rose again. Jesus is your ark."

All of the children cheered. When they looked around, Jaden and Orpie saw that none of the children had a puppet of a person left in their hands. All had

had a puppet that made it into the ark.

The man went on to tell of how the rains flooded the earth. He told of underground rivers that flooded, releasing their water. He said that during the flood many volcanoes and huge earthquakes changed the surface of the earth while the flood took place. Riding in the ark safely, Noah and his family were saved. They saw no one else after they landed.

After he finished telling the story, the man hugged many of the children. Jaden and Orpie went up to talk with him. Orpie said, "James, I know you from the church we both attended. You were a fine youth pastor. My grandson wanted to hear you talk, so here we are."

"Yes, Orpie. I came here ten years before you did. When I got here, I asked Jesus to let me teach children as I had when I was on earth. It's my pleasure to keep on doing what I did then, and help children grow and learn here so that when their parents come, they will recognize them. Now this is your grandson? I didn't meet him on Earth, but I was at his party. Jaden, I'm glad to see you."

"I'm happy to see you too. I asked Grandma how I could get to see different people. When she asked who I wanted to see, I mentioned you. See, I heard a lot about you and wanted to meet you and learn from you. I know I'll want to come here a lot."

"I'm surprised you heard about me. Maybe your brother and sister talked about me. Anyway, since everything's about God here in heaven and on earth, we'll be talking a long time about His wonders. Don't forget, we're in eternity now. Time no longer limits us."

"Thank you, James. I think I'd like to find out other ways to meet people today, too. It's been really fun here. I know I'll be back."

As they were leaving the building, Orpie talked with Jaden about one of the other things on Jaden's list. "You said you wanted to find out how to go across heaven to meet people from other countries who never left their countries?"

"Yes. People who learned about Jesus from missionaries, people from other countries."

"I got a guidebook when I arrived here, when my orientation school was almost over. I think you are ready for it. Let's go to my mansion and look through it." With that, a path lit up for them to go back to the mansion. It was less than a second Earth time it when they got back there.

After they had a lunch, he looked at the guidebook, studying it as well as he could, asking for help with words he had not learned yet. He jotted down some of the answers from the guidebook next to his questions.

Then he thought of going back to the Composers' School, and a path lit up. Following the path, he found himself in front of a door in a different section of the building, with a sign, "New Musicians' Entrance."

Entering, he saw a receptionist, a bulletin board with class times, and names of teachers under instrument names. Looking at the list, he found Rosie's name under recorder and Yosef's name under piano. Seeing the names he was writing down, the receptionist told him just to look at the room numbers and he would find himself in the teacher's room.

Jaden decided to go to Rosie first. When he looked at her room number, he found himself in a brightly decorated room with many different recorders, some seeming to be very old, and some seeming to be like the one he brought to Rosie herself. Rosie was sitting in front of a music stand, playing from a music book titled *Songs of the Spirit* by Ada Songstrom.

After Jaden listened for a while, she looked up from the music. "Hi, Jaden," she said. "I'm glad you're here. It's a good time to get you started on the recorder. Here's a music stand to use here. Sit down while I get you a recorder to start with and the music to start on."

She brought a wood recorder with small holes, and a book of music titled *Hymns for C Instruments with Ornamentations and Accompaniments* by Risella Dormier. When Jaden held the instrument for the first time, it felt like it had been made just for him.

During this first lesson, he was shown how to make sounds, then how to finger some notes. After he played for a while, she began teaching him some note values and other things a musician first learns. "Jaden, I want you to set a regular time to practice. I won't tell you how long. If you really love music, your practice time will seem to fly. You may come to my mansion for your lesson if you want it before next week this time. Other than that, just come here about every seven days."

After finishing the lesson, he took the recorder and book with him, and thought about Yosef's room number. He found himself in a piano studio lined with music books.

He could see titles from early hymn writers such as Palestrina, old masters such as Haydn and Handel, hymn writers such as Isaac Watts and Fanny Crosby, twentieth century composers such as Gershwin and Carl Schalk, and many composers not recognized by people outside of heaven because they were not published on earth for reasons known only to God or had long been forgotten by the time Jaden was born.

"Hi Jaden," Yosef said. "Would you like to go to the throne room with me? Heaven is so new to me I just want to soak up the throne room atmosphere today and maybe get some instructions on how to teach you and others. I was thinking also about seeing how violins are made while I was it.

"Rosie took me to Orientation School and then to Composers' School right away, but she said there are many other things to learn in Orientation School. I want so much to be where the action is today, don't you?"

"I do want to visit the throne room a lot, and I was thinking a little like that." With that, they found themselves near the back of the throne room.

On either side of them as they walked from the back to the front of the throne room, they saw rulers sitting on their thrones, reading messages and talking softly. They heard choirs in the background, as Jaden had heard so much from the time he got to heaven, but the voices were more intense in the throne room.

Chairs were placed throughout the room. As they came to the front, they saw Jesus had a chair next to him, the Father had his arms stretched out in Jaden's direction, and the Holy Spirit had a visitor from Earth talking with Him near Jesus. In the middle of the action, Jaden saw angels behind the Father and next to Jesus as he ran up to the Father and sat in His lap.

The Father held him in His arms. He had a fragrance like the earth after a rain shower. While he was with the Father, the Father said to him, "I'd like to share some things with you that your earthly Daddy asked me to have you do and see because your time with him was short."

So while Jaden was talking with the Father, he began to see visions of things he could make, people he could visit in other countries, and leadership training he could take.

He saw his Dad praying and asking God to let Jaden experience things he had not been allowed to experience on earth because his time was so short.

Then he saw where he could go in heaven to see and do the things his Dad was talking about. Most of all, though, he saw that the Father was pleased with Jaden's Dad's prayer.

The Father then set him down and told him to get lunch outside the throne room on his way back to Composers' School, where he had his first piano lesson and was assigned practice times.

He went home to Orpie's mansion, and after visiting with Jeb and Rosie decided to take his bicycle out for a spin. Orpie had told him the bicycle was his, just like the car was hers to use. So he decided to go riding. Thinking he remembered how to ride a bike, he just started pedaling towards the River of Life branch that was in their neighborhood.

Pedaling along, he realized he was going much faster on Earth, but not as fast as when Jeb took him here. He stopped pedaling for a while and found he could in fact go more slowly. But when he wanted to stop at the river, he got confused. The brakes he was used to were on the bike, but he couldn't get them to work.

When he saw someone coming by on another bike, he waved his hand at the person. "How do I stop this bike?" he said. "It's my first time riding one here, and the brakes don't work like the one I had on Earth."

As the person got near to him, he saw it was Jeb. Jeb pulled up alongside him, reached over, and showed him how the brake worked. "I guess I thought you knew current bikes on Earth when you came here. Anyway, now I'm able to show you the rest of the doodads on this thing. Do you want me to show you that before or after you take a dip in the River?"

"After," he answered. So they went for a swim in the river. Seeing some inner tubes on the bank, they rode in them. After floating on those for a while, they just sat in the water and talked. Every so often, they would reach out and pet a passing fish or eat a piece of floating vegetation.

Following him, Jeb showed some of the other gadgets on the bike before they pedaled back to the mansion.

They got there in less than a second Earth time. Both were hungry, and Orpie and Rosie had put out plates and utensils for all of them. It smelled like a good roast beef, with mashed potatoes and honeyed carrots.

After they were finished eating, he gave Rosie her gift, but still had not talked with his teacher for Jeb's gift. For a while, he wondered when he would make it, but realized that there was a time for everything. After Rosie received her gift, they played a few games, including "Walk Through the Garden of Eden" and "How to Enjoy Heaven More."

Later, after Jeb and Rosie had left, he spent some time practicing the recorder, working through several of the songs before he got tired and went to sleep in his room.

Chapter Eleven First Assignment

He woke up thinking about what the Father had told him. He was to go to the Library of the Nations and look up two—Crete and Liberia. This puzzled him, because he knew when he left earth his reading skills were just a little higher than fifth grade level, according to what the teacher and his parents told him. He was not sure how he would understand what he saw, but the Father knew what he was doing.

He was to look at the book on the planet which he had checked out from the Creation Library, and made notes about what planet it really was and how he discovered that. He was to make notes about the creatures as well. Then he was to compare what he discovered with Crete and Liberia about the history of the nations.

Finally, after all that, he was to go to visit the two countries in the Portal Building, and follow it with a visit to the people here who came from them. The Father assured him that he was up to this task, and that he would not be alone in working on it, as He had assigned two helpers to work with him on this task.

As he was hungry, he decided his first order of business was to pray over his breakfast and then eat it. He smelled something like cheese and eggs in the kitchen, and found that Jeb had brought breakfast and a guest with him. He set the table for four people. Soon Orpie came in, and the stranger led the blessing of the food. As they were eating and talking, they did not say anything, for they soon realized it was Jesus, come to fellowship with them.

As they were talking, Jesus talked about the beauty of creation, and God's great love for people, especially for children. He mentioned that while Jaden lived with Orpie until his parents came to heaven to stay, he was adopted by the Father to be His own child.

The Father gave Jaden special care so he could grow to be what he was made to be. All the children in heaven were watched with tender care by specially selected people and angels to watch them in play and teach them the way they should go. Jesus loved to meet with each child to let them know how greatly they were loved. Each came to know Him in a way that was different from the others.

Near the end of the meal, Jesus said to Jaden, "The Father wants you to start your special assignment now. Your music practice times will begin at the end of this assignment. Are you ready to get started?"

Jaden smiled and said, "You know all things, Jesus. I've got my notebook ready, and I'm just waiting for the go ahead."

"Then let's go." And with that, he took Jesus' hand and they floated away into New Jerusalem. When they landed, they were at the Library of Nations. Jesus left him there, and he looked up the nations of Liberia and Crete and checked out two books, one on each of the countries. A map inside the library directed him to the Hall of Nations for further information.

When he found the Hall of Nations, he saw a big sign outside the door proclaiming, "Come see the goodness of God for your country! See the movement of God in the nations of the world! Explore nations of the past. See the future of the world. See the past in the light of heaven! God's goodness smiles down on you from the cultures of the earth!" A guide on another sign directed him to Europe for Crete and Africa for Liberia.

At first when he got into the Hall, he just looked at the sights and listened to the sounds in the building. He heard music, laughter, and talk in many languages.

Anyway, that's what a listener on Earth would have heard. But on this day in heaven, he began to realize even more that now there were no language barriers. Even though Yosef had called Orpie liebschen, Jaden understood that Yosef was saying to Orpie that he loved her like she was his child. In the same way, Jaden was able to sort out what was being said in this building.

He had not gone more than a few feet into the building of nations when a person in a Roman toga came up to him. Though the toga was from an ancient time in Earth's history, it suited the man who came up to him and gave him an air of great dignity.

"Jaden," he said, "the Father told me that you are to view the history of Crete. He also told me about Liberia, but I am not to guide you for that. As you look at the presentation you will find that you are viewing actual events from the country, as if you were there.

"You may call me Demetrius. I was a missionary to Crete not too long after the Resurrection of Jesus. It was a great honor. Since I came here I've been asked to share with others about my island experience.

"The Father said your earthly father wanted you to know some of your family's roots and to visit Crete in some way before he comes to live here. Here you will be taken through your family's ancestry even after your ancestor left Crete. Do you feel up to doing this?"

"Yes," Jaden answered. "The Father told me a little about this assignment and said I was ready for it. So whatever you want to start with, let's get to it."

Demetrius led Jaden down a long corridor, but in earth time it took less than a second for them to get to the open door of a room marked "Crete." The room was unlike any building Jaden had seen, even here in heaven. It had pillars, glistening white marble, paintings embedded in the walls, and pictures of animals and people unlike any Jaden had seen.

"Jaden," Demetrius said, "this room is much like a room I lived in when I was at home on earth. When I was sick for a while, after I was persecuted for my faith, some friends took care of me in their home, in a room like this.

"Here we'll watch some movies made of families who lived on the island of Crete. Get comfortable on one of the cushions on the floor, while I get you food like I used to eat. After we've had our fill and then some, we'll start."

Demetrius came back with grapes, figs, cheese, dolmadas, bread and honey, and grape juice. Soon the pictures came to life and Jaden saw everyday life from long ago. Looking in all directions in the room, he saw many activities come to life on the walls. He saw hunters, farmers, shepherds, and seamstresses and tailors.

One person seemed to shine in the scene. Watching him, Jaden saw him moving among the shepherds, directing the flocks. As he grew older, the wall scenes changed. Jaden saw the man's wife and his children grow older. Then he watched one child marry and have children. He saw the second child persecuted for the faith, suffering many trials and preaching the Gospel. His children were persecuted as well. But they persevered.

The Gospel spread throughout the island as he watched. He heard sermons about persevering in trials and tribulations. In this way he watched many generations of the family. Some suffered much for the faith. Some were healed of severe illnesses. Some raised the dead, some died martyrs and some preached the Gospel with signs and miracles following.

As he watched, the scenes kept changing. Once in a while, a three-dimensional person or scene came to life around him. He kept looking in every direction, experiencing what these people were going through, yet only observing, for he never left the room.

After watching many generations of the family, he saw a natural catastrophe overcoming the island. Members of the family, one family unit, caught a boat and found their way to another island. On that island, they preached the Gospel some more. One person left the new island and settled in the main part of Greece. As he watched the family's life, fashions changed, houses changed, and life changed. It began to seem more like his life on earth.

He saw the family in Greece grow larger, watching one missionary family move to Germany, so much different from Greece. He saw them learn the language and grow in number, seeing a bright light come on a girl as she became a teenager. It was Orpie, helping one family at a time, one person at a time escape the Holocaust, a time when so many lost their lives.

The shape of the room became the shape of a ghetto home in one of Germany's Jewish sections. He watched as she and her family hid people, getting many out, sharing the news that the Messiah had come, and watching many suffer and die for their faith. Yosef was one that she rescued, and Jaden saw him play many concerts in the little home where they lived and hid until he was sent out of Germany. He saw Orpie and others sailing to America, now safe from persecution.

Jaden now found that during the film he had actually been transported to America in the Building of Nations. He remembered that he was to research Liberia also. When he thought of that, he saw that he was now in Africa, in a room like a hut. The pictures were like etchings on the wood of the hut, with men and women in very few garments.

"Hi, there! Are you looking for somebody in this room?" A man wearing slacks and a shirt was asking the question.

"I was supposed to look at the history of Liberia, and found myself in this hut," Jaden replied.

"Well, you are in the right place, and the history of Liberia includes part of an experiment involving people from Africa who came to the United States and then went back to Africa. I know it sounds confusing, but you'll see what it's about as we watch."

"You're my guide for Liberia, right? We didn't get that far in school, but the Father said that my Dad wanted me to learn this stuff and do some things before he joins me in heaven. It's been lots of fun so far. So what about you? Looks like you had hard times. When were you there?"

"You've got a lot of questions. Well, my nickname was Short Stuff as a child. I like that much better than the name my slave master gave me, so you can call me that. I went to Liberia to live, but I started life in the United States on a plantation. Most all the ancestors of the people who went to Liberia came from Africa to begin with, but not many from the area of Liberia. So we'll start in Africa with my ancestors and take it from there."

"First I want to bring you some snacks from my plantation days, at least the vegetable and fruit kind, with some juice. Then we'll get started."

In a short time Short Stuff came back with a plate of peanuts, some peaches, some greens, and some juice. Jaden wasn't too sure about the greens, but he thought he'd better try some anyway. His taste buds had changed since he got here.

"Before we get started, tell me about these greens. I don't remember them from Earth."

Laughing, he said, "Jaden, not too many people away from the South have made greens just the way we used to. When I got here, I had to get used to using different seasonings. These are collard greens. They taste like the bacon I liked on Earth. No meat for dinner most times here, not ever pork, but somehow the Father got the collards tasting like my favorite dish."

As they sat down to watch, the African scenes came to life. They saw a coastline area, with huts not far away, perhaps twenty or thirty of them. They watched a man and a young woman come from another tribe. The man brought some cattle and a pig with him and spoke with the chieftain in the main hut.

As they watched she went into the chieftain's hut, and the other man left. The chieftain and the woman raised a family of five children. Others in the village came and went over the years. One of the chieftain's sons was made chieftain on the death of his father.

Later chieftains from nearby villages began to fight the chieftain and his tribe. Some people died, and Jaden could see their spirits leave their bodies, some to heaven, but more to the lake of fire. He could hear both rejoicing and screams, but the rejoicing was louder than the screams, as he saw the righteous dead come to heaven, greeted by friends and family.

When the fighting ended, he saw the chieftain of the coastal village, his hands tied, being led with his warriors into his own hut. They saw a bright light around him like a protection. After a few days a ship's boat landed near the hut. People in it brought many things to trade. The chieftain from the inland villages bargained for the trade goods. When they settled on the price, in goods, all the captives from the coastal village were brought in chains to the ship's boat, even the chieftain with his bright light around him.

Ship's slave masters brought the captives to the ship and forced them to go down into the hold. Their suffering lasted for many days, with some being buried at sea. The video they watched only showed some of the days, enough to see that all were tortured. Some were beaten. The chieftain had marks on his body where a whip had struck him. Yet whenever he was struck he did not scream or whimper. Jaden wondered about him, but he didn't say anything yet. Even though it was hard to look at, he knew the Father wanted him to see it.

After many days, the ship landed in a port in a warm land, but not as warm as where the warriors came from. As he watched, men beat the warriors and the chieftains with sticks, forcing them to get out of the hold in chains. They were blinded for a short time by the sun, having almost forgotten what it looked like.

People who spoke a language they did not understand dragged them to a market. Men forced them to take off shirts and stand in front of others in shorts. Men and women came and looked at them, speaking in a language Jaden understood, but the warriors didn't. Bargains were made, and the chieftain and two men were forced in chains to follow one of the men.

Now they saw that man's home life as well as the chieftain's life in the new country. It was difficult. He was forced to marry a strange woman at gunpoint. Even so, they grew to love each other, and had many children. Some of the children stayed with them, but more were forced to go to another plantation. Some died early.

The man made him go to what he called church services. After time, the chieftain began to understand what people were saying. He learned English, the language of the Bible the preachers read. He learned how to love his wife. He began to realize that what the preachers were saying was right. He needed the God of the Bible. This was the same God who had protected him and shown him what he needed while he was in Africa.

After the film showed him the chieftain, as in his Crete experience, he followed one of the chieftain's children, then a child of that child, and so on, until he saw a baby born in 1805. He knew that year, because he was shown a newspaper from that year in the hands of the father of the child.

The father was a slave owner, and the mother was a slave, a great-great-great grandchild of the chieftain. On the day the slave was born, the father called the child Onesimus. The mother called the child Short Stuff, for he did not grow very tall.

She saved money from work she did after working in the fields. Then she started doing fine needlework and saved scraps of thread and cloth left over from sewing for the master's children and her own children. She sold small items at other plantations. Her skills at needlework were in heavy demand. After fifteen years, she had saved enough to purchase Onesimus's freedom, but not her own. She went to the master with the money.

In the video Jaden did not see the transaction, but he saw the result. Onesimus left the plantation, and went to another part of the country, for his mother pushed him away, saying he needed to be free to follow God wherever God sent him.

Jaden watched as Short Stuff, as he called himself, worked for low wages and heard he could go to school and learn many things. He saw him listening to the Bible. Soon he was preaching the Bible himself. He read the Bible often, and began to hear about an opportunity to have land and freedom in a faraway country.

Now the film showed Short Stuff going on a wagon train to a coastal city, and getting a one-way ticket to Liberia, Africa. All he had were five changes of clothes, one pair of shoes, a blanket, a pillow, a Bible, and a case to hold them in. He was given the equivalent of one hundred fifty dollars to find his way to settle in the new country. The year was 1830. The Civil War for freedom for all in the United States was thirty years away. He was free, his liberty not threatened by any man. And because of his faith in God, he was free on the inside as well.

Unlike his ancestors, Short Stuff was allowed to go anywhere on the boat he pleased. He talked with his fellow passengers about his hopes for the new country. He shared with them his faith in Jesus Christ. Some said they didn't know Jesus. Some said they were members of a church, and they named the church.

Short Stuff reminded these people that they needed to know Jesus, and that attending church was not enough to get them to heaven. Many came to know Jesus through the Bible studies he led on board the ship. Others learned to read for the first time because of his teaching. Still others paid attention when he shared his love of God and his hope that his master might come to know Jesus for real.

All too soon, it seemed, the boat got to a harbor in the country that would be called Liberia. In the room they were in, they watched Short Stuff's younger self unload his one suitcase and help others with their things as they got off the boat.

Short Stuff told him, "The man who met us was a cousin who became chieftain the same year I was born. I didn't find that out for a while, though. I was just so excited to get there. It was very hot there. My clothes weren't much use in the heat. I had to find a way to keep myself covered without getting too hot.

My cousin later showed me a good way to do that."

As they watched, the landing party broke up into groups. Relatives who had come on an earlier trip ran up to greet the new arrivals. Those who didn't know anyone were greeted like long lost buddies. As with many of the boats that dropped off settlers for Liberia, a few families were aboard, some single men and women, and many who had become friends while on board ship.

One or two of the boats that dropped off colonists over the years traded with other countries. They watched his boat trade dollars for goods, goods for goods, and produce for goods. Almost everyone who came to meet the boat had something to sell.

They watched the colony of Liberia grow and form a government patterned after the United States. While this happened, he noticed that Short Stuff's children and grandchildren held positions of leadership in schools and churches after Short Stuff was welcomed into heaven.

Many schools were formed in Liberia. The teaching of the Bible held a prominent place. Presidents came and went. Gradually the United States dollar was replaced with the Liberian dollar for the currency.

Jaden saw that the many changes in the schools helped bring about a long period of peace in the country of Liberia. The government made distinctions between people who were white and people who were black. White people, who were very few in number, were not given voting rights through the constitution. Only the majority, the black people, had the vote. But these seemed content.

Many learned to read and write. The teaching of the Bible was a part of education for many years. Yet Liberia was not known to have the power of God at work in the country.

After more than a hundred fifty years of a peaceful government, Jaden began to see a spiritual darkness come into Liberia. He could see both God's angels and evil beings trying to talk to people.

Those that knew God refused the voices of evil. Those that did not know God listened to the voices of evil. The government was overcome through a type of civil war with much bloodshed. Even with the bloodshed, he could see that God had left a voice in the nation. He saw the Bible being taught in the schools. More importantly, he saw Bible preachers preaching with signs and wonders following, in small areas of the country.

After the civil war, God began to show them some of His plan for the country. He wanted missionaries to go from Liberia to other parts of Africa with the Gospel and signs and wonders following. He showed a plan for Bible schools, even as there had been elsewhere.

Then God showed them the man in Liberia who he had in mind for this plan. At the time of the civil war, God showed them a small part of Short Stuff's family. There was a boy about ten years old at that time. In a village nearby, there was a girl about five years old. Her family moved into his village, and she grew up near his family. When they were old enough, they were married.

Many people from the surrounding villages began to bring orphans to them to raise. The couple began to teach the orphans Bible stories. They taught them ways to pray for the sick. Most importantly, they showed the children how to listen for the voice of God as they went about their daily life. They also showed them how to support themselves with their own hands while they taught others about God and prayed for the sick.

God began to do signs and wonders through

their children. A revival of the Word of God began to spread from Liberia to surrounding nations as people were drawn to hear the Word of God that these children preached.

Short Stuff said, "Not all of this has happened, but God has shown what he intends to do shortly." Jaden was so excited, he asked God to let him visit the people from Liberia and Crete who were in heaven right away. Before he finished the thought, he found himself on the way to that part of heaven.

His first stop was the island of Crete. He saw great mansions, many of marble, some of great gems. Here, as in New Jerusalem, the pavement was of gold. Some of the mansions were almost finished, some were in beginning stages, but most were already inhabited.

On one of the mansions, with many pearls on the walls, even had a sign on the door, "Demetrius Welcomes You to Visit Today to Study the Bible in Greek." Other mansions had olive trees, orange groves, eggplants, and cedars in glorious profusion around them.

As Jaden looked, he saw an orange as it was falling to the ground and decided to catch it and eat it. He knocked on the door with the sign, or started to, but the door was quickly opened.

"Hi, son. I was expecting you today. The Father told me you were coming to visit to meet some of your people on this side of the world. Well, I'm one of them. I came up here long before Orpie did. I was one of the people that urged others to preach the Gospel on a new island before going to Greece. I heard you looked at the history of Crete."

"I guess you could say that," Jaden replied. "But there's still so much to learn that I wanted to meet some people from there."

"And so you have. Well, I'm Demetrius, and I can walk you around this part of heaven. There's a part here that looks a little like the island did when I lived there, but better. And you can enjoy a festival as you visit the people."

As they walked around the area Demetrius talked about things that were different in heaven from the island of Crete on Earth. He showed people making things very much like he was used to using when he lived on earth, and some people making things using tools that had not been invented when he left Earth. As they walked, they neared the center of the island.

Outside an area like an outdoor ampitheater signs said, "Festival today. All welcome. The love feast of Communion celebrated like we on Earth, but better." People wearing robes of many different styles were coming together. Festival foods were on platters and wooden boards and seats across an area the size of a football stadium. The seats were on the sides of a hill surrounding a stage. A throne and several chairs around it were in the center of the stage. Sounds of ancient melodies filled the air as excitement built up in the crowd.

Finally, a voice was heard from the stage. "Welcome, children of the Lord," the speaker shouted. "We are glad you're here to celebrate the coming of the Lord to your island. It was a great pleasure for our Father to send people to bring the gospel to you. In a few moments you will see and hear some of these messengers, but for now we will sing and worship the Lord."

As if they were one voice, the crowd burst out into song. Melodies in many styles filled the place, spilling out into the area around, and reaching the throne room of God. As their voices were raised in worship, it seemed as if the voices reached down to Earth with the glorious shouts of the redeemed as those still on Earth also seemed to join them. The angels hearing their praises looked on in wonder at the songs of the redeemed.

Their praise was so great that the very throne of God descended on top of the cherubim onto the stage in front of them. Jaden talked with God about his desire for his family on earth to know how many were waiting and watching for them, that there really was a great cloud of witnesses, including him, watching and hearing them. He was filled with the joy of the Lord. God showed him how pleased He was with him.

Finally Jesus himself spoke to the crowd. "Welcome to the love feast these people have set before you. We are commemorating the many things I have brought you through to bring you to myself. We are commemorating the great love I have given you for each other. We want you to eat of this meal with joy and laughter. We are not yet at my marriage supper, but the time is short. The number of your brothers the martyrs is not yet full. Continue in my joy."

Jaden did not get to visit Liberia in heaven on that day, but near the end of the day he asked the Father to show him how to get back to Orpie's mansion. The way was lit up for him, and he found himself escorted by several of his relatives and friends from the festival. On his way there, he discovered even more delights: games, festivals, parks with new rides and equipment to try, and other things, too many to relate.

When he got back to the mansion, he did practice some on the recorder, and found that he could play some of the melodies he had heard that day.

Chapter Twelve Spare Parts Room and Other Places for
Getting Answers

Jaden woke up the next day excited about all
that he had seen in Liberia and Crete, about his and
Short Stuff's family history. He thought about the
miracles and wondered about things he saw when the
miracles took place. At times he was seeing body
parts coming down from heaven as people grew limbs
or fingers where there were none, or even crooked
limbs becoming straight. So he asked God about it.
After breakfast he got directions for a place to go.

"Orpie," he said, "I've got directions for a place
called the Spare Parts Room. Want to go with me? It
sounds like something a lot of people could use."

"Sure," she replied. "I often wonder about some
of the ways God answered prayer. It seems to me that
sometimes when the lepers were healed he gave them
new fingers and noses to keep them from looking so
strange. But a spare parts room? That sounds like
something an automobile shop might have, or a
factory. Let's explore."

As they were talking, a path lit up towards New
Jerusalem. They went to a gate they had not been in
before. In front of the gate there was a sign posted
reading "New Pool of Bethesda. Waters stirred as you
step in. Don't wait for the waters to be stirred. Now is
your time."

People from Earth were milling around in front
of the pool. A gentle man was whispering words of
encouragement to each one. Some heard and their
eyes lit up. They immediately stepped in or crawled in
and found themselves healed, restored to full health.
They went on their way rejoicing, and Jaden saw them
go back through a portal to a service on earth where
an evangelist was praying for the sick.

Others continued to stay around the pool, shaking their heads and looking as those who were healed returned to Earth well and telling of the goodness of God. Finally five more were healed, and all went back through the portal. Immediately another portal opened and many others came through and were encouraged in the same way. He continued to watch as still more received their sight or started walking.

During a very brief break, the gentle man said to Jaden, "This goes on all the time where people gather in the name of Jesus. Not all are ready to receive, but all come through a portal to receive healing at the Pool of Healing. Enter through this gate and you will see more."

Doing just that, Jaden and Orpie went through the gate. On one side of the gate a sign said, "Wheelchairs, crutches, canes, glasses, and other unneeded appliances reworked into your choice of furnishings while you wait. You were healed. We make these beautiful for your mansion. Show others the goodness of God in bringing health to you." They walked inside a building decorated with before and after pictures of wheelchairs of every description. No after picture looked like a wheelchair. Instead, there were bicycles, unicycles and chair cushions. Eyeglasses were made into lamps with prisms showing more colors than rainbows. Crutches and canes were made into chairs or bars and pulleys for exercise rooms. Everything was reworked into something much more beautiful than before.

The path lit up yet again. They found themselves on a walkway leading through a park with benches and flowers, fruits, herbs, and other plants with healing properties. Again, they saw a portal open and another gentle man walking with people.

He took them through the park, giving them parts of certain plants, urging them to eat what he offered them. Some, finding it bitter, shook their heads, but he kept on urging. When they ate what he offered them, even the ones who were offered bitter herbs were strengthened.

After he had given herbs or other plants to them, he led them to benches where he urged them to sit for a while. As they sat, he kept on offering parts of certain plants to them, and occasionally leaves from the Tree of Life. Again, if they ate, they were strengthened. If they refused to eat, they simply rested and took much longer to get strength. As at the pool of Bethesda, some went through the portal unhealed. Those that ate the plants given to them went back in full health.

When they got to the other side of the park, they saw a huge building. The sign in front of it said, "Do you want new parts for your body? Are you expecting God to transform parts of your body so you can function better on earth? Enter and find what you need. Receive it here."

The door was mahogany, and reminded Jaden of rocks in his collection on earth. Yet it shone with the brilliance of the glory of God and the Lamb, like everything in New Jerusalem. It showed the marks of many fists from people who had not known the way in. But for Jaden and Orpie, the door was opened before they got to it. As with other buildings of New Jerusalem, they were let in because they were on business for the King of Kings.

When they walked in, they saw how huge the building was. Instead of being labeled by body part, it was labeled by country, then tribe, then language. Under each language, there were sections by family, and rooms by person.

Directions for visitors living in heaven were just

inside the door, but they could see people coming in through portals from earth directly to their family section. If they were praying for a family member to receive a new body part, an angel lifted out the body part and brought it down to Earth through the portal putting it into the person they were praying for.

For people for themselves, the angel led them into the room labeled with their name and selected the body parts needed. There the heavenly surgeon performed a transplant. No surgical scars showed on their bodies. When the surgery was finished, they returned to earth by the same way they came.

Jaden asked the gatekeeper to take him to his family's section and to their rooms. The gatekeeper smiled and said, "Why, you have received all your new body parts because you are now living in heaven. People on Earth will get their new bodies in their rooms, but they will not remember the time in their rooms, for it will take place in a moment only."

"My friend Pascal has something wrong with his eyes. May I see his room?"

The gatekeeper smiled, and guided them to the section for Pascal's family. In Pascal's family section, they saw rooms marked Pascal, Sylvia, Norman, and many others they had not met. Seeing a window on each door, he ran up to Pascal's room and look in. Besides eyes labeled right and left, he saw many other parts that looked a lot like Pascal.

"As your friend grows, the replacement parts grow in size. When he is healed on earth, he gets some replacement parts then. When he comes to heaven, he gets a whole new body. That body will be waiting for him in this room, even as yours waited for you."

When they left the building, they looked around to see the end of the building. Looking past the corner, they saw it stretched for miles on the side.

Going back to the front, they saw that the front stretched for miles also. When they left the building, Jaden remembered he wanted to find out how God started to answer prayer. As he thought it, a narrow path lit up, just wide enough for him. "Orpie, it looks like I have to go alone. I'll see you later."

With that, he began walking on the path. As he got further down the path, it narrowed. Finding thorns and thistles next to the path, he used an ax he saw nearby to chop up the weeds. The more he cleared, the wider the path became.

Seeing a tall beautiful blue building at the end of the path, Jaden almost stumbled in his eagerness to get to it. It seemed to beckon him with the reflected glory of God and of the Lamb. The more he chopped away thorns and thistles, the more glorious the building seemed to be.

Finally the building was just a few feet away. The path widened in front of him. As he stumbled, his steps grew stronger and firmer. Finally he was no longer stumbling. He was strengthened, and was no longer scratched.

A brilliant man with a bright blue sash embraced him in his arms. "Come, child. Come into the hall of answered prayer. Here you will discover some ways God starts to answer prayers. Some of the ways He does not show anyone.

"But to those who persevere as you have, He shows Himself, and they find one answer within God Himself. Come into the banquet room. Discover the goodness of God. Discover how He starts to answer prayer."

Jaden found himself alone once more. He could hear many soft voices in the room asking God to come and whisper to them. He heard an answering whisper surround them and him.

As he was doing, many were seeking God in the

stillness of His power. They asked God to come in fullness into their lives and the lives of those they knew. They asked for His mercy to be shown to others. Sometimes God's whisper was "Soon," "Not yet," sometimes "Now," sometimes "It's been done, but you have not seen it yet," and sometimes God just wrapped his arms around them.

Afterwards they, as Jaden did now, just feasted at God's banqueting table, whether fruit, as Jaden ate, or meat, or a full course meal. Whatever it was, they were filled and were satisfied, content to go back to their lives, knowing that God was at work.

After his experience in the House of Answered Prayer, he went back down his path, and found a path lit up to go to Orpie's mansion. There he met a teacher who would help him make Jeb's gift. They made plans to meet at the school the next day and work on it.

After that they all had a light supper of yogurt, fruit, and coconut milk.

When they were finished, Orpie got out one of the dictionaries from her room. They played a game of charades, or at least tried to, but found out they were talking out loud when they thought they were just thinking the word they were trying to show. Finding that out, they tried a game with blindfolds and found out that using a blindfold with a game would not work very well because it was always light, even under the blindfold. Finally, they got out a game of checkers. Jaden won two games, Orpie one, and the teacher one.

After talking with the Father for a long time, he went to sleep with a smile on his face, thinking about their games. He had to laugh as he remembered Orpie trying to make her word hard to guess. She had made just one gesture and he got it. It happened the same way with the blindfold game. No matter where he hid something, they found it right away. No matter where the picture was, he could see it, even if it was in back of him. When he was spun around, he wasn't dizzy. He knew where he faced too, because it was so much different from Earth. They would have to make up some new games for here. Maybe he could check out one of the stores.

Speaking of Earth, he thought it was Sunday, a day of rest there. He had seen what went on in a small part of heaven while people on earth celebrated the Lord's Day and while they prayed for other people's needs.

He'd watched his parents' church from the Portal again. Many of those who came to the Lord at his funeral began to trust God for miracles in their lives and in the lives of others. Some stood up to testify in the service during the brief time he watched.

He saw his parents wipe tears from their eyes as they rejoiced at what the Lord was doing in the midst of their tears. He saw angels remind them of the Father's love while He wiped tears from their eyes.

Chapter Thirteen Sorrow Turned Into Joy

On Earth at his parents' home, Jamal and Susan were visiting them. Jamal asked Joanna, "Mom, how can you stay so happy? You just buried him a week ago, and yet you're humming along like nothing happened?"

Joanna went to Jamal and hugged him. He was crying, and buried his head in his arms. "Honey, I don't know myself how it happens.

"All I know is that when I think of Jaden all the hymns about joy and 'Power in the Blood' and God wiping tears from our eyes start going through my mind like the angels are singing them to me. Every once in a while it sounds like he is singing right along with them. It's so beautiful to hear I just can't stay sad."

Tony, Jaden's father, chimed in. "Sometimes I can smell something that's like moussaka or lamb and I think maybe he's been eating that. Those were his favorite foods. I think that God would let him have those as often as he wants."

"Mom, there's a guy I know at work. He's upset over the accident. He thought we should press charges. I told him that wouldn't bring Jaden back. And besides, we know heaven is much better than here. He'd be crazy to want to come back. And he couldn't any more, anyway."

"Jamal, we need to pray and ask God to show you what to say to him. Remember, we want our lives to be a witness of God's forgiveness, even though right now we don't always feel we can forgive. Tony, would you lead us in prayer?"

Tony prayed, "Father, we don't know what to say to people to tell them we forgive the driver who killed Jaden. We know he's with you, but right now we're missing him. Cause us to feel your arms around us in our time of sorrow.

"Turn our mourning into the joy that only you can give to us. We forgive the driver. We ask you to give Jamal the words to share with his coworker, showing your love and forgiveness for the driver and our love and forgiveness for him too. We thank you for the years he was with us and the testimony he had that he truly loved you. In Jesus' mighty name we pray. Amen."

Sometime during Tony's prayer, Jamal began to smile, his eyes lighting up. "I think I know who he's with a lot. Grandma Orpie. Remember she's the one who led him to Jesus. I wouldn't be surprised if he's waiting in Grandma Orpie's mansion for all of us."

"When he's not on assignment from the Father," Susan put in. "He's always one to want to work for the guy in charge, even if he hardly knew him or could reach up to him. Remember the time when he tried to lift up your toolbox, Dad?"

"Yes. He was only two years old. He climbed on a chair when he thought I wasn't looking, reached onto the workbench, and tried to lift the handle up so he could carry it to me."

"I saw you run to him and stand behind him so he wouldn't fall. I saw the look on his face when he couldn't lift up the handle, let alone the toolbox. You could hear him all the way in the kitchen, Mom said."

"I was making lamb for dinner that night, and ran because I thought he'd hurt himself. When I got there, I nearly cracked up laughing. Jamal, you must remember that."

"Sure do. There Dad was, hanging onto Jaden's pants with one hand, and balancing the toolbox with the other, so he could think he was lifting the toolbox, even though the handle wouldn't come up. It was such a funny sight."

They all laughed, remembering their part in that incident. After reminiscing about many things he had done, some funny, others not, they shared other memories.

"There was one April Fools' Day at school when you and two guys moved a whole classroom next door, desks, bulletin board, announcements, teacher's notes and everything. Then the whole class sat in the new room. The teacher went to his classroom and saw no one there. Remember, Susan?"

"Jamal wasn't there a time you took an IQ test that wasn't done too well? You had to choose an answer with a name that didn't belong with the others. One answer made it all Greek gods, and another answer made it all names of planets. Bet they had to redo that one."

"Right, Susan. I really don't know if they straightened that one out. I wrote a note to our teacher about the question and filled in the circle the one about the Greek gods. Maybe they were looking for the all-planet answer, though."

"They were probably a little red-faced at being shown up by a high-school kid."

Not long after that conversation, Jamal and Susan left to go to their homes. Their mother went back to Jaden's journal, looking at some more entries.

Jaden was remembering his ninth day. He had talked with Jeb about Little League starting on Earth not long after Easter, telling him he'd wanted to be part of it and had been looking forward to baseball for the first time.

"Well, son," Jeb had said, "we do have sports here. In fact, some of the coaches for baseball hereabouts were part of the group that helped start baseball in the United States. We also have some very good coaches from later years. Maybe even some people you know."

So he had found himself playing with his friends and learning baseball from Joe Nick and Albert Strange, who were from the Negro League. Hamstring Spruce from the pro league at the time of the Second World War coached him briefly, then was replaced by Bob Hammersmith, who had worked a short time for an American League team, and then gone on to coach a Little League team.

This was now his fourth day trying baseball. Already he caught most of the balls thrown to him. He played outfield most of the time, and saw that the grass was much greener and brighter than anything on Earth. When it came to batting, well, he just knew he could learn how to do that sooner or later. He was having a lot of fun in the outfield, though.

Hannah played catcher sometimes and pitcher other times. Chong, he thought, was the best batter they had. He could place a ball anywhere in the field, and usually fouled until the count was two strikes and three balls. Then when he saw how the outfield was placed, he swung and sent the ball past their heads or in for a bunt, getting a hit every time he was at bat.

He asked him, "Chong, how do you get a hit all the time?"

"I'm not sure," he answered. "I just know that every time I get up to bat, I see the ball coming at me and I know when to swing at it and how high to swing. Most of the time the swings I take mean foul balls, but always on the last one I connect in a way that fools people. Let me know if you figure this out. I just think that God is letting me be really good at this. What do you think?"

"I think that you could teach me something about how to know when to swing and when not to swing. You seem to have that down pat, and I need to get it better."

So this was the day that Chong became his

coach for that "all-American" pastime known as baseball. It seemed that almost all their baseball time became a lesson from Chong on the art of swinging a bat well and placing the ball away from the opposing players.

Now he was at school after morning Bible story time. He and his friends had brought in their kits and looked around the room for their chairs. Seeing his was in front of the teacher he had met the day before, he said, "Hi, Mr. Anderson. I'm glad you're helping me with Jeb's gift."

"So am I, but you can call me Zach. Let's see what you've got."

"I'm not sure yet. I haven't opened it, but I had thought he might like something made from wood. I see that you have some hammers and other wood things here. So I guess that's what we have."

When they opened the kit, they pulled out instructions, a hand saw, pliers, and some small tools. After getting the wood out, Zach began to show him how to check to make sure he made straight lines on the wood and sawed through at a good angle. He showed him how to sand and make it level. They finished it to the point of gluing, sanding and nailing it.

When they looked up, they saw that others were only partly finished with their projects also. But, in the center of the room they saw some tables with many types of foods to the side of the work areas. "Time for a break," a teacher said. "Your families brought in some food and asked to stay with you for the rest of the day."

Orpie and his family joined them at the table. "We have a surprise for you," she said. "Zach is also part of the family. You didn't see him before today because he was on errands for the Father. He's one of your uncles going back a ways on your mother's side."

"That's right. So you'll be seeing a lot of me all through eternity."

Finishing the project after a lunch of grapefruit, almonds, Swiss cheese, and nut bread, he took it home to the mansion.

Remembering piano studio time, he picked up two of his books, thought of the School of Composers, and went to practice piano there. He had been practicing faithfully, and Yosef often told him how much progress he was making when he passed by the practice room.

After finishing at the piano, he went home and practiced recorder in the mansion. Orpie sat down with him, using the second music stand, and played the oboe Jaden saw the first day at the School of Composers. She had a copy of the same book that Jaden was using for practice, and she often played the second part for the duet that he was working on.

That day she told Jaden, "For working with the recorder only since last week, you are doing very well."

"And I didn't get to practice very much, because of all the other things I did."

"Well, you practiced, and God used that time to give you some good skills very fast."

With that, they both laughed, and went to eat. Soon he was in his room looking through the books he had checked out and making notes from them, comparing the animals from the planet book to the animals he knew from Earth. Not too long after he began that task, he began to realize something.

"Orpie, I'm looking at these pictures in the planet book I checked out. Some of the animals look like animals that were in cartoons I saw. These strange-looking creatures look like something I saw on the Internet not too long before I came here. Does this mean that this planet I'm reading about is earth by a different name?"

Orpie looked at the book, then at the author's name. She also flipped through the contents of the book. "I think you're right. When you look at some of these pictures, they look a little like things I saw through a microscope.

"The author's names are Leeuwenhoek and Foster. Leeuwenhoek was known for his studies on the effects of germs on illness and Foster was known for astronomy and for looking for odd animals. Both of them are here in heaven. This book was written after they got here. Leeuwenhoek did not speak English, though. So a book where he was the main author would not have a name you know."

"People told me about things like this that I could read when I got older. I saw some books with pictures of weird animals in them that they called science fiction. The animals in this book seem a lot like them. That's why I wasn't too sure. I'm glad I got to look at this."

Not too long after he was finished making notes, he decided to go to the throne room before he got sleepy. As at other times, the pathway to the throne room lit up for him, and he got there in less than a second, earth time. All the things that he did while there would have taken many hours in earth time, but when he got back to the mansion, the light had not yet changed.

On Earth, Joanna had finished reading his journal. "Hon," she said, "how about making copies of this and sharing it with people who knew Jaden? Don't you think that they'd like to know about this?"

"Good idea," Tony said. "Then they can understand why we're not so sad, because we know we'll see him. I could get it copied and bound after we know how many copies to make."

So they began to make plans for doing that, and made lists of people they thought would want a copy.

Putting together these lists brought back many pleasant memories of time spent with friends, neighbors, loved ones, and church people.

It seemed like such a wonderful project that later Joanna called Jamal and Susan to get them involved in making their own lists. While she was talking to them about her listed, she mentioned some of her memories to them and talked a long time.

Chapter Fourteen Loving the Lost

Jaden woke up smelling eggs and cheese, and hearing the clatter of plates. Looking toward the wall, he saw a crown with a note on it resting on his pillow. He looked at the note. It read in part, "To Jaden, to give to Orpie, for her part in winning others to me. [Signed] your best friend, Jesus." He also heard a different chorus of voices in the kitchen. One of the songs he heard was "Loving the Lost no Matter the Cost." Another was, "What a Friend We Have in Jesus," but with different, joyful words, reminding him of the times on earth when he felt Jesus' love throughout his day.

When Jaden went into the kitchen, he took the crown with him, holding it carefully in front of him. A jeweler would have told him how scarce the sapphires and emeralds on the crown were on earth, but he simply knew that it was a gorgeous, bright crown. It didn't remind him of any crowns he had seen in pictures on Earth.

Somehow when he looked at it, though, it reminded him so much of Orpie that the crown itself seemed as light as a feather, although on earth it would have weighed more than fifteen pounds. He looked around, and found that while he woke up in his own room in her mansion, as he walked into the kitchen he had been transported to the throne room of heaven. He also saw that she was there with him.

As they came up to the throne, Jaden carrying the crown, voices around them rose in great applause. "Worthy are you, Lord, for you have chosen your beloved to carry your love to those who never knew you. You drews many to yourself because of her great love for you. She chose to let you shine through her to many. You are great, Lord, and greatly to be praised."

Around them were many other people carrying crowns with someone standing next to them and both worshipping God and kneeling before the throne of God.

"Arise, you who have been bought with a price, redeemed from every tribe and nation. You who have carried my love to the lost come forward and receive your crowns." Many came forward to receive their crowns.

"You who have asked to be allowed to crown these, come forward with their crown as you have asked." Many came up with Jaden and stood next to the person who had brought them to Jesus.

"You who brought the crowns step forward and face the one who showed you Jesus. Talk to them as you wish and lay the crowns on their heads after you have spoken with them."

He stepped forward with the crown and faced Orpie. He shared with her how greatly his life had changed after knowing Jesus. He reminded her about how because of her leading him to Jesus, Pascal got to know about God's love for him. He told her how Pascal had been talking about going to Bible school after he finished regular school.

Orpie took his face gently in her hands and kissed him. Lost in that moment, he did not notice when the crown was taken from his hands and placed on her head by Jesus himself. He was too busy praising God for His wonderful love in bringing him to Jesus through Orpie.

If he had even looked at others, he would have seen this was the way with all those being crowned. Jesus himself took the crowns from the hands of those who wished to crown the ones who had won them to the Lord and placed the crowns on their heads as they each shared the goodness of the Lord in their lives.

Lost in the wonder of worship and praise, they

felt like many minutes had passed. Perhaps so, but soon they found themselves back at the mansion. Around them they saw Jeb, Rosie, and several others he recognized from Orpie's video. Each had brought a dish to share. Together, they had a feast in the mansion kitchen to begin their day.

Afterward, he wanted to visit people from Crete and Liberia in heaven. As he thought about it, a path lit up toward a boating dock. In less than a second, earth time, he found himself on board a colorful boat with the words "Liberian Cruise Line, Heaven Branch" on it. The captain resembled Short Stuff, but was a little taller. "So you want to meet people from Liberia," the captain said.

"Yes," Jaden answered. "I saw much of the history of that country yesterday. Now I want to meet with some of the people and learn about how they got to know Jesus while they were slaves. I also want to know how they got other people saved."

"Sounds like a tall order, but we got all eternity," the captain chuckled. "Good thing to know is that you can find out a lot today, and tomorrow, and tomorrow, and tomorrow..."

"I get the picture. So are we ready to go or what?"

"Seems God wanted a special cruise just for you. It's like he's got something in mind for you to learn, and I know just the folks here who can teach you what you want to know. It seems that some money your folks sent to help people get to Liberia helped some of these people get saved, and you'll get to find out how."

While they were talking, the boat flew across a great amount of water in what seemed like a matter of minutes. In Earth time, well, since a day in the Lord's eyes is as a thousand years, and a thousand years as a day, let's just say we don't know how much time really had passed. The water itself was like crystal, and Jaden saw a number of fish when he first got on the boat and even more when they pulled up at the dock on the other side. He asked the captain, "Could I go for a short swim first?"

The captain answered, "I don't see why not. Thinking of playing with the fish, aren't you?"

"I don't know about that, but I just want to swim. Swimming is so much fun up here." So he went for a short swim, and some of the fish led him out a little ways. One rolled over belly side up, waving its fins, and nudging his hand. He stretched out his hand a little, and rubbed the fish's belly. "He's smiling at me. I heard him say 'ah, that's it,' like he was enjoying it."

"Could be. You seem to have a way with animals. Ready to go on shore, now?"

"Yep. Lead the way."

When they got away from the dock, he recognized the land from the film. But now where the chief's hut had been there was a big shiny building. Glittering in the light of God's glory, the mansion's gemstones seemed to blend in with the trees around it. As they drew closer he could see the edge of the building and the reflection of the trees on the building. Short windows gleamed near the top. There was no roof, as the whole mansion was open to the sky.

"Now this here's where the hut I grew up in stood. My grand pappy raised me about where that little fruit tree is. I more or less stayed outside in a tent most nights when it was too hot to stay inside. The grass roofs didn't keep the rain from coming inside, but sometimes they helped us keep cool. You want to peek inside? They built me a building before I got here, just like they're building you a building up here."

Seeing his astonished eyes, the guide said, "Sure, you're getting a mansion for yourself too one of these days. We all get our own mansions. Some just have to wait a little bit, like until they're grown up. But here it seems like no time at all when you get it. Maybe after your mommy and daddy come."

"I'd like to look at your mansion." The guide took him inside it. The light shone as bright as outside. They could see columns like trees every twenty feet, with walls like tall partitions between them. There were many rooms with large decorations in each. A rich red throne stood in the center of the first room they saw.

As they left the mansion, several people came to meet them. All wore white garments, of course, but the styles were distinctive. Looking more closely, Jaden could see stripes woven into the fabric, loose belts, and crowns that seemed much like the hats that slaves had worn in the heat of the day.

Instead of straw as in the film, the crowns were gold decorated with gems of rare colors, unlike anything he had seen. Looking closer, he saw gemstones where wounds had been in the film. All had great big smiles of welcome and reached out with hugs and handshakes.

"Jaden, son of Joseph, son of Itsak, welcome to the land of some of your ancestors. Your parents have not yet learned this, but they will. Welcome, and come eat bread with us."

"So tell me, how did you get to know about Jesus? You're calling me a child of some Bible people, right? Tell me about that."

"After we break bread, child, after we break bread."

Laughing, Jaden said, "Oh, I get it. You're Jesus, the host, and this is a family reunion."

"You got it," He said. "At first I hid my identity from you, just like I did sometimes while I walked the Earth, so people could get to know me by faith. But many of these people are really related to you, from way back. They'll tell you their stories during your visit here."

While he visited there, and it seemed like several days, what with all the people he met and the stories they told, he got to know many people. They came together from many parts of Africa to this wonderful gathering. He saw chieftains and common people from many tribes. Some were from the tribes in the middle of Liberia.

Jaden asked a tall man, "How are you related to me? Jesus said it's a family reunion, but my parents never talked about people from other countries besides where Orpie was a missionary."

"I'm Itzak, and I come from people that heard the Gospel long before many of our people were taken. When Joseph was born to my wife Pearl, we moved to another part of Africa. We did not know many people there. People said we were in Egypt. While we were there, we heard that the Messiah who had come and that we should believe he was the Promised One.

"Some people from Israel had told our ancestors to start looking for the Messiah before that time. So that's how we heard about Jesus. We did not go to the United States, but some of Isaac's children (Joseph's son he was) came to the United States on a boat. Later they escaped slavery and settled near you. Two centuries later, Joanna was born, and you were born to her, one of three children she had."

"So you're my grandparent."

"Yep."

After the feast, there was dancing and celebration for a while. Then the captain came to Jaden. "So, what do you think? Did you learn a lot here?"

"Sure did," Jaden answered. "It seems to me my Mom and Dad didn't tell me who all they were related to when I lived with them."

"Or maybe they didn't know who all their ancestors were?" the captain replied.

"Something like that."

They got back on the boat after he played with the fish again. It seemed like no time before they got back where they came from.

"Captain, it seems like we were there a long time. The party was so much fun. Was I there all day, or just part of the day?"

"Child, I really don't know that. Here we just don't pay attention to time sometimes. We have all eternity to learn what we want to know. Course, you know on Earth the millennial reign of Jesus hasn't started yet, or we'd be back down there."

"Oh, yeah. They were saying something about that in one of our church services. But they said that it was what another church believed in, and they weren't too sure about it. So that's how we'll be able to know that everyone that's going to be with Jesus has been born. At the end of the Millennium, right?"

"Right. The Father will show you when he thinks you're ready. I don't rightly know how that will happen, because I haven't seen the preview yet, just what I read in the Bible. But I've seen a lot of the Bible films already."

"I thought I'd be ready to see Crete yet on this trip, but I'm getting a little tired. I want to go to the throne room and talk to the Father."

As Jaden he said this, a path lit up for him, with a chariot pulled by a huge horse on it.

"Jaden, this is your chariot for this part of the day. The Father longs to talk to you as much as you are long to talk to Him. Come up."

Jaden looked at the driver of the chariot, and as he looked at him, he felt himself flying into it. "Wow! I'm not tired anymore," he said.

"That's right," the driver said. "This is the chariot for those who are weary after a day of work on the Father's business. For you it seemed like a long time, but it was half a day. You need strength to go on to Crete."

As he said that, the chariot driver set the horse flying over the city of New Jerusalem. They landed just outside the Throne Room building. He could hear the increased singing around the throne. He had got used to hearing singing all the time from when he woke up until when he went to sleep. Now he remembered other visits. The music was just as loud now as before in the throne room.

He ran to the front of the throne room and knelt, taking off his crown, shouting, "Jesus, you're worthy. You brought me out of so much. You brought my people out of so much. Give me something to do that would help bring more people to you. I want to have a part even now. Let me encourage your people."

Jesus said to him, "Child, it is not for you to go back to earth. I have a plan for you. You will encourage people who visit here. You will help them learn what they need to know so they go back refreshed. It gives me great joy for you to ask for a task so near to my heart."

While Jesus was speaking, the Father came over to talk with him. "Son," he said, "you are near to my heart. I have known you from the beginning. I knew that you would have a short time on earth, shorter than many. You were faithful in the little you had. You will have a part in some places where my people need encouraging. Take heart in this, for it can be done even though you do not live on Earth."

He looked up. In front of him was an angel with a small loaf of bread. The honey on the bread was a deep gold color, so thick it was hard to see the bread itself.

"Eat this bread, Son. It will give you knowledge and help with the skills for this task."

He ate the bread as he was told. He didn't share with others how it tasted, for they also had eaten it. After he ate, he stayed in the throne room, worshiping for a long time in both heaven's and Earth's time.

Leaving the throne room, he stopped at a park and swung on the swings for a while. Afterward, he climbed on a jungle gym in the shape of a crown before heading to the mansion. As he got inside, he smelled his favorites, roast lamb and moussaka. Remembering how they were made and all that went with it, he joined Orpie, Jeb, and Rosie in eating another festival meal that day.

Remembering his assignment, he wrote down some of the things he learned during his visits, journaling his thoughts about them before he rested.

Chapter Fifteen Crete

Waking up after his rest, Jaden thought about his visit with the people of Liberia, and his new home. It was much bigger than his home on Earth, but still it seemed that every time he woke up from his rest it had got bigger somehow. He didn't know how it happened, but he was so glad to be there that he didn't really think about it very much.

His breakfast was scrambled eggs, mango fruit on toast, and a glass of what tasted like chocolate strawberry milk. He felt ready for anything.

Soon he heard Jesus' voice outside the door, and the laughter of the children he was seeing during the first part of his days. He ran to meet them at the door, picking a piece of fruit from the tree at the front on his way out.

Jesus asked, "Children, what did you think of your trip to a strange country here in heaven?"

After thinking about it, he answered, "I was excited to meet all the people and try their food."

Chang said, "I didn't know I had ancestors in so many countries."

Others talked about boat rides and trying out different toys. Then Jesus answered some of their questions by saying, "You remember how after I was born Herod got angry and wanted to make sure I didn't live, right?"

"Yes," they all said.

"Well, my earthly Abba took me to Egypt, another country, where I lived for several years. He was warned in a dream to take me there. After Herod died, we went to Nazareth, a town in Galilee, where I grew up. An angel talked to him both times in a dream. Now I know some of you had dreams. Do you remember them?"

"Sometimes; not always," were their answers. "Some on Earth were scary."

"My Father used dreams, the Bible, and the prophets to talk to people. Many times these ways were to guide them and keep them safe. But with Moses He talked face to face. Moses really wanted to get to know my Father. He didn't just ask for guidance. He wanted to know my Father just for Himself. Did you know the Father wants each one of you to get to know Him? That's why we're all here with Him now, because He loves His children so much."

After talking about this and other Bible stories, they parted, some to play under the watchful eyes of angels, and others to go to places in heaven they wanted to visit.

As he went toward New Jerusalem, a path lit up in front of him, and Jeb came up to him. "Son," he said, "I want to go with you as you visit the people from Crete today. There are some people I know from way back in that part of heaven."

"Sure, the more the merrier. I wanted to have someone with me yesterday, but it seemed that you two had other things to do."

"Often happens that way. Sometimes God has us on different assignments at times. Never a dull moment here. There's just so much that we can do and see. Not to mention that we can see everything going on in Earth right now if we want to, and it won't seem like it takes any time to see it. Anyway, Son, I want in on what you're doing today, and I think the Father is mighty pleased with all of us right now."

"Yes. We talked about visiting the places our ancestors came from and then visiting with people we saw from our films here in heaven yesterday. Are you saying that some of our ancestors other than Orpie came from Crete?"

"Orpie is your ancestor and she's one of my many great something grandchildren. It could seem confusing sometimes to people just learning what those words mean on Earth. But you're catching on faster than you would have on Earth."

"Okay, got it. So how do you think we should go meet them?"

"Here comes one of my friends now. Aristarbus, meet my great something grandson, Jaden."

"Hi, Jaden. Glad to see you in Heaven. I watched you some while you were on Earth. I heard your Daddy when he prayed you would get to meet your ancestors and people from places they were missionaries to. Well, Crete was both of that for them."

As they were talking, they arrived at a dock with another boat waiting for them. The letters on the boat were Greek, but Jaden understood them right away. The name of the boat was "Wings of Eagles." It had many windows with oars leaning outside of them, but no people were sitting at the oars, as Jaden could see when he looked through the windows.

"It's just like pictures of a Roman galley that I saw in a book once," Jaden exclaimed. "But nobody's rowing it today."

"That's right. Here people don't have to row these boats. The boats have oars because some people who rowed boats like this are here. The oars remind them of God's goodness. When they get on the boat, it goes faster than the wind, just as it will for us when we get on it."

With that they boarded the boat. Those on board greeted them, and it was only seconds before they got to a beautiful island, better than the island of Crete in the film Jaden had seen.

While they were on the sea, beautiful birds flew over them and flying fish frolicked in front of them.

Jaden laughingly petted a fish that landed on the deck and gently dropped it back into the sea. As before, the fish seemed to smile as he petted it. A bird landed on his shoulder and rubbed its beak against his cheek before it flew off again.

While they were going to the island, Jaden saw that the seats with the oars were in front of tables spread with many kinds of food. As they landed, the captain invited all the passengers to take some of the food onto the island with them.

Jaden picked up a basket near one of the tables and loaded it with fish, bread, fruit and cheese. Others took baskets like his, as well as olives and assorted vegetables. Still others took other goods.

Even though they took much with them onto the island, when Jaden glanced back, he saw that the tables looked almost as full as they were when they first started toward the island.

All the people on the boat wore many clothing styles. Some were dressed like the pictures of ancient people Jaden remembered from pictures of caves in encyclopedias, but the garments were white. Others wore clothing like the people of ancient Greece. Some were dressed like paintings he remembered seeing. And there were some dressed like people from the film of Crete he saw when he first learned about his family history.

All were talking at once as they landed, bringing the food with them. On the island there seemed to be hundreds of people greeting them. He could see people from all ages meeting them. But most people he saw were men who seemed to be wearing small caps under their crowns and women wearing gold coins and headdresses like pictures he'd seen, but appearing to be woven into their crowns.

"Who are all these people?" Jaden asked. "I don't remember seeing so many people in the whole film of Crete. It looks like everybody I saw on any of my family films and quite a few more besides came to Crete."

"That's right," a man nearby answered. "Many people traveled to Crete and heard the Gospel as they traveled there. Some refused Jesus when they first heard the Gospel. Later, when they got back to their home country, someone else watered the seed in their hearts, and later they came to know Jesus.

They are here to celebrate the home coming of one of their own. This person is a descendant of one of the people who passed through Crete many years before you were born and is not related to you. They were so greatly touched by her that they asked to be notified when she came."

As Jaden watched, the crowd grew silent. A great rowboat was flying toward the island. In it was one passenger and one person steering the boat. There were oars, but just like Jeb had not seemed to pedal at all when he brought Jaden to heaven, even so the person doing the steering did not seem to use the oars at all.

As the boat landed, he watched as people cheered and danced and sang and laughed as the person landed. From the middle of the crowd, Jesus came forward, followed by many people who looked like the small woman coming out of the boat.

These people were also dressed in many different fashions, for they too were from different countries and times. She shone brighter than many people there, but was not as brightly as that of Jesus.

When she saw Jesus, she did not run to embrace him, as others did. She knelt before Him and said, "Lord, thank you for those you gave me. I wanted to bring more, so many more. Take me, and let me serve those you have given me, for my love for them is so great."

Abraham emerged from the crowd and said, "Daughter, welcome to heaven. Rise to meet the one you have served with such love." As he was speaking, Jesus firmly grasped her hand and raised her to her feet.

One of the people closest to Jesus asked Him about the woman's crown. Jesus said to him, "Not yet, son, for those who came to me because of her asked that I give a feast in her honor when she came. Daughter, come feast with me and these who wish to welcome you."

Those on the shore and those from the island set their baskets all around a big table. The table seemed to take up the whole island, for he could not see the end of the table. Yet, this was not the wedding feast of the Lamb and His bride. This was the welcome home feast for one of Jesus' own.

Jesus chose to meet her on Crete, heaven side, for it had been her home on earth for most of her youth. In later years she went out and won many to righteousness.

As they were feasting, she kept getting up and talking with many of the guests, for she knew so many of them. She also kept trying to serve them food and other dainty things she saw. Laughing, many told her, "No, this is our time to serve you," or, "You have served so many, allow us to serve you."

Jesus himself said to her, "Daughter, I have a plan for you for all of eternity. This is your welcome-home party. You will yet be allowed to serve, but you must wait a little while for that."

With that, she left her seat at the table, and knelt before Him yet again, and worshiped Him. As she was kneeling, Jesus wrapped His arms around her and wiped tears from her eyes, for not all her tears were of joy, but some were of sorrow for what had been while on earth.

During the time he was allowed to be close to the new person, he saw that he had not seen her in the film either. Yet he had seen many other people while he watched his family history on Crete. He asked a guest, "Who is this, that there is such a big feast for her today?"

The man answered, "She is someone who spent much time reaching out to the poor. Some here learned about Jesus for the first time through her. Others had heard before. All were touched by her life. Many touched by her have not yet come here. Most of us never heard her name. I did not learn her name. We only knew her as The One Who Loved Us."

"Does she have a name?"

"Listen, and you may find out at the same time as I do."

After they were finished eating, one of the people who had come with Jesus to greet the woman said, "Janetka, I am your grandmother. You never knew me, because you were little when I came here. Jesus let me watch you many times. Let me hug you and take you to my mansion to visit." One by one, many others at the table followed the grandmother and said much the same thing to her, some reminding her of the part that she had in their lives, others simply weeping with joy at being near her. Not one was turned away.

These greetings may have taken hours on Earth, but in heaven conversations can be very rapid or slow, and there really is all of eternity, so no matter how long they took, it still was day when all had gone except for Jaden, some of the people from the boat, and Janetka and some of her relatives.

"Friends, please join us at Janetka's mansion while we show her where she will stay. Then we will all go to visit with Father Abraham at his welcome party for her and others." They followed her grandmother to a beautiful mansion made of diamonds in many different colors set in gold like the pavement of New Jerusalem, so pure earth could be seen through it.

"Janetka, dearest, I reminded the Father that your favorite gem is diamond. He let me watch the builders make your mansion. Every one of these diamonds represents one you helped bring to righteousness when you were on Earth. So many of them wanted to come to your welcome party."

Jaden stopped counting diamonds when he reached a thousand, and this was on one outside wall of the mansion. The door to the mansion was of bright mahogany set in cedar. Inside were many pieces of furniture gleaming with such beauty that he could not have described to Orpie or Jeb.

Suddenly Jesus was with them. "Daughter," he said, "the Father needs you at the throne." With that, a path opened up to New Jerusalem, and Janetka and all those with her followed Jesus to the throne room. They arrived there faster than the speed of thought, or so it seemed.

All arrived at the throne room. As the new arrival was led through the throne room, Jaden watched angels bring a throne very near the throne of Jesus. On the throne was a crown set with rubies and emeralds, and all kinds of precious stones.

She did not see this, for when she saw the Father on His throne, with the flashes of lightning and the rainbow, and heard the thunder, she knelt and worshiped before the throne, as did all those with her.

While she knelt, Jesus left the Father's side and picked up the crown from the throne the angels had brought. Standing over her He said to her, "Oh woman full of wisdom from the Father, careful to listen to the Spirit of Truth, you have been found faithful in the little that you have had and have not neglected My

Word, but have spoken it no matter the cost! Because you have been found faithful in a little, I am giving you rule over many. Continue in the love and wisdom you have shown as you rule here the way you were shown on Earth."

Much shouting and joy and praise to the Lord of All rang through the throne room. A few had seen what she had come from, and all had seen what she had been since coming to the Lord, for they had been invited to see the film of her life when they heard she was coming.

More cheers rang as she was led to the throne the angels had brought out. Jesus led her to sit on the throne. She got up from the throne and knelt to worship Him. Others went to her after she got up from worship and asked her questions about many things. She answered them with great wisdom, and they understood much that had troubled them while they were on Earth.

After watching her for a while, Jaden left the throne room and picked up a plate of food outside it. After he chatted with some people, a path to Orpie's mansion lit up, and he went back to it.

On his way there, he saw a park with a merry-go-round. He hopped on the merry-go-round with other children and was pushed around by a kindly man who seemed to be in charge of the park. When he felt tired, it slowed down long enough for him and others to get off. Some more children got on to take their place.

Leaving the park, he wondered why he hadn't seen it before. "My son, the man you saw managed a park like that on Earth. He asked to continue managing one after he got here. He is not the only one running it, but he just started soon after you got here." The Lord's answer came before he even asked about it.

In seconds after that, he was at the mansion.

They chatted for a while and watched the video about Jeb. Seeing it for the first time, Jaden asked, "I see him talking to a big man there. Haven't I seen him somewhere here?"

Orpie answered, "You met him at Orientation School. Remember Zach? Well that's who it is. Not too long after that conversation he went and made some things for a small church near his home, like pews and kneelers."

"No wonder he was able to teach me."

Not long after that they both went to sleep, as it seemed a long day, and perhaps it was, but it could have been just a few seconds on Earth time.

Chapter Sixteen Wonderment

When Jaden woke up the next day, the whole atmosphere seemed charged with excitement. He smelled something like ham and eggs, but when he got to the kitchen he saw that it was a dish made from a fruit he had not seen before. A lot of other foods were put out also. He saw Jeb and Rosie at the table with Orpie.

Outside children were ringing bells and playing instruments like harps, horns, trumpets and oboes. He ate some of the fruit dish, finding it tasted just like ham and eggs, swallowed some juice, and ran out to see what was going on. The others followed him outside.

He saw a parade like none he had ever seen before. He and his family were almost the only ones looking on. A man wearing a huge robe sat on a horse leading the parade. The robe flowed over the horse's back, with birds holding up its sides, making it appear that the horse had wings. Even with the man riding that way, he could not see the man's feet.

From all the mansions nearby, people came running out to see the procession, for it seemed that's what it became. Donkeys pulling golden carts and camels loaded with barrels and baskets and rich cloths followed the man, led by people dressed in luxurious garments.

He could see that the whole procession was going to New Jerusalem. He knew that he was still in heaven, and he knew that it was not yet the time of the Millennium or anything like that, but it seemed like something very different from what he had imagined.

The last cart had on the front of it a sign "Offering from the King of North Bolivia to the King of Kings for All He Has Done for My Country." Now not too long before he died, Jaden had heard about Bolivia. When he heard about that country, he heard that it was one land, not two.

But before he could ask about a king of only part of a country, he heard from the Lord, "My people are rewarded for their service to me. It pleases me to give them kingdoms I know they can rule. This man governs ten cities in North Bolivia. Mayors rule under him. When you come down to Earth in the Millennium, he will rule there also."

While Jaden was thinking about that, he also thought about the things that in the carts and on the camels. Besides pottery and large jewels, he saw many kinds of fruit he had not seen before, crowns, sheep, goats, yarn, cloth, spinning wheels, and many different metal toys.

He decided to follow the procession. But before he did, he asked Orpie, "Would you wait for me, I want to get some stuff for the King of Kings, too." And he ran inside the mansion, to his bedroom. He saw next to his drawings and paintings, his diary from on Earth. Finding a backpack, he put everything in it and joined the others.

Following the procession, he saw others come in line behind them. Many of these also had carts and rode horses, and people with them led camels or horses or donkeys. He asked the Lord what was going on.

The answer was, "This is a festival. Although the feast of Pentecost has not yet come, these people did not want to wait so long to celebrate their day of Pentecost. When I rose from the dead, Pentecost was fifty days later.

"My disciples were in one place in Jerusalem, and were baptized in the Holy Spirit that day. That same day 3,000 people decided to follow me and change their ways. After that I began to pour out my

Spirit on many people. Even here people celebrate feast days to me, and this is what these people are doing."

So he followed the people into the city of New Jerusalem. It did not take long, for in heaven everything can move much faster than on Earth. Everyone in the procession had a great big smile on their face as they talked about their own Pentecost experience when the Lord anointed them to preach the Gospel in some way. He did not notice that his family was with him in the parade.

As he neared the gate, which was the one he and his family usually came through, he saw more and more processions approaching the gate from several directions. As they came close to the gate, he saw that there were several kings followed by a number of people in each of the processions.

Looking nearby, he saw the duck from his garden, several other ducks, and a number of other animals following his group. In fact, it seemed like one huge procession was gathering at the gate.

Even though many people and animals were in the procession, there was room at the gate for all to enter, each in their own groups, without bumping into each other.

He could hear the music growing louder as the groups came together. He knew that not all his neighbors were coming, but some had come with them. Thinking about that, he remembered many people had special duties, like Jeb coming to Earth to bring him to heaven.

As groups from every gate came together, he could tell that they were near the center of the city of New Jerusalem, near the throne room itself. He heard the Lord call him by his new name. "Here I am, Lord, and I brought the duck and other animals you gave me to thank you for what you have done for my home town and my family."

"Son, I am well pleased with your offering. You may keep charge of the duck and her family as long as she wants. She will know when I have another assignment for her and will tell you then."

"Thank you, Father. Here is my work. It is little, but I give it freely to you." And with that he gave the Lord his drawings and his journal writings from his time in heaven. He also gave Him the diary he wrote while on Earth. "Father, I don't know how you brought this here, but I give this to you. Make other people see you all through this."

With that, the Lord took his offering and gave it to librarians and shopkeepers. He saved the Earth diary and some of the drawings from Jaden's time on Earth and hung them in a special room. He went to the room later. In it, he found his name in big letters. Nearby he saw Orpie's, Jeb's, and Rosie's rooms. Looking for Hannah's and Chong's rooms, he didn't see either of them, but then he realized that they were not from the same family, and that Chong was from a different Earth country.

As he left his room and the building, he saw that the building's name was "The Father's Children Treasure Room." When he left, he noticed many coming and going. When he got further away from it, he turned back and looked at it again.

His duck came back to him, quacking excitedly.

"You saw your ducklings?" He asked. "They came with other people and then came back to you?"

She quacked some more. A parade of twenty ducks, now fully grown, came to meet her, all quacking at once. He answered, "Of course I'll teach you how to worship the King. We can start at the temple now, if you want."

They all quacked once, and followed their mother and Jaden into the temple. Because it was their first time in there, it seemed like they were there a long time. Perhaps they were. But as always, it was still light out when they headed back to the duck pond in his garden.

It seemed like no time had passed when they got there. Every so often he shook his head in amazement at how the ducks had responded. The mother had helped teach her ducklings the moves she had learned: how to bow, how to cover her face, even how to kneel, duck fashion. From the one time he had shown her, she was now his helper in teaching her children.

Sitting on the porch after he got to the mansion, he wrote down his experiences for the day. He wanted to remember the procession so he drew, then painted some of the scenes from North Bolivia's ruler's procession. He started planning a painting of all the processions coming together. First he sketched in some of the lines coming toward the gate and the part of the jasper wall he could see. Later he would put in details, such as some of the other kings.

After he was done with this, he was ready to rest. He had been so excited by his day that he had gone on the strength of the morning fruit most of the day.

When he entered the mansion, he saw Orpie. "Greetings, child," she said. "Wasn't it great to be part of that procession? I saw your duck and all the things you had with you. Then I saw you give them to the Lord. Somehow you got to keep the duck. I know you loved that."

"Yes, it was fun. That's why I brought the things. He put most of the things in my room, but He gave some to a library and put some in a store. After that, I went into my treasure room, and saw where He put the things that went there. It seems He really likes my diary. He's got an angel to show people around my room. He put my drawings on the walls, my paintings on easels, and He's got pictures of me feeding the ducks by Pascal's home and everything.

"Could you take me to see some horses? I keep hearing that one horse nearby. It might be fun to watch the horses or maybe even learn to ride them. You know I lived in the city on Earth."

"Why not," she answered. "I know where Roy Rogers and Dale Evans have their riding stables."

"Who are they? I never heard of them. Are they someone famous or just ordinary folk?"

"That's hard to answer. In their time they were famous for singing and for a television show, but people didn't talk much about them after they left Earth. He rode a horse on their show, and rode it in real life too. When they got here, that's one of the things they decided to do. They seemed like ordinary folk on their television show, too."

She was saying this as they left the mansion. It wasn't long before they got to a ranch with a huge mansion in the center of it. The sign in front of it said "Evans and Rogers' ranch and riding lessons. Demonstrations and lessons for beginning riders, Trail riding for all skill levels."

As they came through the gate, they saw an arena with many people watching. Some were demonstrating show jumping on one side, and others were showing how to saddle a horse on the other side. In the middle they could see beautiful horses of every description, with a teacher standing next to each horse. Some were demonstrating to students, and others held signs showing they were ready to teach beginners.

"Let's go to the center," he said as he ran up to one of the teachers. The teacher put him on a palomino, adjusted the stirrups, and showed him how to hold the reins while he was led on a short ride around the ring.

"That was fun," he said, "but I'd like to learn how to ride alone, too."

The teacher said, "We can do that too. First we teach people how to get used to being on a horse, how to talk to it, and how to get used to being so high. Some of this takes time. The next time you'll ride your horse with someone riding alongside you and showing you how to use the reins to steer your horse. Then there'll be group rides at that time also. You'll learn.

As he went to sleep, he thought about all the people he had seen. He also was amazed that God had such a big room with all his things in it for people to see. It had been huge, bigger than Orpie's mansion. And his journal from earth was in the center of the room, highlighted, with the angel nearby, ready to explain to people what he had done on earth for God.

Chapter Seventeen Fearfully and Wonderfully Made

Jaden woke up still thinking about the procession, but hungry. Not smelling any breakfast, he looked on the counter in the kitchen and found nuts and fruit there. He ate his breakfast and while he was eating, he found a note on the table.

"Come with me to New Jerusalem," it said. "There's a building that shows why you have a big room celebrating you, [signed] Granny."

Now Jaden really wondered about that, because he had not met his Granny, even in heaven. He knew he had two grandmothers, because everyone did, even if they had not met one of them while they were on earth. But his Granny had died when he was a baby. Every once in a while his mother had talked about how she missed Granny, though. So now he was going to meet his Granny!

When he finished his breakfast, he heard a knock on the door. "Come in," he said as he opened the door. "I saw a note and I didn't know much about my Granny..." Then he looked up and saw a tall woman, so much like his Dad that he knew she had to be his Granny.

She knelt down and picked him up and swung him around, dancing a little and kissing him before she set him down. She shouted, "Thank you, Father, for little Jaden. You had me on your business when he came here, but now you've let me come and see my little grandchild, who's grown so much since he was born." And she laughed and cried all at the same time, wiping her tears with her robe, not caring that they were also dried by the Father.

"Granny," he said. "I'm so glad you got here after all. I cried before the Father wiped my tears because I didn't see you. Show me everything about you, your mansion, your life, everything."

"I'd love to now, but the Father wants to show you wonderful things about you first. Afterwards we can do that if you still want to. We really have all eternity to get to know each other. Let's go."

While she was saying this, she was still holding on to him and they were leaving the mansion, following a bright path to New Jerusalem. It was as if she could not get enough of him, trying to make up for all the years since she had been on earth, the years when they were apart.

"Since I got here, the Father has had me take people from all ages to this Hall of Science we're visiting. I started writing down people's names and things about them that were special, and the books are in the libraries.

"I ran out of room for those books even though I kept giving them to the Father. This last offering was more than four cartloads, two donkey packs, and four horses' worth, besides what I had in my hands. And the people who led the animals looked so happy to lead them! Some were people I showed this building to. I was so happy to give their books to the Father."

They were now at the building. It was taller than some buildings he had already visited in New Jerusalem, and stretched out past what he could see even with his renewed eyes. The sign on the building read "Hall of Biosciences. We Specialize in Showing You What Makes You Unique."

They came into the Hall. While he looked at some of the exhibits, she signed his name to the registry. "Now Jaden, when I watched you on Earth, I noticed you liked the ducks and you had an insect collection. What else was there?"

"Well, I was just beginning to look through a microscope once in a while, and I climbed through the heart exhibit at the museum."

"Hmm. It seems like you were just starting to look at what is called biology, the study of living things. Did you find out anything about how to take care of yourself?"

"Just a little. Things like hand washing, keeping from getting sick, and making sure we had things like meat or protein vegetables, regular vegetables, fruit, milk or cheese, and bread or grains at each meal, things like that. They also wanted us to exercise more."

"Well, you know that here we don't get sick any more, and things like vegetables are really fun to eat and sometimes taste like meat. We eat differently here, anyway. Let's start out with the outer you and work our way in."

"This sign says, 'How God Created You.' Is that what you mean?" he asked.

"Sure is. We'll come in here." When they went through the doorway, they came into a huge room. In the center of the room a machine projected images like holograms. While they watched, they saw a hologram of the Father form in front of it. He was sitting on the throne with flashes of lightning around Him. They saw the Father's arms, shaping a child. After the child was formed, an angel took it from the Father and brought it to a home on earth.

"Granny, the angel's going to my home."

"That's right. On the day that your Mommy knew that she was going to have you, the Father had already sent you to her and you were growing inside her. That angel was assigned to watch over you and to go to the Father on your behalf for as long as you were on Earth. So that angel never left you the whole time you were there."

"Wow! That's special," Jaden said.

"There's more to you than what your parents saw when you were born. Not only did you have the angel, but you had some special things inside of you that made you different from all other people. God made us all unique, and we're here to look at how you are different."

"Now that's something I'd like to see, Granny."

"Let's get to it, then."

While they were talking, they went down a hallway to a huge room with a sign "The Inner You." Inside, he saw a map labeled with "parts of the body", "systems of the body", "chromosomes", "genomes", "molecules", "atoms", and "inner space".

"I never knew there was so much in my body. Are we going to be here a while?"

"Only as long as you want to be. Remember, right now we're in our spiritual bodies only. At the resurrection of our bodies, this is what we'll be in, but without sin and without what made our bodies die. So, where would you like to start? Remember, we don't have to stay here. We can keep on visiting as often as you want."

"I don't know what some of those words mean, but I do know that my body has many parts. Let's start there, like maybe my heart and what goes on there. Sherry Ann had something wrong with her heart. She couldn't do much."

So that's where they started. After they saw a hologram of the heart, they saw it getting magnified, so they could see into the blood vessels and see cells inside the vessels. Then the cells were magnified and they saw closer and closer. They saw one of the cells, a white blood cell, wrap around a dark cell and eat it up. Then they saw inside one of the cells in the wall of the blood vessel. They saw the membrane around it. It seemed so real that he tried to feel the membrane, but he didn't feel anything.

While they looked at the cell, it seemed like they were going toward the center of the cell. Now when they looked at the hologram, a single cell, it felt like the whole room was the cell, and at the center of the room were many strands tightly bunched together.

"What am I looking at now, Granny? I don't get it," he asked.

"Well, what can I say? I think God wanted to show you this stuff without giving you the names of things, just so you could see how some of your body works. You wanted to see the heart and circulation, and we saw that.

"Now we are seeing inside a cell in your body. It's the most basic thing in a body at the biology level. Or at least that's what people learned in high school. But you weren't in high school. So we're looking at it now and perhaps we'll learn the names later. Some of what we'll see doesn't have a name on earth yet."

When Jaden asked the question, the hologram stopped for a while. As they watched, labels began to appear on the things in the cell. They walked around the room, looking at the shapes and names of everything they saw. When they reached each part, they saw it work, then stop as they moved to the next part.

They went inside the center, labeled nucleus. As they watched, some strands unwound as other strands came from outside the nucleus. Then they saw these strands come together and work with each other.

"Hey, Granny! These strands have my name on it. They say Jaden's chromosomes."

"How about that? You know, if you look carefully, you might be able to find some parts labeled on each of the chromosomes, or maybe save it for another time. On Earth scientists spent several years mapping out these strands. They called that the genome project. We have all eternity to look into this. Do you want to continue or should we go on to something else?"

"You mean there's something else here to see now? I know I learn faster here than in school, but I want to write down and draw some things I saw. Maybe later?"

"Well, you saw quite a bit today. So I'm not surprised you want to draw it and journal about it. Should we go to my mansion after all?"

"I was hoping you would say that."

With that, they found themselves outside the building. The brighter path led to the gate towards Orpie's mansion, but when they got near the mansion, it veered off to a place where people had many orange groves and other colorful trees surrounding their mansions.

Near the middle of this area was a mansion with pink and green stones, like the stones in the walls of the city of New Jerusalem, colors in between and gold doors with gold shutters surrounding crystal windows. In front of the mansion stood a magnificent oak tree with a family of squirrels, sheltering a lilac bush and several mango trees.

He started to go past the mansion, when he noticed that Granny was turning to it. So he turned with her. A swing hung down from one of the branches of the oak tree, large enough for two people. She got into it and motioned for him to sit down.

"Jaden," she said, "it's time you heard from me how I got to be here and why you're here early. Most children grow up on Earth, but you're going to do the rest of your growing up here in heaven. People will tell your Mommy and Daddy that they should have asked God to bring you back. But God told them you wanted to stay here, and that's what you're doing."

"I love it here, and I know this is my home for all eternity. Heaven, that is. I know my parents miss me, but I also know God is wiping the tears from their eyes, because he lets me see them every once in a while."

"That's right. God had a plan for you on Earth, and it did not stop once you got to heaven. All the things you've been doing here are part of His plan for you for eternity. He showed you part of it, and I got to see some of His plan when you were born and much more later. Remember watching your funeral?"

"Yes, I do."

"I watched mine, too. It wasn't as pretty a sight as yours was. People were moaning and groaning about how they were going to miss me. They were saying they knew how much good I'd done when I was so young. They forgot how mean I got later on. Then when I finally got right with Jesus, there wasn't much time left for me. I didn't know it at the time, of course. No one knows the date of their death on Earth, or they would be living for Jesus much sooner than I was.

"Now when I was born, I was the middle child of five, two girls and three boys. They didn't get round to naming me until I was a few months old because I was so sick. So for a while I was called Squirt, but my name is Rosanna. They named me after I got healed from that awful sickness.

"During the time that I was so ill I got to see lots of things here in heaven. I got to see where the spare parts for my body were. I asked the Father to put in the spare parts so I could tell the good things he had done. Even though I was a baby, somehow I was able to remember being here at that time. I got to spend some time on Jesus' lap, and it smelled so good. I also remember playing some games with other babies. Angels watched us while we did that."

"You were in heaven while you were a baby?"

"Yes. At night when I was sleeping and while I was so sick. The first time an angel came telling me to get out of bed, I said I couldn't because I couldn't walk. He said just try, and sure enough, I was able to get out of bed after all. I saw myself sleeping, though. He came for me many times. Hey, I even remember seeing you visit heaven after I came up here. But the Father would not let me visit you then. Even then I was showing people how they were made."

With that, she got up from the swing, lifted him up again and swung him around, spinning him effortlessly, set him down, and led him inside the mansion.

"Here's where I am when I'm not about the Father's business. The Father had so many of my relatives working on this, I didn't know what to think when I got here. The beauty overwhelmed me, and I never stop thinking about how good He is. I even asked Him to give me a portal where I could watch what is going on in earth and maybe even participate in some miracles there."

"How do you do that?" he asked. "I didn't think I could work with something like that here in heaven. After all, there is that great gulf like between Lazarus and the rich man, between here and hell, and then we're not allowed to go back and witness to the people we know because they wouldn't believe us. Tell me about it."

"Instead of talking about it, let's just go to the window for the Sudan." With that, they were off to New Jerusalem. When they got there, they saw huge angels near the throne room, dressed in gold. Jaden craned his neck and kept looking up, but could not see the heads of the angels.

After they worshipped in dance, both together and separately, they talked with the Father and got instructions. Then they went to the Portal building. After showing their assignments to the doorkeeper, they went to a room with many others in heaven. As they looked at Earth through the portal, they saw they were viewing a part of Africa that was very poor.

Indeed, it was the Sudan.

While they looked, they saw the people who believed God shining with a great light, fighting dark beings. Angels stood alongside them. They cried out to God, crying out "Jesus!" often. When they did, the angels were strengthened, and the dark beings got smaller.

When one of the shining ones faded, Rosanna or Jaden handed an angel some bread. After getting it, the angels spoke to the people who were fading and getting weak. When these people ate the bread, which had a cross on it and the words "Bread of Life" in big words, from the angels, they got up quickly and went back into battle. When the battle was over, the shining ones knelt in worship, as did Rosanna and Jaden. While all were worshiping, another crew of angels came on the battlefield. They chained the evil beings and gagged them, escorting them away to a prison.

Then the battlefield took on a great glow. Many people were drawn there. As all were worshipping, those who came started asked the shining ones what they had. Those who listened told them how Jesus had bought them the victory.

As they were speaking, angels were encouraging those who listened to the shining ones. While Jaden and Rosanna watched after worshipping, they saw the people come to faith in Jesus, and saw blind eyes opened, the deaf hearing, and the lame walking.

After what seemed a long time in Earth time, they left the Portal building and went back to Orpie's mansion. On their way there, he asked her, "You said you asked for a Portal for yourself. Does this mean you have one in your mansion, too?"

"Yes," she answered. "But most often I go to the one at New Jerusalem so I can be with others there. Sometimes people come to visit me when I'm at my portal. Then they join me in watching and acting on our prayers."

As they entered Orpie's home, they smelled the fragrance of honey and flowers and other good things. Orpie and Jeb were at the table with Hannah and others, yet somehow there was still room for the newcomers.

Chapter Eighteen Rosanna's Portal

Jaden woke up the next day thinking about what Granny had said about having her own portal in her mansion. From what he knew of Orpie's mansion, there was no portal in it. So after a light breakfast, he set out for Rosanna's mansion. His path lit up as he closed the door of Orpie's mansion. As times in heaven went, his journey was leisurely, but in earth time, he took less than a second to get there.

On the way to Rosanna's, he passed a park that he had not noticed the day before, as he had been thinking about what she told him. Seeing a small mountain for climbing, he climbed to the top, then slid down a slide that was built into it. He saw a small pond with a diving board in the center, and reminded himself to look at it closer later. Seeing a walnut tree with ripe walnuts, he picked three of them, and got back on his path, which was still lit up for him.

Walnuts in hand, he got ready to knock on the door of her mansion. Instead the door was flung open for him. "Jaden, I was hoping you'd come by," she said. "I've been at my portal. But first let's get these nuts ready to eat for later." She got out a small hammer, showed him how to crack the nuts open. Setting aside the nutmeats, she led the way to a room with an inside window, a bookshelf with an assortment of books, and some chairs.

"What does it look like? Something like you saw in the Portal building, but maybe better? Or just different?"

"Different. So show me how it works for you."

"The first thing I do is talk to the Father. I don't always go to the throne room building, but could. Instead, I ask Him to show me His will for that day. Some days, as you saw when you first met me, I don't go to this portal or any other at all. I may spend the whole day or part of a day with someone the Lord wants me to guide.

"But on the days I am supposed to help give wisdom to someone on Earth, I usually do it from here. This way, there is privacy for the person I'm working with, as well as privacy for me, if it's needed. Usually not, for the Lord sends people here to learn. Then when they go to their own mansion, they may find an additional room labeled Portal, one which they had not seen before.

"Here's my project today." She led Jaden to the window. As he looked at it, he saw a mountain scene, snow still deep in spots, shallow in other areas. In the center of the scene was a group of men wearing parkas, plodding along with poles on skis.

"These people are on a mountain in the Alps, not the highest mountain, but there is some danger to what they're doing. Let's listen in."

The men were talking with loud voices. Both viewers understood what was being said. "I'm not concerned with what they're talking about," she said. "Let's look at the whole scene."

When she said that, the view expanded so they could see the mountain on all sides at once. The men were working their way toward the sunnier side of the mountain. There was snow on an overhang on the path they were walking on.

"If they keep up this loud talking, one of them will be buried by the snow in an avalanche. It will come from that overhang on the sunny side. Father, we ask that you remind them to be at peace with each other."

When she said that, they saw three angels in the form of other climbers join the men. "Men," the lead angel said quietly, "could we interest you in joining us on our hike? We heard of some beautiful formations on the north side not too far from where you are."

"We would like that," the man who had been talking the loudest said. "Maybe you could help us with a discussion we're having, about which of us is better at climbing this mountain than the others. I think that I am, and the other two guys say that none of us is that good. I've been to rock climbing and mountain climbing schools, and these other two haven't."

The lead angel smiled and said, "Let's listen to the mountain as we go see these formations." They followed the angels around the side of the mountain, at a higher elevation. There was a smooth path, just right for their skis, not too steep, with many places on either side to place their poles.

As they were climbing, the men jumped when they heard a loud groan and whoosh coming from near where they had been. "What was that?" one of the other men asked.

One of the angels answered, "That was an avalanche on the other path, where you were heading. Gentlemen, I think you will agree that the formations you see in this place were worth the effort. Please look at the view before going on. We came here just to look at them and then return where we came from."

Looking in the direction the angel pointed, they saw a cave glittering with icicles like diamonds. Next to it they saw a rock formation that reflected the shape of a cross in the sun.

The men stayed in the cave and ate before they, too, went back down the mountain. When they got to their former path, they saw that they had to make a detour, for the avalanche had landed near their planned path.

"Guess God was protecting us from my loud mouth. One of the things I learned was avalanches start because of loud noises. Can you forgive me?"

"Always. Hey look! The only tracks here are from our skis and poles. Think those other guys were angels?"

"Sure seems like it."

"They stopped shouting," Jaden said.

"But too late to prevent the avalanche. That's why the angels came. The other showed me part of his plan for the guy that was shouting. Once his temper is under control, he's going to be a tour guide, and maybe even a preacher."

"Are all of the things you do at your portal this exciting?"

"No. Sometimes I watch your brother and sister and their families. I want their children to grow up to know Jesus, so I ask God to protect them from the enemy's attacks. I get to see the results of my prayers for people that I knew on Earth. I've got videos to watch about my family and about the people I've prayed for. Every time I watch them there's something different on them, as God answers prayers."

Before Jaden went other places, they watched a video labeled "Answered Prayer in Rosanna's Family." He stopped her after they got into the third full video." "Wow!" he said. "A lot of your prayers have been answered."

"After a while, you'll see your own video like that. That will be something great for you to watch."

As Jaden practiced the piano and the recorder, played baseball with his friends, and visited the throne room through the rest of that day, he thought about the men they had seen.

During his quiet time with the Father that day, he asked for a Portal room to be put into his mansion for when he moved into it. Until then, he thought, it would be fun and exciting to watch through Granny's portal, maybe even share in her prayer adventures.

Chapter Nineteen Babies Who Were Martyred or Stillborn

The next day Rosanna knocked on the door of Orpie's mansion and came in when Jaden answered.

"You have food to share with your Granny, Jaden? I left my mansion before breakfast. I'm so glad the Father is letting me be with you. I want to show you some more things today."

"We sure do, Granny. We have fruit that tastes like mangoes, breadfruit, and oranges all in one. Then there's also yogurt and nuts."

"Great. Hi, Rosie and Jeb. Let's all go together after we eat. This is an area everyone should look at, and some of us have gone back many times because they heard of someone new coming there so often."

"So, why the mystery? Why not tell me the name now?"

"When you see where we're going, you'll want to ask all sorts of questions, and I'm not ready for that now. But some of your questions will be answered right when we get there. The short answer is that it's part of the main Nursery, but set apart from other nurseries in that building."

"Now you've really got me curious, but I can wait."

While they ate, they talked about other things. When it was time to go, he grabbed his drawing book and his journal from his room. The whole family looked at each other, picked up some small things from the mansion, and left following Rosanna.

As they went along, he noticed some women were with them, some carrying small dresses, some small shirts, and some small toys. A few shouted names, thanking God for those people who helped them. Some held clothes against their cheeks. Still others were held up by angels who gave them water and bread.

As they ate the bread and drank the water, they gained strength and soon were walking on their own. When these gained their strength, the angels went to give bread and water to others. Behind each one he could see several people, calling out to them and encouraging them, some walking alongside one of them.

They gathered together at a gate just inside one of the big gates. Over the gate were the words, "Rachel's children: Nursery of the Martyrs." Another sign over a gate almost across the way from the first had the words, "Nursery for the Stillborn."

Rosanna said to Jaden, "These are the homes of some special children. You see our Lord loves you very much. You are precious to Him. Even as you are precious to Him, so the children in these nurseries are special to Him.

"I know that these two signs are not easy to see, but these children came to heaven very early. I am not to take you inside these nurseries, but I would like you to wait here by the gate of the Stillborn while I go and ask someone about some of the people in there."

While Jaden was waiting, he saw some women entering a building between the gates. The sign over it read, "Nursery Workers and Visitors Entrance." He asked Rosanna, "Could I wait inside the visitors' building instead?"

"I think that would work out. But I do know for sure you should not be in the nurseries right away. Okay?"

"Got it. Must be something I'm not ready for yet, and I can wait." She lifted him up, gave him a big hug, set him down, and went through the gate of the Stillborn Nursery. While she did that, he went into the Nursery Workers and Visitors Entrance.

As he entered the building, he found himself in an entryway. There was a huge guestbook, with headings on each page. Next to the guestbook stood an angel wearing a gold sash, with dark brown curly hair and ringlets hanging down in front of his ears. Even though he seemed very powerful and ready to fight off anything, he had a broad smile on his face as he greeted Jaden.

"Welcome, child," he said. "We knew that you would want to come here and check on things here. Did you know that you have a sister nobody in your family met?

"Your mom was hurting before she found out you were on your way. Then Jesus wiped away her tears and she got to know you. She still misses the little girl she never met."

"I didn't know that," he answered. "Will I be able to meet her now?"

"I don't know. Your mother would like to be the first one to see her, then others later, but the Father allows people in heaven to see these children in His timing. I have not been told when you will see her. I can have you sign the guestbook. Then you will be able to see some films about her and maybe other babies after they got to heaven. Perhaps later one of the mothers will bring her child to meet you."

With that, the angel led Jaden to a chair and brought the guestbook to him. At the top of the page, he saw the heading, "Brothers of Lost or Stillborn Babies". There were many signatures. Near the top of the page was Jeb's name, a signature so familiar to him already from his few short days in heaven. Next to Jeb's name was another name, Josetta, with Jaden's last name spelled in Greek letters.

"Who is Josetta? It looks like her name was different from Jeb's. Was he visiting his sister?"

"Yes. Her mother is Greek, and is Jeb's mother, too. We don't know why, for the Father did not tell us why, she rejected His Son, but their mother is not here in heaven.

"When that happens, the Father chooses a mother who has asked Him for a child, and maybe never had one on earth. Before the mother arrives in heaven, the child stays in the Nursery of the Stillborn or the Nursery of the Martyrs until the mother arrives.

"Then the mother works with the nursery workers for a while until she is ready to take the baby home to her mansion. Do you remember the women who were with you on your way here?"

"Yes, there were a lot of them. Some called out names. Some could barely walk and needed help, many had toys and clothes with them."

"These were the mothers that had cried out for their missing children. They got to heaven today and wanted to see their missing children right after they saw the Father. Another worker takes the mothers chosen by the Father for the babies of the other mothers. Now it's time to see the video."

While they were talking, Jaden signed the guestbook near the bottom of the Brothers' page. Immediately after he signed it, a name appeared right next to his name. When he saw the angel close the book right after he signed it, he realized that he was not permitted to talk about the person's name right away.

After the guestbook was put away, he looked at the back of the entry room and saw a scene on the wall. While he was looking, the people in the scene seemed to come to life. He saw that he was in a hospital room, looking at his own mother. She was crying as she looked at a tiny form, wrapped in a blanket but not moving.

"Hon, what did we do wrong that this baby came

so early that it died before it was born? The doctor said he could do nothing for its heart and it was too weak to survive. We asked God to heal her, and look at her. She looks so peaceful, but she's not breathing. Her heart couldn't beat outside my body. What did we do wrong?"

"Joanna, we did nothing wrong. God chose to receive her to Himself. We don't understand why. We just have to trust Him."

"I'm hurting." His father reached out to her and just hugged her. Together they wept.

While they were weeping, he saw the baby, perfectly formed, and moving, in Rosanna's arms. She gently held the little girl as they traveled as on wings and arrived in heaven. He saw her bring the baby to the Father.

Then he saw the Father talking gently to the child. He told the baby, "Well done, good and faithful one. You have been faithful over a little. Come into my joy." He saw Him whisper her name to her. He told her that there was a mansion for her, but first she had to grow up. Then he saw Jesus carrying the girl, his sister, into the Nursery of the Stillborn.

After seeing Jesus carrying his sister into the Nursery of the Stillborn, he suddenly realized that's where he was now. In front of him was a cradle with a name on it. She did not look much bigger than she did in the video, but he could see how well she was.

When he looked around, he saw that he was in a mansion with babies and small children. He saw some of the mothers who had walked with him picking up their babies and kissing them. For them it was a grand reunion, filled with laughter. All were thanking Jesus for the chance to watch these little ones grow up and to take care of them as they had wanted to when they were on earth.

While he was looking for the nursery worker for his sister, Jaden saw Rosanna come up to him. "Who is taking care of my sister until my Mom comes?"

"Why, Orpie, Jeb, Rosetta, I, and all your relatives that wanted to do so have come and played with her and fed her. To her it's felt like only a few days since she got here, but you were born after she came here. Because she was stillborn, the Father gave her some extra growing time, gave her some replacement organs, and is letting her rest until your mother comes. So your mother will get to raise her. She named her Hannah, just like the girl you go to Bible story with, but she isn't the same person.

"Come to think of it, you do look like you aren't very old, but much older than I am."

"For children, that sounds about right. Care for a game of tag?" He saw that she was surrounded by children.

"Sure." And he tagged one of the boys. Soon they were chasing each other all through the nursery grounds. At one point, Hannah became "It" and tagged him. Then he tagged Chong.

After the game of tag, they all sat down to an apple, some yogurt, and nuts. Instead of being sour like most yogurt he had on Earth, it tasted like a sweet-sour pudding. The nuts reminded him of his favorite cereal, with honey flavoring a blend of walnuts and cashews.

Then Rosanna said, "It's time to head to the throne room. Jaden, I know you love to go there because it's your favorite spot. How about leading us?"

"Sure." And a path to the throne led them past the nurseries, near some baby carriages, and into the center of the city. In fact, it seemed that the throne room was so near the Nursery of the Stillborn and the Nursery of the Martyrs that they were there in less than the time it took to say those words.

They worshipped and talked with the Father, dancing with each other, with Jesus, and with Father Abraham and whoever else was nearby. Soon after that, they went to the tables at the back of the throne room, ate whatever they wanted for a snack, and went to their own mansions for a time of rest. Jaden chose a sweet orange that tasted like it had honey on it for his snack.

Chapter Twenty University of the Bible

When he woke up in his own mansion the next day, he was remembering his visit to the nurseries the day before. Seeing his sister's body on Earth and then alive in the nursery made him realize how different he was now from what he had been.

Meanwhile, he could hear voices in the kitchen. Orpie was talking to someone new to him, and there was the clatter of dishes and the fragrance of cut papaya. Leaving his bedroom with his journal and pencil in hand, he saw her with a man in biblical costume. As with all people in heaven, he looked young and stocky, with a huge smile on his face, carrying a harp in his hands. Seeing him, he was glad he brought his journal.

"David," she said, "please sit down. I found out your favorite foods, and we have fruit and vegetables here that taste just like the finest you had on earth, perhaps even better. Jaden, please sit down and try some of this, too."

So he put his journal and pencil on the counter and sat at the table with the visitor. He saw on the table a small plate with something smelling like roast lamb on it, wedges of fruit tasting like honey bread, and milk sweetened with honey. After David blessed the food, they ate and talked all at once.

At one point David brought up the idea of the University. "You know, Orpie, it's not too early to start Jaden learning at the Bible University. Remember, you took my classes on some of my psalms? He can begin to understand some psalms I wrote, the ones I wrote when I was a lad, tending the lambs and sheep, getting the best one ready for Passover."

"Yes. That was soon after I got here. But he's just nine. Won't he be with grownups?"

"Not for these classes. The University has classes taught by people who wrote part of the Bible, as you know. Each of us teaches one or two classes a month just for children, beginning with children his age when he arrived here."

"Hey, Jaden, how about that? Sounds like we can get you into Bible study with other children, and you can learn from people like King David, here, who wrote some of the Psalms, and other writers of books of the Bible, whenever you want. Let's check it out."

"Sure, Orpie. I really think I'll like school here. Instead of learning everything all in one building, I'm getting to go all kinds of different places and learn from many different teachers. Remember how that math teacher got me started learning math the easy way? I like this way a whole lot." With that, David, who really was King David, led the way to a series of huge buildings, bringing them to the center building, Bible University School of the Psalms.

"Now here, if you're starting as a child, like you, Jaden, you don't have to register for classes. All you have to do is show up at any time listed in the building you want for your children's class, and it starts right away. You see, anytime someone comes to one of these buildings, the schedule changes immediately. God is so eager for His children to learn the Bible that He wants all His children to be able to learn from all the authors, even those that just wrote a few paragraphs."

As he said this, they entered the School of the Psalms. One sign listed room numbers for each of the authors: David, Asaph, Solomon, Ethan, Moses, some Korahites, and others whose name were not mentioned in the book of Psalms. Another sign pointed to the children's auditorium and a general auditorium.

As he led the way to the children's auditorium, the noise level increased. The children were shouting,

"Tell us more, Moses. You did so much for the children of Israel. We love what you did when you parted the Red Sea. It was great when you told us about hearing God speak to you so much."

"I love talking about that, too, but God is the one who parted the Red Sea and all the things you think I did. Anyone who wants to draw close to God can hear Him speak to them often. Do you go to Him often? You can go to His throne room any time and talk to Him."

"Yes, Moses. We'll do that."

"Now for those of you who want to go right now to the throne room, there is a messenger outside this building ready to take you there." There was a great round of applause and then many children went right by them.

After the children passed, David led the way into the auditorium. They found seats near the front. As they sat down, they looked around and saw that the whole auditorium was full. Yet it seemed that each child had a front row seat, for all could see without much effort.

David bounded up the platform and started playing on his harp. Gradually the auditorium quieted down as the children realized he was playing and singing. The song was Psalm 23. When he got to "Yea though I walk through the valley of the shadow of death," everyone sang the rest of it with him, changing the last part to "and I am living in the house of the Lord forever." The building shook with the sound of their praises as the angels with all the people joined in the song.

When they were finished singing, David said to them, "When I wrote that song, I was watching the sheep as a little boy. I was not much older than you were when you came here from Earth.

"Even then I protected the lambs and their

mothers from the lions and bears that were after them. As I fought those animals, I was able to use my slingshot.

"With God behind me, the slingshot was as strong as the swords warriors used in Paul's days on Earth. Yet it was not big. Here's a slingshot I still use."

With that he took out a slingshot from the pocket of his garment. It was small, just a little bigger than his hand, yet all could see it. "The stone that I threw at Goliath was the same size as one of these stones." And he showed them a stone no bigger than his hand.

David talked a while about how he took care of the sheep. The children asked questions about how the sheep followed him, what they ate, and about his life.

Soon some of the younger children seemed to be yawning. So David said, "How about we just take a break and come back again at another time? We have all eternity to learn much more. Remember this, though, God is watching you like I watched over the sheep. He loves you very much, and so do I."

They left the auditorium with the others and went to a nearby park, where they sat and ate fruit from the Tree of Life, for they were near the River of Life. When he tasted the fruit, it was like orange flavored lemonade, but better.

After eating, he asked, "Is there a library near here? I'd like to look at a book or video about Israel in King David's time." He was still speaking when they saw a path light up at the far side of the University of the Bible. So they followed the path and looked inside the building it led to.

When they got inside they saw a sign, "Experience Israel throughout history or just choose your interest." He keyed in "King David as a child."

After he did that, they found themselves in a room with many different scenes on all the walls. While they watched, they saw a baby being held by its mother, with many brothers and other relatives looking on. They saw the parents naming David, teaching him and his brothers, assigning all the brothers different tasks as they grew up. None of the brothers showed an interest in animals, so David was assigned to tend sheep.

They watched as David carefully checked each sheep day after day, taking burrs out of the wool, tending the ewes at the birthing of the lambs, shearing the sheep, and leading some of the lambs to his father to take to the temple for Passover.

As the video ended, they saw David trying on Saul's armor before going to battle Goliath, and tossing it aside as he picked up the five smooth stones before killing Goliath.

"Wow!" he exclaimed. "I didn't know that shepherds did all that stuff for the sheep. David was so good at it. He even went after the sheep if they started to go away. And he took his harp with him every time he went out to take care of the sheep. It looks like he had a lot of time for singing."

"It seems that way, doesn't it? But he loved the sheep and he loved the Lord. You saw how he sang without the harp and called each sheep by name. They knew he cared about them. You saw how they didn't listen to anyone else."

"Yes, that's a lot to think about." While they were talking, they saw Jesus leading some children to them.

"Jaden, I brought these children so you could join them for a late afternoon Bible story time. Orpie, I love how you take care of him. I want you to join us, too." So they all sat around Him. He talked about what King David said about the coming Messiah in the

Psalms. He asked questions about how the shepherd took care of the sheep. He also reminded the children that one of His names was the Good Shepherd.

When they were finished, Jaden saw that while Jesus was talking with them, they were coming back towards the mansion. He was at the same place where Jesus led his group in morning Bible story time. After Bible story time, he and Orpie went into the mansion for their evening activities.

A card table rested next to the wall. Taking it out, he put a chair on each side of it. After that he took a puzzle from his room out of its box. Together he and Orpie began to assemble it. After getting half of it put together, they called it a night.

Afterward, he did much journaling and drawing about what he saw and did that day.

Chapter Twenty-One Experiments

When Jaden woke up the next day, he glanced through his journal, seeing the questions he had written down during his early days. He remembered wondering what the colors of the sashes people wore meant, especially the blues or the greens that most people seemed to be wearing. He knew that he did not have one, but that didn't bother him, because he still had some growing time, even here in Heaven, and schooling to take, before he could fully do what God had shown him when he first got here.

Now, though, he thought he had some of it figured out, and wanted to test his theories. He wrote down all the different colors people wore, and he wrote names of the people wearing it. He also wrote down the color of the sash Jesus wore, purple, and noted next to that color, "only Jesus."

Starting with King David, whom he had seen just the day before, he wrote down that David wore an emerald sash, green like someone else he had seen, but he wasn't sure who it was. Then he remembered seeing Moses that day also. The color of Moses's sash was different, and he was not sure what that color was called. It was not like the colors he painted with. He'd have to ask Orpie about it. So from those two different colors, he knew that there was something different about their purpose in the Kingdom of God or their fruit, both in heaven and on Earth. King David had been a ruler on earth, but now only Jesus wore a purple sash, so the new color had to mean something different.

So he wrote down some of the things each person he knew did now or had done on earth, also writing down a fruit that he thought they were known for. Since Jesus was the only ruler over everything in heaven, Jaden thought that His purple meant that He was royalty, and no one else was royalty in heaven.

Next to Moses' name he wrote a question mark next to color name, and then wrote a list of the things he knew Moses did. The main thing that he really starred was that he talked to God face to face.

Next to David's name he wrote emerald. The things he wrote after that were "man after God's own heart," "took good care of the sheep," and "sang about longing for God in the Book of Psalms."

When it came to other people he had met, Jeb was next. He had a green sash, but not the same color as David's. He wrote down some of the things he knew about Jeb and wrote down what he thought that green meant.

By the time he wrote down all the people he knew and all the color names for the color sashes they wore, there was a long list of names divided into more than twenty columns for colors and subdivided into about three different meanings for each color column.

He thought it would be good to run an experiment to see how close his guesses were to being correct for each color. Right after a breakfast of cinnamon apple, he set about testing his ideas, almost scientifically, except he had not heard of scientific methods yet, just that it seemed like a good way to get to know more about heaven through other people.

He began by looking for Jeb. So he asked the Holy Spirit to guide him to where Jeb was at that time of day. He saw a path lighting up away from New Jerusalem and toward a small lake. Beside the lake he saw a park, some swings, a little girl, some sheep, and a donkey. Thinking it was a little odd, he got a little closer. He saw Jeb, sitting down with her. A few of the sheep were around both of them, rubbing their noses against them. Jeb was humming a little tune while she ate a small apple.

"I wanted to ask you to tell me about the time you got that green sash. I mean like when you first came to heaven or whenever it was that you got it," Jaden said, without paying attention to the little girl or anything around them. "I'm trying to figure out what all these colors mean, like maybe telling me what people do, or something."

"I was wondering when you would get around to this question. Seems to me you always wanted to know stuff about people."

"Even before I got here, you mean. Right?"

"Yes, Jaden, even then. I remember watching through the portal when you were just a little tad, seeing all that curiosity and wondering what it would all lead to.

"So now you want to know about these sashes. Well, let me see. It wasn't long after I got my heaven messenger job, picking up people on Earth and taking them to heaven, going place to place here, and running errands for the Father to and from Earth."

"I didn't think people were allowed to visit Earth after they died."

"They aren't really. But every once in a while the Father allows them to go on errands, fix up things a little bit here and there, things like that."

"Like what?"

"Remember that time when your dad thought that he was really lost and almost had to stop for directions?"

"And someone showed up at just the right time to rescue him? Yes, I remember."

"Well, I wasn't on Earth, but I asked Father to send one of his friends to get him back on the road. I don't know whose prayers were answered. I think it was what Jesus called the prayer of agreement.

"For a while I was his prayer partner on this side, while a lot of other people on Earth were praying for him when your family was running late. So it may have been a lot of people praying for your Dad right then, not just my doing, and your Dad got the benefit of the Father's love for him. His friend was really great in helping straighten out his sense of direction."

"Now, when I was on earth, stoplights helped traffic, and green meant go. Do you think that's why you got the green sash?"

"Well, messengers get to go a lot of places, and stoplights stand in just one place. Know what I mean?"

"How about this for an idea? My main job here really isn't about watching portals and the prayer of agreement. When I was on Earth some things I did for God had to do with getting people's lives changed around. After work sometimes I'd preach in little meetings where the people really had messed up lives. Not too long after I started talking to them that way, they'd change for the better.

"Before I knew Jesus, I was messed up with things like alcohol also. You know that can make lives miserable."

Jaden wrote these things next to Jeb's name on his list and said, "Thanks, Jeb. Who's this little girl here?"

"She's a great-great granddaughter of a friends who didn't get his life straightened out. Her life on Earth was shorter than yours. The Father made me one of her foster parents while she waited for her mother to come to heaven."

"So you're helping her with her new life here. I wonder if your green sash has to do with helping people get their lives together, or helping them with their new life in Christ."

"Could be. You could talk to some other people about what they do to help you figure that one out."

"Thanks, Jeb. I'll probably do a lot of that today.

Of course, that could take a while, and eternity is a long time."

When he left Jeb, he thought about Orpie. Right away, a path lit up, but it did not lead to the mansion. As he went down the path, he noticed that the mansions were a little like the Greek homes he saw from Orpie's parents.

He came to a mansion with many diamonds encrusted in the walls, and clear diamonds instead of glass for windows. Before he even knocked on the door, it was opened by someone he remembered from the film.

"Welcome, grandson," the man said. "I was expecting to see you today. The Father told me you had a special project you were working on."

"Well, I don't know how special the project is, but I wanted to find out what all the colors meant for these sashes. You're wearing blue, and so is Orpie."

"That's right, child, and we were married to each other when we were on earth. I got here first. You may not know this, but sometimes our mansions are put in different places from other family members so we can spend special time with each other and get to know each other better than we ever did on earth.

"So, since I got here first, I got this mansion, and Orpie stays with me quite a lot. But you hardly see that, because she leaves her mansion while you're sleeping sometimes or when you do your errands. That's when she stays with me."

"So you're my grandpa Eddie. You look a lot different from the picture my Mom has of you. I'm glad I finally get to see you. I don't remember you from my party, though."

"I had a lot of bad things happen to me when I was young, and I got old and had gray hair. Now I'm in my youth for all eternity, and all those scars are gone, never to return. But some of those scars were turned into special mementos because of how I got them."

With that, Eddie showed him a place on his arm that had a diamond, and one on his wrist with a ruby. Jaden tried to take it off his grandpa, but it was firmly embedded. He could only touch it.

"When I was in a concentration camp for my faith, before we got to the United States, my hand and my arm were wounded very badly, and I almost did not survive. They healed, but there were terrible scars where these gems are now.

"God healed my heart, so I could forgive the people who did that, but I asked Him to let me have something to testify of His goodness, and these were what he gave me.

"The diamonds on the walls of my mansion are for all the soldiers and others that God brought to himself while during my life.

"So it was like what you did in life was God's grace for other people to get to know Him."

"You could say that. All I know is that I saw a lot of people get to know Him. But I had to learn to forgive them.

"As for not being at your party, I was on errands for the King, and didn't feel it was the time afterwards to come. But now was the time for us to meet."

"God's grace for you led you to forgive and led these people to accept and follow Him. How about Orpie? Was she like that before I knew her too? Except for the scars, because I didn't see any, I mean?"

"She was my example in forgiving those who were not lovely and were difficult to forgive. The hardest thing, at times, was to forgive those who hurt me. By God's grace I did, otherwise I wouldn't be here.

"But Orpie, even during the times when we were separated from each other because of that terrible war, you always shone with the grace of God and forgiveness for all, especially for those who betrayed us after we befriended so many.

"When she's not with you or me, she's with babies who were martyred or stillborn, showing God's great grace and power for all of them. She and Rosanna watched hundreds of babies from the time they got here until the time they got either foster parents here or one of their parents came here."

Jaden made notes next to "blue sash" and added a column for diamonds and rubies as well. "Wow, Grandpa Eddie. That's a lot to think about. Did the Father tell you about the project?"

"Yes, child, almost from the day you were born. The Father wanted us to be ready to answer your questions, because He has a special plan for this experiment you're doing."

"Oh, I'm so glad. It just seemed so exciting to be doing something like this."

After talking with his two grandfathers (Jeb being several generations before Eddie), Jaden went on to talk to many people that day.

One of the people he talked with, Benjamin, showed him how to make a kaleidoscope. Together they made three of them, so he could give two to friends. The colored bits of paper inside the tubes were immersed in something to strengthen them, yet remained translucent. When he held them up in the light bursts of color formed crowns, roses, tulips, angels, and many other shapes. He sketched some of his discoveries from these onto drawing paper before making paintings of them.

Before he headed to his bedroom, he and Orpie finished the puzzle they had started the day before. The picture was a beautiful castle, almost like a mansion.

By the end of the day, when he was so tired, he

felt like he had barely started this project. He wrote down some ideas for continuing it.

But before he went to sleep, he talked with the Father about the day, shared his thoughts about the experiment, and got some names for people to visit. He jotted down some things he would ask them, as well as where he would find them.

Chapter Twenty-Two Love

When Jaden got up the following morning, though in heaven it is hard to tell when it is morning, he thought about what everyone had shared with him. The aroma of food was so overwhelming he ignored his journal. Instead, he went into the kitchen first.

Rosanna was there, visiting with Orpie and Jeb. "Hi, Jaden! I didn't think you'd mind if I tag along on your project today. Anyway, I'm here, and we can talk about it during breakfast."

Orpie handed him a plate of fruit. From it he took what looked like an apple and a small section of pomegranate. Eating the apple first, he found it tasted also like cinnamon nut bread with another flavor that he couldn't put his finger on. After he finished that, he ate the pomegranate, enjoying the crunch of the seeds on his teeth, and washing it down with milk.

"Tastes like coconut, not much like milk."

"As you know, the Father likes to surprise us with some of our favorite flavors in new ways. What do you think about Grandma Rosanna's idea?"

"Sounds great. Maybe she can give me some pointers. Don't I have a music lesson today at the conservatory?"

"Yes, you do. You can ask your teacher some of your survey questions. I know he's been given a lot of time to teach you this week. I think maybe he has some idea that you're really gifted."

"Did you know that he already has me on book three of the series he's using? Last week we went through all of book two. He said I played well enough that we might get into some of the slower Chopin etudes, or maybe some music he wrote."

"That's farther than I got before I quit when I was a little girl. I found I enjoyed cooking more than music. Now, you can run along. You and Grandma Rosanna have a lot to talk about."

"So, Granny, what do you think about the music? Yosef's been working with me for only about a week now. Last week, after everything else I did, sometimes in between, he let me come in for special lessons. I only met him last week, too. It's like he's got just me as his student. But I know he has other students."

"Well, Jaden, you are special. In God's eyes, even though your life on earth was so short, you are very special. He's got you learning a lot so you can do a unique task for him. Didn't He show you some of it during your first week?"

"Ye-e-e-e-s. It just seemed like there would be a lot to do and that I would have to learn a lot and all that."

"It seems that Yosef is one of your special teachers for this task. In fact, I think I would like to meet him and maybe learn some things from him too, maybe even music. You know how much I dance, right?"

"Yep. So let's go. I have to get my music and my journal, and a few other things, too."

After Jaden got his things together, they left Orpie's mansion and found a path lighting up for their visit to the Conservatory of the Composers. While they were going, Rosanna took him on a side trip to some mansions.

One mansion they visited was on a path near a forest with a lot of deer. In some ways it looked like the castle from England, like the one in his puzzle, complete with turrets and flags, a moat gleaming in the brilliant light, and many bridges leading to many gates in the building.

"So who lives here?" Jaden asked. "I'd sure like to meet them."

"That's why I brought you here first. The people here are people you would not have looked at twice on Earth. They lived in a bad place in London before they came to the United States, and got there while it was still colonies.

"When they got here, they wanted to live together as the husband and wife they were on Earth. Families there were separated for so much of the day that they could not spend their time together.

"In England before they got to the United States, they worked for people in castles. Every day they went home and struggled to find food. When they heard about living in America, they went on a crowded boat. But they had to sell their labor to get there."

"So what did they do? When they got to America, I mean?"

"Maybe they'll tell you their story. Remember, even if you don't find out today you can find out later. It seems like they're busy today."

With that, they arrived at one of the many doors to the mansion. They found all the doors were open. People were going and coming through five different doors. Those who came in brought gifts of many different sorts. Those who left carried exquisite garments of many different styles, some never seen in a fashion book or recorded in history, for the designs had not yet been released on earth. All were talking of all that they had seen.

"Granny, what is all this? So many people are coming into these people's mansion. How many people live here?

"Just the two people I told you about. God gave them their heart's desire, which was to live together and show others what they had wanted others to show them while they were on Earth.

"They never received from others on Earth, but now they're receiving more than they ever dreamed.

And they're giving out much more than they ever dreamed they could give. They are so happy, they don't seem to know that most of heaven's people are beating paths to their doors."

"Wow! They must be really special."

"People on Earth decided that these people were just someone to give orders to. If you saw them on Earth, you would never have talked to them, when they were alive. But now, all talk to them and seek their wisdom."

While they were talking, a man came up to them. "Hello, Jaden. I didn't know when you'd come, but we're both glad to see you. This is my wife, Geraldine. We both live here, and are so happy you came."

"I didn't bring you anything special, but these are some pictures of my duck and her ducklings. It was so great watching them all worship that day. She asked to come here with me."

"Jaden, Tommy and I are so happy you came. We love to meet artists of all kinds. We can see how God wanted you to come here when you did. Come in, come in."

Many others followed them in, but it seemed as if Tommy and Geraldine were only focused on him. They led the two of them into a grand hall having a long table set with many foods. "Rosanna, you will have the seat of honor, for some of the children you have helped raise have asked to serve you today. Jaden, we are asking you to join us in this celebration, for some of these children will join you in some of your activities here."

With that, five people sat on either side of the table, with Tommy and Geraldine at either end of the table. There were other chairs next to them, and before long the table was filled.

Jaden was seated next to Tommy and Rosanna next to Geraldine. The feast had the aroma of roast chicken, but he found that the dish was made with several types of beans and grains, and a vegetable he had not seen before.

During their meal, some people left the table, others sat down, and many more stopped to chat with Tommy or Geraldine, sometimes Rosanna as well. All the while they ate, people kept bringing in dishes to try.

Finally, when all at the table had had their fill, he saw that they had close to thirty people sitting with them, with more people standing behind each person at the table.

"Granny, who are all these people? I didn't know you helped so many people."

"The people standing behind these chairs are all people who were children when they got to Heaven. I carried many of them from Earth to heaven and was honored to help them get to know heaven and to learn while they were waiting for their fathers and mothers."

"The people sitting with us at the table are some of their parents and grandparents who got to care for them after they got to heaven," Tommy added. "We were delighted to be appointed a way station for parents to meet their children after they came here and for the children to honor the foster parents who helped raise them.

"And now, for the guest of honor, Rosanna."

"Thank you, Tommy, but I am not who this party is for. Jesus wants us all to come to a concert at the conservatory, where you will be able to hear the seraphim and your favorite composers and musicians play for you. Before we go, here He is to speak to us." When they looked towards the door, they saw Jesus wearing His kingly robes and scepter. They all fell down and worshipped Him. Jaden looked at Jesus' eyes and saw pools of love. It seemed as if Jesus and he were the only ones in that great room.

Before they realized it, they all found themselves in the great auditorium of the Conservatory of the Composers. Instead of being a musician, as he had been when he first came, Jaden watched Yosef play a concerto with a beautifully made viola an alto singing every note with him and praising God with a psalm.

Following that, he saw another violinist take up a cello and lead the whole string section in a symphony for strings. A choir joined in singing praises to God with another psalm. One of the flute players directed the entire flute section as they played a Mozart flute concerto while a soprano sang with the flutes.

A tenor sang with the cello section while they played a cello concerto. Next, a bass sang with the basses, keeping up with all the notes in an intricate bass concerto.

The concert closed with a concerto grosso, the entire orchestra showing its abilities, and voices of every range, in the audience and on stage, joining them, singing praises to God, and many matching the orchestra's harmonies. He had never heard his parents describe a concert like this, and wondered what people on Earth would think if they heard something like this, especially the concerto grosso ending with only one player playing the final note. All these thoughts flashed through his mind as he joined all the musicians and the rest of the audience in kneeling to worship Jesus.

"Children," He said, "once again today you have pleased me in worship. You give me great pleasure when you worship and praise me, for your hearts are pure. You have small tasks to do today, and you will not find them hard, for they will bring great joy to those around you.

"If you have not yet received today's instructions you are invited to the throne room for fellowship with the Father immediately. If you have your instructions for the day you are invited to come when you are finished. Go now in the Joy of the Lord."

He saw he had taken everything with him from Tommy and Geraldine's mansion. Seeing that he was prepared, he left the auditorium and went into the student entrance of the huge Conservatory of the Composers building.

Quickly he found Yosef's room, but didn't see him there. Finding a note he read, "Jaden, come to the stage in the auditorium today. We have to practice for a concert." Shaking his head in wonder, Jaden went around to the players' entrance and walked onto the stage. In front of him, he saw Yosef, some of the Korahites he had met at the Conservatory, Rosie, and others he had not yet met.

Yosef began by saying, "Jaden, for this concert, you are to play the piano, as you have practiced. Rosie will play several instruments, depending on what piece we are playing. Some of these musicians will play biblical instruments and the other musicians will play instruments they started learning recently.

"This is our first rehearsal. For this concert, we will play by listening with our hearts to what the Lord would have us play. Because some of us are not familiar with working without music in front of us, we must have two rehearsals, and then we will play for others."

Rosie continued, "Our first piece is 'My Soul Magnifies the Lord and my Spirit has Rejoiced in God my Savior.' The singers will listen while we play and then they will start singing when the Lord shows them to sing. They will sing a fresh melody and fresh harmonies, even as we play them, as the Lord directs. Let's begin by listening to the Lord for the music and the instrument we need to use. When we have heard His answer, we will begin."

After a few moments silence, they each picked up an instrument, Jaden sitting at the piano, and began playing. Hearing a few bars of a new melody, the drummers began playing softly while instruments embellished the melody, passing it back and forth. He played chords, which signaling the entrance of the singers. Soon all were singing and playing the Magnificat to a new melody.

After this song, they went on to several other songs. Sometimes Rosanna danced to the music, and other times she sang or listened. After rehearsal was over, Yosef and Jaden talked for a while. Then Yosef said to Rosanna, "We are forming a small company to show musicians how to play and sing together without music to look at, as we did just now. You are welcome to join us whenever you like."

"Yosef, honey, only God likes my singing, and that is good. That is why I prefer dancing. I sing only when the words are so great I can't help but sing." They all laughed at the remark.

"Okay, Rosanna, I get the hint. But when everyone sings, you join us in worship, okay?"

"Okay, I agree. Maybe like I did just now, as the Holy Spirit leads."

When the rehearsal was over, Jaden got out his notebook. But before he said anything, Yosef asked him, "Jaden, what do you think of this? I got this sash that goes across from left to right, like some king, right? But I'm not a king now. And I wasn't a king on earth. I don't think I was that special on Earth, either. But when I get to heaven, I find I'm wearing this sash. Tell me what you think about it."

"Well, it's red, and God says in one of Peter's letters that He made us kings and priests to our God. So, doesn't it mean you rule something?"

"I don't know. You tell me. When I got here, I met Rosie, and she showed me some things here. I went to Orientation School, and I guess I'm still in that, but I got all these children coming to me for lessons, and I find myself directing an orchestra. What color red is this?"

"Brighter than the red on the flag. I don't know. I thought I saw one of the angels wearing a bright red uniform, almost like this red, but with gold buttons. Did you have to maybe do some preaching or praying or something like that?"

"I did a lot of praying when things weren't going well on earth. I don't know. I had to pray because a lot of people got sick and there was a lot of bad sin where I lived. I had to ask God to protect my people a lot.

"Some of my people were in concentration camps, too, and there was a spiritual enemy there. I led people in prayer against it. Maybe that had something to do with this sash?"

"I don't know. I'll see if that's like other people wearing red sashes. I think that Granny wanted to take me to visit other mansions, but Jesus changed what we're doing."

"He sure did. Yosef, would you like to join us at the throne room now? Or do you have something left from the assignment the Father gave you today?"

"I'm free to go to the throne room. When I was on Earth, I spent a lot of time there in prayer."

With that, they found themselves in the throne room in less time than it took to say these words. When they got there, there was a combination of a party and worship service going on.

Those that just came in, like Jaden and Yosef, laid their crowns in front of them and lay prostrate before the throne, closing themselves in with the Lord and listening to His voice in the middle of the party.

As they got up, they began seeing some newcomers among the people there. It was then that Jaden realized they were now in the Welcome Center. After worshiping, these people were gazing at the sights, hugging people they knew, meeting others, and dancing every once in a while with Father Abraham and the others.

"Children, these came out of great tribulation to enter here. They are not the last of those who are to come after much tribulation. But their number is nearly complete. Welcome them and join their party."

With that, He led a conga line with some of the people, and Abraham led others in a dance similar to Hava Nagila. Even though a conga on Earth has a rhythm unlike Hava Nagila, the lines looked exactly right. As the music sped, more and more dropped out of the line, until only the leaders were dancing.

Again they were back in the throne room. Yosef and other violin players played a song of praise, and all joined in, some playing other instruments, others adding their own words to the melody or harmonies as they saw fit.

Jaden saw that some were kneeling alone, in awe over being in God's presence. He went to join them, adding his voice to theirs. While there, he saw prophetic visions of his family's future. After seeing the visions, he went to the Holy Spirit to ask Him to protect them and cause them to remain true to Him.

After these visions, he went to see South Africa through a portal. As he watched, angels surrounded the Christians. He saw some missionaries leave the country and go to other continents. He saw great clouds of darkness over parts of the United States. As the missionaries and others prayed against the clouds, the clouds over their areas became smaller and pockets of revival broke out.

Again he looked, and the portal was changed to another African country. He saw a man arrive from Germany and begin preaching to many people. Many small churches formed as they heard the Gospel. They took small portions of the Bible they had and looked for more parts of the Bible. People copied out parts of the Bible by hand when they could not buy it. He saw people in other countries, even other continents, copying out the Bible, some hiding it in their home, writing it out longhand, and handing out the copies to other Christians.

He saw a nation with a demonic king with many tentacles spreading out the tentacles from near the Middle East to many parts of the world. The king whispered in the ears of many people, saying their god was the only true god.

Then he saw angels going to the leaders of those countries, showing them the truth of Jesus Christ. He saw as one by one they came to Jesus. He watched as these new believers stood their ground. He saw some taken up into heaven, and he recognized some of these believers as people he had just met in the dances Jesus and Father Abraham had led in the Welcome Center.

After seeing these things through the portals, Jaden went back to the food table, eating a plantain, and then went into the throne room again and knelt down in worship. When he got up, he saw that his mother duck and some of her ducklings were also worshiping in a row right behind him. He held out his arms to them and talked to them for a little, calling them by name.

Before long, he and the ducks returned to his garden as the path lit up for them. Seeing the swing in the garden, a gift from Jeb, he sat on it, just enjoying how it felt, and drifted off to sleep. He did not notice as someone walked up and dropped a note.

In his dreams, he went to the throne room again. This time he watched the angels who were taking papers to the room for his home town. He watched as Pascal's mother's name was written down. He joined the people who rejoiced, returning to the swing again and smiling in his sleep.

Chapter Twenty-Three New Friend

When Jaden woke up, it was a new day, both there and on Earth, but to him it did not seem that way. As he rejoiced over Pascal's mother, he noticed that while he was sleeping, someone had tucked a light quilt around him, and left a note for him. "I'm glad that you're in your garden today," the note said. "When you finish reading this, go into the school building, pick up the kit you see at your chair, and meet me by the pond. Jeff."

Jaden remembered the day he had met Jeff. When he was in the auditorium hearing about Noah, he had sat near Orpie, with two other boys. Jeff seemed older, maybe twelve or thirteen, but he clapped and answered questions just like the other boys and girls. Jaden thought he could become a good friend. After all, he had all eternity to get to know anyone he wanted to know.

Getting up from the swing, he walked the short distance to one of the many doors in the school building. Like on any heaven school day, a smiling, tall angel stood near the door, greeting the children and teachers as they entered and left the building.

As he entered the building, he thought about how much he liked to learn in school, but it was like a dream, a shadow of what he could learn here. Looking around the school again, he saw that it was so very different every time he came here. His chair still had his name on it, and was still in the same place, but now it had some carving on it, especially around his name. While he looked at it, he remembered the note and went up to it.

Near the chair was a kit with a picture of a boat on the outside. It seemed to have a lot of wood in it, two knives, as well as other things. Seeing an angel nearby, he asked, "What can you tell me about this? I need some help with this, too."

The angel answered, "Your friend Jeff will show you what it's about. It'll be fun. John here will help you carry it." Even as the angel spoke, a man came up to him, tying the large end to his own hand and the small end to Jaden's hand. Lifting up his end, he followed Jaden out the door.

At the speed of thought, they came to the pond in his garden. He saw Jeff there, swirling the water with his fingers and splashing the ducks. The ducks were splashing him right back. The quacks seemed more like laughs than duck language.

"Hey Jaden, ready to start?" Jeff asked.

"Whenever you are," he answered. He turned to say, "Thank you, John," but he was already gone.

"Okay, here's the deal. We are going to make a boat for your pond, not because you need one here, but because boats are pretty and sometimes you like to ride in them."

"Like when I rode from one end of a lake to the other and it seemed like no time before we were on the other side."

"Yes, like that."

So they each got out a knife. Following the diagram in the kit, they joined the pieces of wood together. When they got to the inside of the boat, they saw that the instructions were to carve pieces like the pictures in front of them. But Jaden was hungry.

"Let's pick some fruit and find some tomatoes," he said.

"Well, I'm fond of chicken and wouldn't mind some berry pie," Jeff answered.

With that they found a fig tree and picked four figs, then picked two tomatoes.

"Well, what do you know," he commented. "This fig tastes like roast chicken and the other fig tastes like the best red raspberry pie I've ever eaten."

"One of mine tastes a lot like the best cheesy lasagna I've ever tasted. But the other piece tastes like red raspberry pie. Did you eat your tomato?"

"Yep. Nothing like what I had the last time I ate one. It tastes like fried green tomatoes."

"Mine tastes like pepper and tomato mixed together. I always liked the way Mom served that at home."

After they finished eating, they went back to work on the boat. Soon they had it ready for a trial run.

"Hey Mama Duck! Want to go for a ride on the boat?"

Jaden heard her say in duck language, "No, but I'll swim ahead of you." He laughed at that, and laughed even harder when he looked at the boat.

"Know what?" he said. "We didn't make the oars."

"So that's why there's so much wood left," Jeff laughed. "Guess we'd better work on that." They carved the oars using the directions in the kit and attached them to some oarlocks they had made. After that they went on the trial run, and found that they were on the far side of the pond in two strokes.

When they landed the boat, they saw that they could not see the other side of the pond. "Hey, look at that!" Jeff exclaimed. "We really went far. And there's your mama duck, swimming to meet us. We're so far away from her. Do you think she'll want to us to wait for her?"

"No, I think she just wants to swim for a while. Let's go exploring."

They were going into a small woods as they talked. As they looked around, they could see some bees busy around their hive, some leaving to visit flowers, others coming back into the hive.

Jaden could hear them singing. It sounded something like, "Gathering pollen, that's the thing to do. We gather for love of man and young. Our gardener sees our work for all. We praise God he's here for us."

"Do you hear the bees' song? Isn't that something? They'd sting us on Earth. Now they leave us alone. It sounds like they're glad we're here."

"I found that out when I got here. You see, that's how I got here. I was stung by bees, and they couldn't get me to a hospital fast enough. By the time my body was taken there, I was here, celebrating with Jesus. I got here not too long before you did. So you could say I'm in your Orientation School class. How about going to my mansion?"

"Sounds great." While they were speaking, they saw a big building, bigger than some of the mansions Jaden had been in already. Jeff ran up to it, taking big strides. Jaden flew to catch up with him.

"Hey, looks like you're learning to use your wings already."

"Guess so. Tell me about your mansion."

"This is where I live until I get into my own mansion. I'm not grown up yet, but almost. So I live with my aunt who came here before I was born. Every once in a while I go look at the mansion my parents will have and see my own mansion being built. It's almost ready."

"So let's go inside."

"Sure. That's why I brought you here." So Jeff opened a large carved door by touching the side of it. The carvings had gems inlaid in them, including cameos of various flowers, jewels in rings, and many other things that Jaden did not recognize. It looked like it was designed many years before, yet its design was unique, unlike anything he had seen so far.

"Wow!" he said. "First time I've seen jewels on doors! It's like I'm looking at my Mom's jewelry box, only bigger and better. Did your aunt tell you anything about this?"

"Not much. Just that when she was on Earth there was so much pain she'd gone through that Jesus decided to show her that in her mansion He turned it to beauty for her. She said something about it being made into building material. The pain that wasn't building material, though. It was how she let Jesus shine through her."

"That says a lot. Wonder what your own mansion looks like."

"Plenty of time to see it after it's finished. It's being done by some people who know me. They asked the Father to let them finish it for me after I got here."

While they were talking, they came into a magnificent parlor. The couches looked like they came from Buckingham palace, but were brighter. Windows opposite the door showed a garden with more varieties than he had seen anywhere, surrounded by the mansion itself. On both sides of the parlor open doors led to more halls and rooms. Across the garden, they could see a balcony outside a bedroom with a table and chairs on the balcony.

"That's my bedroom for now."

"Your aunt must have been someone really special."

"Not really, Jaden. I just followed Jesus and loved Him. I'm at the throne room so often I don't see this very much." He turned and saw a short woman with a huge smile. She hugged him and lifted him up.

"I'm so glad Jeff brought you here to visit. I'm Oxalana and on Earth, well, you wouldn't look at me twice. I did things like washing, ironing and housekeeping. It was fun, because Jesus and I did a lot of talking during that time. It also hurt, but now I forget the pain because it helped me lean on Him. Now let me take you around my home."

With that they toured the mansion, ending up in a grand kitchen where they ate vegetables and fruit that tasted like borscht, pumpernickel, chicken and baklava, but seasoned better than anything on Earth.

Afterward, Jaden went back to his boat and rowed across the pond in two strokes again.

Thinking of Orpie, he saw a path lighting up to her mansion and went home to it. "Orpie, could we go to that amusement park again and take Chong with us?"

"Sure," she said. "Maybe his grandpa would like to go with us. We can ask." They took a detour to Chong's mansion. It was almost Oriental in style, but with some accents at the windows that showed scenes from Jesus' resurrection, set in diamonds.

Before they knocked on the door, Chong came out. He said, "Grandpa told me about an amusement park and wants to go there."

"That's why we came here. We've got tickets with us."

"We do too!" They both laughed. The boys led the way, talking excitedly, and sharing the rides they had gone on.

When they got there, Jaden and Chong decided on the "Trip around the World," while Orpie and Chong's grandpa joined some others on the "Yesterday's Gone" ride.

The boys' ride took them on a flight to Earth. They visited cities on all continents, always from the air, stopping to look at animals in remote parts of the world, and looking at mountain climbers on a remote mountain. At one point they asked to be let off to move a rock that was about to fall on a climber. When they got back on the ride, they were flying over the Yukon when their vehicle brought them back to the amusement park.

The "Yesterday's Gone" ride took Orpie and the others to Bethlehem at the time Jesus was born. All on the ride wore biblical costume as they watched the Messiah's parents being turned away from the inn. They joined the shepherds, helping with the sheep, getting their clothes dirty. When the angels announced the birth of the Messiah, they went to the stable and worshipped. Then they were taken back to the amusement park. When they got there, they noticed they were again in their heavenly garments.

The boys shared their experiences with Orpie and Chong's grandpa, then the grownups shared their experiences with the boys.

After they returned to their mansion, they talked about their day over a meal of yogurt with bananas, other fruit, almonds and walnuts, snow peas that tasted like roast beef, and milk.

They played some oboe and recorder duets before calling it a night when Jaden started yawning as they chose their music.

Chapter Twenty-Four Hall of Bible Knowledge

Jaden awoke to the aroma of eggs and toast. When he got into the kitchen, he saw many of his family there. The table had been expanded to make room for all. Rosie, Rosanna, Jeb, Eddie, and Orpie were all there, and some others he had not yet met.

Jeb said. "We all wanted to go with you to New Jerusalem today, so we could show you our favorite building in the City, and take you to our favorite rooms. Afterward, you can stay wherever you want for as long as you like while we go about the Father's business."

"And our favorite building is, the Hall of Bible Knowledge!" came a chorus from all.

"But to be fair to you we wanted to give you a good breakfast, because it may take us more than a day to show you all the things we want you to see," Orpie added.

So after an omelet with the flavor of feta cheese, red onion and green peppers, Jaden ate pumpernickel toast spread with fruit that tasted like mango and honey. Some talked while he ate, and others joined him at the table, helping themselves to fruit and nuts.

"Now we all know you've been there, watching God create all things. But that's only part of what He did that's written about in the Bible. I'd like to show you Ezekiel's room." This was from Jeb.

"Well, the rest of us can wait with our favorite room until we get there," Rosanna said, laughing.

As they left the mansion, they found themselves almost flying to get to the building. When they got there, they stopped right outside one of the doors.

Rosanna said, "For this part, Jaden, I'm the tour guide. Construction on this building began before Adam and Eve were created, maybe about the beginning of time, but God would be the one to tell you that, if he wanted. Let's back up to see if we can see the top part of the door."

So they all backed up to the middle of the walkway, but couldn't see it. When they tried halfway to the River of Life, Jaden said, "I see it, but it's really far up. And there's an angel next to the door. I can see his face near the top."

"Yes, he's a tall guard, isn't he? Now let's go around to the side of the door." And they did just that. "Rosie, how about continuing? I think you should go first."

"When I came here, this was already my favorite building. I just didn't know it at the time. If you look at the outside of the door, there's not really anything special to see close up. It's made of fine mahogany and has huge carvings. To see what they say, you'd have to be miles away or in Orpie's car farther up. But on the inside, well, just look."

They had reached the edge of the door, they went into the building. "Now look back at the door." When Jaden looked, he could see ornate lettering that seemed to mention books and people of the Bible. He stepped back a little more and could see carvings of a big garden, filled with many creatures and plants, with a man inside it. As he watched, the carvings came to life. He watched as the animals were brought to the man and got their names. He heard God say, "It is not good for man to be alone." Then he watched as Eve was made from Adam's rib.

"Now you know why this is my favorite room in this building. It shows where it all began. Adam and Eve were perfect. All of what you see in this room is from the book of Genesis. You could spend days in this room and still not see everything there is to see here. But Jeb wants to show you Ezekiel."

As soon as she mentioned Ezekiel, a hall lit up

through a doorway from the first room, with a sign in Hebrew lettering on a door lit up on one side of it.

"That's right, son. Now what excites me about Ezekiel is that he was shown a lot of things that were wrong, but he got to see some exciting things that were right. Here's his room. I didn't know Hebrew, but I do know where his room is, and I read it in my Bible, too.

"You'll notice we passed a lot of rooms on our way here. They're the rooms for the books of the Old Testament before Ezekiel. We passed the other prophets when we left Genesis. The first set of halls from Genesis lead to the rest of the history. The second set of halls from Genesis is Wisdom literature and Psalms. The third set of halls from Genesis is the Prophets, like Ezekiel. And the last set of halls goes from the end of the Prophet halls to all of the New Testament in four different halls."

"So it's arranged a little like the Bible, but each part shows how it links to Genesis?"

"That's right, Jaden. But God has not shown me why this building is made like this. I just wanted to get to Ezekiel and stay there for a long time when I got here. There's something about the dry bones getting flesh...Well, I'm getting ahead of myself. This might not even be your favorite place here, anyway."

When he finished saying this, they were in the room. It was huge, seeming to be much larger than any of the rooms they had passed, even though it was not the longest book of the Old Testament. It had many alcoves, with at least five dictionaries in each alcove.

"I want to look at these dictionaries! At least that's what I think they are," Jaden exclaimed.

"And so you may. Let's look at it together." With that, Jeb took Jaden to alcove 37, for they were numbered, and took a dictionary off the shelf. "Now when we look at the book of Ezekiel, we read all these verses in each chapter. What's your favorite verse in the whole Bible?"

"John 3:16," Jaden answered.

"When you get to John's room you can experience something a little like what we experience here. Open this dictionary anywhere. What do you see?"

"Each word in Ezekiel 37:3 is like a picture. But it's not the words that are from the English Bible, either. It's like I can see a thing instead of a word. And it's moving around on the page, sometimes joining up with one word on the page, and sometimes with another.

"I'm seeing a movie. It's showing what these words can mean in this verse. Then I see parts of the movie getting added to the verse to make another movie."

"Well said, Jaden. Every time we visit this Hall, we can look at dictionaries in each room we visit. Or we can look at the whole picture, like we saw on the back of the entry door to the whole Bible, for a section of the Bible.

"When I look at these verses, I see more and more of what God did to bring me to life in Christ. I see that in the Old Testament here, and I see in the New Testament with some of Paul's letters, too."

"Now you're talking about my favorite section of this Hall." Orpie came up and gave Jeb a big hug and said, "Let's go into the New Testament and let Eddie lead the way with Matthew, since that's the entry."

"You're right, Orpie. That's my favorite book of the New Testament. And here's the room it's in."

The door, as were the others, was already open for this room. As they walked in, they saw many bright scenes in the room. There were inviting alcoves with couches and chairs, tables, and displays everywhere. As with Ezekiel, this room was huge.

Three sets of dictionaries were in each alcove and many names were on each piece of furniture.

Without a glance at the other alcoves, Eddie led them to the sixth alcove. "When I was on Earth, this was my favorite room, and you could say this was my favorite alcove then, as now. Of course, I did not know at that time there was an alcove. Jaden, what do you notice different here?"

"Lots of places to rest and talk to other people. Like a library, but better."

"That's it in a nutshell. Let's take a look at the displays. Orpie, why don't you take over from here?"

"Eddie and I come here a lot to talk about his favorite parts of this book. Then we look at the dictionary. Take one and look through it, Jaden."

He took one, but noticed that the other two were different from it. "Hmm. This one has pictures but at the front it says Aramaic Words in Action. What does that mean?"

"Jesus and the disciples spoke Aramaic. If you think about it, they knew three languages, Hebrew, Aramaic, and Greek. Their Aramaic words were translated into Greek. Greek was the common language of Jesus' time on earth. Take a look at some of the words."

"It's like the other dictionary. The words are pictures. I can see in the pictures what they mean. These pictures show a lot more than I knew in this passage."

"Which one are you looking at?"

"Six Verse nine, 'Our Father, Who are in heaven, holy is your name.' The pictures aren't moving around so much. I see God on His throne, then getting up and showing a list of all His names in the Bible, and Jesus doing something for each of those names.

"He's only doing one thing at each of the names. But He's got a whole list of other places to go. When I get there I can look for what else He did. And it's for each one of those names. Then He shows just a little bit of what it means to be holy. I even skipped over the picture for Our Father. He's saying I could be here forever. That's a lot to learn just in this one place. Not counting the whole Bible. This verse says a lot. And that's only one verse in the Bible. Wow!"

"Now you know why Eddie and I like to be in this room so much. But there's more to see. This is Eddie's favorite room. My favorite is a smaller room, but it has a lot of information." With that, Orpie led the way to Ephesians. It had six alcoves, and had just one dictionary in each alcove.

The displays included a small throne, a footstool, and a full suit of armor, in the style of Roman times. Each piece was carefully labeled with a Latin name, a Greek name, and the name it represented for God's people.

"They watched as one soldier came and put on each piece of armor. Other soldiers joined him, putting on their armor in the room. In no time, they were in battle array. They watched as an enemy soldier came in. But even before it could speak the small army spoke, "You are defeated in the name of Jesus." They heard the enemy as if from the distance, screaming as an angel quickly gagged it and took it to a faraway place.

"And now for my favorite room," Rosanna said. "Revelation. Jesus Christ as John saw him on the Isle of Patmos. Some alcoves were current time when John wrote it, some have happened since, but most of it has yet to come." As she spoke, they went down the one hall that had only one room at the end of it.

Like other rooms they had been in, it had many alcoves, but here there were more than one for each chapter book. Each alcove held just one dictionary, some already open to a page, as if inviting them to look into the book immediately.

Jaden ran to the alcove labeled 11B. "This is about the two witnesses. My Dad talked about them, how people would see them from far away, like the whole world at once. I want to look at the dictionary for this one, and see what it really says about this."

"Help yourself, Jaden. I like the last part of Revelation myself," Jeb said. "I think it's really plain to understand. [Rev. 22:17-21] 'And the Spirit and the bride say, Come. And let him that hears say, Come. And let him that is thirsty come. And whoever wants, let him take the water of life freely. For I testify to every man that hears the words of the prophecy of this book, If any man shall add unto these things, God shall add unto him the plagues that are written in this book: And if any man shall take away from the words of the book of this prophecy, God shall take away his part out of the book of life, and out of the holy city, and from the things which are written in this book. He who testifies these things says, Surely, I come quickly. Amen. Even so, come, Lord Jesus. The grace of our Lord Jesus Christ be with you all. Amen.' I think that says a lot of what we're expecting even while we wait for the others we know."

"Jeb, of all of us you've been here the longest. Yet for me it seems like it's just been one long day full of fun, rest, worship, greeting, excitement, even work. What has it seemed like to you?"

"Rosie, it seems like minutes since I got here, but I know it hasn't been. I've been seeing so many things and doing so many things. Yet it seems like I do everything all at once. I travel fast. I think something and there it is.

"I want a certain kind of food and the food's there for me to eat with the rest of my meal. I want to teach and I get to teach. I want to worship God every time I think about why I'm here and I get to do that a lot. There's just nothing that I want to do that someone says no to. That's because my desires are in line with God's will all the time since I've got here. This still amazes me, no matter how long I'm here."

Jaden said, "I'd like to stay in this room for a while and explore some of the rooms you didn't get to show me and then go to the throne room. Thank you for showing me your favorite rooms."

As they left, he looked at some of the pictures in the first alcove, especially the dictionary pictures showing Jesus in His glory. As Jaden was looking he found he was taken to the throne room, before he even began to explore the other rooms. When he got there, he looked with fresh wonder at all the things around him, but only after he looked at Jesus. While he was there, he got a new assignment and left the throne room with a brighter glow on his face than ever before.

Chapter Twenty-Five University for Leadership Training

Jaden woke up the next day excited about his new assignment. He looked at his notes again. First he was to go to a welcome party. He was to join Jesus, Jeff, and some people he hadn't yet met at the center gate of the South Wall.

He looked at the name of one person. "Gabriel, goes by Gabe." Seeing that name, he remembered a trip to an emergency room with his mother. A man with Gabe on a name tag cracked jokes with his mother, all the while checking on him. He had told them he was in pre-med and wanted to get admitted to a medical school soon. Could he check out Jaden's ear? There seemed to be something wrong with it. Jaden had said, "Sure." Next thing he knew the man handed him a quarter. "I found this behind your ear. I hope you don't mind keeping it for me." Surely this couldn't be the same man. It seemed such a short time since he'd seen him.

He got to the gate, arriving at what seemed to be the same time as the others. A man with a gentle smile and a pile of books in hand came up to them. When he looked at him, Jaden realized this was not who he saw at the emergency room.

As he was coming, the man said, "Hi. I'm Gabriel, but you can call me Gabe. And before you ask, I'm not the angel. Jesus asked all of you to come here to meet with us. We are part of a welcome party for a newcomer."

Yet another man came to the gate from outside the city. Jesus and all the others came through the gate to meet the newcomer. Jeff and Jaden said, "We remember you. We passed your house on our way to school. We didn't know each other because we were in different grades and we just met each other here. Welcome."

"I was crying one day, and you brought me a cookie and a glass of milk," Jaden said. "You comforted me when Grandma Orpie died. That was soon after I got to know Jesus."

"And you're the reason I'm here," Jeff said. "You helped me get to know Jesus."

All the others shared some things they remembered about the man. Yet the loudest voice belonged to Jesus.

"Welcome home, Ernst. When you left Earth, you thought you left your studies behind. Gabe is here to give you the first of many books you can read if you want. But before we let you get on with your heart's desire, we want you to join us for your welcome home party."

With that, they arrived at the Welcome Center. There they all partied with Abraham and other newcomers, joining in worship at the throne after they were finished partying.

Later Gabe said to them, "I am to show a building to those of you who want to be leaders, as well as Jaden and Jeff. I don't know what's in God's plan for those two, but they are to see this school as well."

In less than the time it took for Gabe to say these words, they arrived at a building in the center of the city. Columns supported archways that at least half a mile high. Carvings and paintings could be seen inside the building through the windows.

The building itself was plated with gold over mahogany, which could also be seen on the inside walls through the windows. Compared to the Conservatory of the Composers, the building was easily ten or more times the size in all directions. So nobody with Gabe could see the whole building.

"Ladies and gentlemen, you are in front of the University for Leadership Training. The people who graduate from this University will have positions of authority during the Millennium and even after the Millennium on the New Earth and other such places as the Father decides.

"As with all classes you have been to so far, away from Earth, nothing is graded. But the skills you learn while part of this school help you learn where you fit best and how to manage people and things in the best way possible. Today is your introduction to this school."

With that, he led them into the building. Inside they could see halls wide enough for two cars to pass each other, with hundreds of people going in every direction down the halls.

Rooms with doors almost as tall as the height of the ceilings in the biggest home Jaden knew from Earth were wide open. Angels stood checked off names on a list the size of a small book at the doorway of each room. It felt like hours, but was just seconds in Earth time by the time the rooms were filled.

Gabe led them past the first two halls and down the third hall off the entrance they had come through, bringing them into an office labeled "Candidates for Leadership Examination Room."

"This is where I must leave you. This is not a test. Pick up the blank sheets of paper and some pencils or pens.

"Sit wherever you like here, and begin by asking the Father to show you what He wants you to do and to show you your heart for the work you love. Write down whatever He tells you. After He's finished showing you this, He will send someone to talk to each of you about your part in this University."

Jaden exclaimed, "Wow! This really isn't a test? He's showing me some things already. I want to go to the Throne Room right now and talk about it, but He's telling me to wait.."

"Remember. You can talk to the Father from anywhere. Wherever you are He will answer you," Jeff answered.

"I get it. Write down the Father's answers however they come and keep on writing or drawing or whatever he tells me to do until He's finished. This could take a long time."

"Hey! Time changed when we got here. We really don't know how long it is in Earth time. The light changes because the glory of God is the light here, but there's also the sun and moon and stars that add to that light. God knows how long it will take, and it will be good."

"You're right, Jeff. It will be. I'm new here and still getting used to things, but then you're new too. How about we sit on a couch and put a small table in front of us to write on?"

"Sounds good." With that they sat down and began filling paper with drawings, writing, and ideas as they came to mind. Jaden's hand seemed to fly across the paper as he wrote and drew. Often he paused and waited as God gave him more ideas. Finally, after filling what seemed to be hundreds of sheets of paper, he was done.

Jeff was finished before Jaden was, and quietly went to another area of the office. He started singing with the background music, lifting his hands in worship, holding up his papers as he sang. While he was singing, an angel gently touched his hand, and led him away, papers and all.

When Jaden finally got up, he too went quietly to another area of the office and started singing praises. The door was nearer than he realized, and while he was lifting his hands in worship he started walking out the door and further down the hall.

Before he got far, he heard a voice right next to him. "Welcome, Jaden, to the University for Leadership Training. I'm here to take you on a tour of the classes you will take when you are ready for the University." Jaden turned, and saw a bright beautiful angel. His wings were folded, and his face shown with a glory seen mostly in the throne room.

"Who are you?" Jaden asked.

"I am one of those who worship the Father and are sent out only to His chosen ones—the ones who are shown their tasks early but must wait and grow through much training before entering into their full assignment. You are such a person."

"Thank you, I think. If that means I won't be in my full assignment for a while, I get it. After all, I came here when I was only nine. So it might take a while."

"Or not. The Father did not show me as much as He showed you." While they were talking, the angel was taking him down the first hall.

He said, "Your first classes will be in this first hall. You will take Introduction to Leadership, Independent Studies in your areas the Father has shown you, and Introduction to Communication Science at the Atomic and Subatomic level. None of these will have tests, and they will not be graded.

When you have mastered these, however long it takes, you will go on to classes in the fifth hall. There you will study Leadership in Animal Husbandry, Advanced Math as Applied to Space, Communication Sciences among Planets, Solar Systems and Galaxies, and Further Independent Studies in areas the Father has shown you. After these classes you will continue with other classes in the eighth hall. The Father has not shown me what those classes will be. Now, where would you like to start?"

"How about with this?"   And he showed the angel one of his drawings, which seemed complex and full of machines.

"Holaka, the professor of cellular mechanics, should talk with you about this." As the angel spoke, they arrived in front of a door labeled "Cellular Mechanics".

The door was flung open as they arrived. "Jaden," the man who opened the door said, "the Father told me you were coming to show me some drawings.   Worshiper of Yahweh, thank you for bringing him here. Come in, come in, child. Show me your drawings."

As he was speaking, he led Jaden to a comfortable sofa decorated with gold embroidery in the shape of many machines. He brought an easy chair over to face him at an angle so both could look out the window of the office if they chose.

"So tell me about your drawings. The Father said they had something to do with your independent studies, and that you could begin your independent study even before you came to this University after your regular schooling."

"The Father showed me these things in visions. I was in the examination room when I asked him to show me my heart. He said he had planted ideas there long before I was born and that I was to design and work with machines here.   He said that when the Millennial Reign of Jesus came, I'd show people how to make machines like the one in this picture. So what does this have to do with cellular mechanics? What is cellular mechanics anyway?"

"Jaden, you're really learning fast here. Your body on Earth had many parts, and the smallest parts unique to your body were found in cells, your DNA. Every living creature on Earth has DNA. Except for viruses, every creature has cells that have that DNA.

"Many of us scientists studied parts of cells. We saw some very complex machines that helped one-cell creatures, which we called organisms. Your drawings show some of these machines. One of these has forty-nine parts to it. If one of them were missing, the cell could not move to get food and would die. We found many machines as we studied. Each one is different, unique. Some people on earth even thought that they could make machines look like animals. Maybe like cells, eh?"

"So where do I go from here?"

"First, you start regular studies at your neighborhood school. After all, you will be allowed to grow as you would on Earth.

"You can learn the basics in all subjects we have in school here. How long it takes you to master these, the Father knows. But it will not seem long to you. You can come here as often as you like to learn what your drawings mean.

"Most of your subjects at the University must wait until after you have learned more at the elementary and high school levels, as you were used to saying on Earth. You will notice that your study in your neighborhood school centers on God and does not allow for alternate theories. You will be happy and will be shown how to learn so you don't make mistakes."

"Wow! A lot to think about, that's for sure. Professor Holaka, it's been great talking with you, for sure. May I sit in on a class today?"

"It may seem hard to you, but I think we can arrange it. I have to teach a class now. How about listening in on that?"

"Sure."

Leaving the office together, they went to a class in the fifth hall. The professor found a place for him in the lecture room. Twenty people were in the class.

Even though the presentation used slides, films and chalkboards, he had a hard time following what was said. His mind wandered to the time his mother talked about her college class.

"Son," she'd said, "I know you want to learn many things. When I got to college I found out things I learned in school weren't what I needed for college.

"I needed to know Spanish, but my school didn't offer Spanish. I needed to learn calculus before college, but my school put me in the wrong class for that. I had to learn those things in college, which was harder for me. Ask God to show you what to learn first. That way when you get to college you will be ready."

He'd tried listening, but at the time he was thinking about going to Pascal's house, and it didn't sink in. After all, he was only eight years old when she said that.

Suddenly he heard Professor Holaka say, "We have with us a young person who can show us one of these motors. It's in drawing form, but I'd like you to see it anyway. Jaden, please bring your drawing to the front."

He got up from his chair, taking the sketch they had discussed, and went to the front. "Please tell us how you got this design."

"When I was in the candidate examination room, God gave me visions of his plans for me and told me some things, too. As you see, I'm nine years old. So I don't know all the words for these things. But I do know how to draw." Taking a pencil, he pointed to various parts of the drawing and showed how they moved or fitted into each other. He also talked about real machines that looked like the drawing.

"So how do you think this type of machine can be made?"

"I don't know yet. I'll have to get back with you after I've learned some more. Maybe in the Millennium?"

They all laughed at that. "You'll be surprised at how fast you learn here. Remember what the dictionaries look like? Everything here is designed for you to learn the way that works best for you. You look a little tired. Have I talked a little bit above your head, so to speak?"

"Yes. But I'll catch on sooner or later. I wrote down some of the things you said with a note to look up what they mean later."

"That's half the battle. We all start somewhere. You're starting earlier than many in this type of class." With that Professor Holaka dismissed him, and the rest of the class left the room not long afterward.

He carried all his notes and drawings away from the room in a folder with his name on it. He had found the folder at the top of a stack near the entry to the classroom, and wondered a little about it. As he left, he thought of Orpie, and saw a path light up.

As he flew down the path, he remembered how much he had learned at the University already, thinking about how young Orpie really looked. He wondered how she got her hair to look so beautiful. He didn't remember seeing it any color but white before. Thinking these happy thoughts, he soon found himself in front of a movie theater.

"Hi, Jaden. I know you've had a busy day," she said. "I just watched a movie about the Millennium. Let's eat these pears in the park, and then head back to the mansion." The pears, flavored with cinnamon, brought new energy for them both. Afterwards, Jaden played with some children there before they flew home. He thought he could get used to the speeds here really fast.

When they got to the mansion, he said to her, "My mom has to get her hair done, or at least cut once in a while. Your hair always looks so beautiful. Tell me about it."

"Hey, I'm glad you asked that. I know someone here who did hair on Earth. Every once in a while I go to her and ask her to fix it special for me. It's such a treat I make a day of it."

"I wouldn't mind watching you go there sometime."

"I won't be going there until long after your Orientation School is over with, but I think that can be arranged."

"I'll put it on my to-do list: 15. Watch Orpie get her hair done."

She ruffled his hair and sent him off to his baseball practice. Later they had something like spaghetti and meatballs for their supper, using spaghetti squash and other vegetables.

Chapter Twenty-Six School of the Sciences

The next day after his morning Bible study with the other children and Jesus, he heard a knock on the door of the mansion. Opening it quickly, he saw a man with wild hair under his crown and a notebook in hand. He saw that the man had written a lot of things everywhere on the cover of the notebook, and across them all he had written the word WRONG in big capital letters.

"Jaden, the Father wants me to talk to you about some things at my school. You haven't visited there yet, but some of your classes later on will be in that school, yes?

"Some of what we teach you will be very different from what people learned on Earth, you see. And I have to guide you through the school and show you some of the classrooms so when you go there later you won't be confused," the man said.

Seeing his look, the man began again, in the same German accent as before. "Okay, I'm a scientist and professor at the School of the Sciences. I studied so much about physics they called me a genius. I wrote many books. They called my formula 'E=mc^2' and the theory of relativity real breakthroughs. Oh, by the way I'm Albert Einstein, not that you've heard of me. You came here so young and all that. Anyway, that's not what I'm here about. You will come with me to my school, okay?"

Orpie came into the living room while he was speaking and just looked. She nodded a few times, and other times just stood, her mouth open.

"I don't know what the Father has in mind, but this is real. This man is who he says he is. I've never met him till now. But if he is to be your guide, go with him. Before you go, both of you take some fruit off the tree. I'm sure he's hungry. In his lifetime he spent hours studying and forgetting anything else."

"Got it, Orpie. Okay, Mr. Einstein. I'm going. Here's a piece of fruit." With that they started on their way to the school.

"Jaden, it tastes like real apfel streudel. Better than my mother used to make, and that's saying a lot."

"Mm. Mine tastes like banana bread. I was thinking about that this morning. The Father is so good."

By this time the path that led to the School of Sciences building had guided them to the entrance of the building. They stood there, finishing their fruit. They didn't bother wiping off their robes, because the juice left no stain on them and evaporated instantly.

"The Father told me something about you that made me wonder. What do you think about the most, besides family? If you had lots of time for studying, what would you do?"

"That's a tough question. I look at things, wondering what makes them tick. I go to the throne room a lot. I see the Father, the rainbow, and hear the thunder and see the lightning. I wonder how it's done, how I hear all the music all around me.

"There's so many tunes at once, but they sound so beautiful. Am I hearing all I could hear? What else could I see? How can I share what I see? When I hear all the sounds, how can I put them to music or into sounds so people can know what God has done with sounds?"

"Jaden, now you know why I came to you. Some of what you are wondering about is found in physics. On Earth, you would not usually study the physics that answers these questions until high school.

"Here, that's another story. In the University for Leadership Training, you can take courses about ways of communicating we found up here before the people on Earth, and some discovered there because the Father wanted them to learn it at that time. Much of what you want to find out came from a paper I wrote before I came up here. But I'm getting ahead of myself. I do that a lot. Let's start our tour."

They started at the entryway. It was smaller and less ornate than any building he had been in. Even the Composers' Conservatory had scrollwork on both sides of the entrance to the auditorium, showing many instruments encrusted with gems, musical notes formed with gems, and all clef forms in relief with gems added at every curve, with onyx stones at the dots for the bass clef.

In contrast, the School of the Sciences had plain walls with lines and dots that seemed to move rhythmically around an unseen point and arrows pointing to shapes and sets of lines. Einstein showed him an arrow pointing to five straight lines. "We're heading in the direction of that arrow."

Mystified, he went with Einstein to a hall. On both sides and on the floor of the hall, he saw five straight lines. On one side of the hall, he saw an open door with a sign, again with the arrow and five lines.

As they entered the room, they heard music. Some was almost shouted, and some was very low in pitch and almost whispered. When he looked around, he couldn't see where the music was coming from, for there were no people or instruments in the room.

"What's here? Where's the sound coming from?" he asked.

"Welcome to my lab. This is where anyone who wants to find out about what makes things tick can start with the sounds they make.

"On Earth we discovered that everything vibrates, which means to make sounds or move around a point. Some vibration makes sounds you hear, and some does not. But you hear more here than you could there. But I'm sure you've noticed that already."

"Yep. I've heard things from what seems like miles away."

"So when you want to, even before you come to this school to take classes, you can come here to learn where sounds come from. As for what's making the sounds, we've recorded various parts of creation. Somewhere in here I have tapes, but I didn't put a label on it. Do you want me to look it up?"

"Sure. I'd like to see what makes these sounds before we move on."

"Okay. We want to first look at the instruments. They are in this cabinet. There. They're a little more advanced than on Earth. Now we get out the computer. Ah. Here it is. The computer is under this microscope.

"Tell me, Jaden. What do you see?"

"I see something wiggling around, with little squiggly things at the center."

"Right. What you're seeing is one cell, with some DNA in the center of it. The DNA has a stain on it, like when you get stains on clothing, so we can see it better. In this DNA is our computer. Some of my students put a code in the DNA telling us where the sounds are from. Now we get some other parts of the cell to make something from that DNA. Something called RNA tells those parts what to do. Do you see what these parts are doing?"

"Yes. The picture's tiny, but the microscope makes it big. Why it's the Earth!"

"The planet Earth makes a sound by itself, one of the musical sounds you hear in this room. We found that out soon after I got here. We got so excited about it that my students and I wrote a book about it. Later on you can find out more about other sounds you here. Now let's look at some more of the building."

They went back to the main entrance of the building. "We who were scientists below like order. We want to sort things out, make sense of it. In some ways you do also.

"All of these shapes mean something. Five lines after an arrow points to music, like the music staff. An arrow and three circles points to atomic structure. But here, I'm getting ahead of myself. An arrow and a triangle point to the God factor that no scientist understood, because only God understands. So there are a lot of symbols, because we like symbols. For now, just remember about the five lines. Okay?"

"Sure. So where do you want to take me?"

"Where I started in science. The arrow pointing to a rectangle with many half circles on both ends. When I was young, in Germany, my father showed me a compass. I saw how when I moved the compass one way or another, the needle always pointed in the direction of north, even when I was facing south.

"So we'll go down the hall and look in that room. From there, we could look at some things about light, because you'd like to learn that. Then I think maybe you want to go, yah?"

"Sounds good. I took notes in one class at the University so I could look up the words. Then I started thinking about stuff I did with my mom before I came here. Finally the professor mentioned my picture that showed the class things they were talking about. All the same, it seemed to take a while before he got to me."

"Yah, when you don't know some of the things it gets hard to follow. God made it easy for me to follow science. I got along well with people. The one thing I didn't want to do was write about myself.

"About God's creation, I could write all day, especially physics. You get me talking about that, and I might not quit for quite a while. What God did is so great, it's going to take all eternity to begin to understand it. He keeps on doing wonderful things."

"I know a little of what you mean. He's letting me learn from some really great teachers already, and I just got here. It seems like I've learned a lot already. They tell me I'm to learn many things before I'm ready for the assignment God has for me."

"Yah, you're one special person, so the Father says. But He's told me I am also. How we can all be so special is going to take all eternity to find out."

So they went to the magnet room, for that's what it was, and they talked a little about things that became attracted to each other through magnetism and a little about what was called gravity on Earth. Here it's called something else, for science had found out another force that kept planets and solar systems and galaxies hung together without flying apart.

Before long, though, he started yawning. "I must be getting tired. It seems like we've been here a while."

"Oh, Liebschen. I forget sometimes that you are a child. So much I've shown you today. So much to learn. Come another time, maybe after you've gone through more basic studies."

With that, he went back to the mansion while Einstein went back to his laboratory and began writing down what he had seen in the cell under the microscope. He had a supper of fruit and nuts.

After talking with the Father, he and Orpie got out a game of chess. She started teaching him the moves for each piece. They discovered a problem with the game. Each could guess the other's strategy so well after a few games that they went into a stalemate. They left the game out on the card table, marked who was to play next, and went to their rooms.

He went to bed feeling excited about what he had learned and about how much he could learn.

Would he ever learn enough to lead where God was showing him he would be leading? Then he realized where he was. Not only was it possible, but God was showing him already how he could lead a group on the job while he himself was still learning the task. Meanwhile, there was all eternity in which to learn everything he could possibly want to learn, and much more besides. With that question answered already, he fell asleep.

Chapter Twenty-Seven Refreshing, Changes, Excitement

When he got up the next day, he had lots of ideas for what to do that day. None of them included visiting a school. When it came right down to it, he had seen a schedule somewhere that said day 27 during Orientation School time (it included all days of the week) was a free day. He was glad of it, because meeting with Mr. Einstein had got him very tired, or so he thought.

When the knock came on the mansion door, he was ready for something different. He'd had his breakfast of something that tasted like scrambled eggs and a little feta cheese. His Bible story group had come and gone. He'd even gone back to bed and rested for a little while.

Anyway, there went the knock again. Yawning, he got up and answered it. "Hey Jaden, how about going fishing or something?" It was Chong.

"I don't know. I had a long day with Mr. Einstein at some School of the Sciences or something. He said I could come visit there whenever I wanted to check into stuff. You mean like with a fishing pole and maybe some worms? I did that on Earth. What's it like here?"

"I don't know, but someone gave me two fishing rods yesterday. I'd like to try them out. We could ask the guy who gave me them. It was Peter's brother, Andrew. Remember we helped them with that catch of fish?"

"Yeah. We could ask him to show us where they fish here. We could just sit and wait for the fish to come. Then we could go to throne room or sing songs, just have a fun time."

"Let's go for it, then. Take a break from all this

school stuff."

"Chong, did you look at schools yesterday too?"

"Yes. The guy who came for me took me to a school of science and talked about animals and how to look at how animals get food and things like that. It was stuff I was really interested in."

"I talked with Mr. Einstein and he showed me stuff I was interested in. Sometimes he got to talking about stuff I hadn't learned yet. I have to do some studying before I can go back there, he said. But I can use his laboratory."

"That's what my guy said, too. But he said it wouldn't take long to learn what I need to know to study animals the way he was showing me."

"Well, let's go find Andrew." When Jaden said that, a path lit up. They followed it and found a quiet river. Andrew was there, pole in hand, watching a bobber float on the water.

"Chong, I've been waiting for you. And this is Jaden, of course. This is a little like you remember on Earth. I have some bait, but it's not worms. It's a vegetable that the fish like. The fish will come to it, eat it, touch the bobber, and then leave. It's a game they like to play. The fish we have for food is not in this river."

While Andrew was talking, they could see the bobber move from side to side or even sink a little. Underneath, they saw fish chasing each other away from the bait after they'd eaten some. After watching a while, Jaden said, "Hey, it's like they're waiting in line to eat their food. That's something else."

Andrew showed the two friends how to tie the bait onto what appeared to be a hook, but really was wood and had no sharp points in it. Instead, when Jaden tried to pull on the bait, he found out he had to pick it up and tie it back on. "You're getting the idea. It's harder for the fish, but this doesn't hurt them."

Chong's bobber was already in the water a few feet away when Jaden cast his line in. He and Chong sat and watched the fish eat from the hook and nuzzle the bobber. When a fish did that, he could hear a soft bell. The bigger fish made a deeper sound than the small fish. Andrew sang a song to the melody they heard. "Fish come eat, swim gently here. We wish you well, sweet life to you here." After he sang it a few times, the boys joined him.

After watching the fish's game for a while, he got up, saying, "I need to go to the throne room for a while. If you want to come with me that would be great."

The others said, "You're right, Jaden. It is time for us to go there. Let's take some fruit with us." With that they all picked fruit from a nearby tree and ate it as they went. Even so, it seemed like no time at all before they got there.

When they got to the throne room, the atmosphere was almost electric with greater excitement than at any time before. The angels in front of the throne, with four wings to cover their face and feet, were flying above, shouting, "Holy, holy, holy is the Lord of Hosts! The whole earth is full of His glory!" [Isaiah 6:3].

When these angels shouted it, the throne room shook as if in an earthquake. They all fell on their faces, saying, "You are holy, Lord. You have taken us out of a people with unclean ways and have cleansed us from our unclean ways. Thank you, Jesus. You are the Lamb who saved us."

An altar with burning coals was brought out for those newly arrived in heaven. Angels took burning coals from the altar and went among the people, touching their lips with the coals and saying, "Now you are clean. Receive the full purity of the Lord."

The Father said, "You who have been touched

and cleansed: Who of you will go and tell an unclean, disobedient people of me?"

As one voice, these, who would become prophets on Earth, said, "Here am I. Send me."

The Father said to them, "Go, then. Tell your people that those who hear must listen and heed. They must obey. The time until the end is short. I am on my way. My Son has not yet been told the day or the hour, but his hosts are ready. He is ready. Prepare your hearts that you may be found ready for my coming.

"Eat the book that is set in front of you. It will be sweet in your mouth. Eat and speak the words that are given you to speak to your people. Let him who sins, sin no more. Let the righteous become a brighter light in their nation. The time of the end is on its way."

The new people ate their book. They found it as the Father said. Then they returned to their assigned places on Earth. Because they were from many places, they seemed to cover the whole earth. The people in heaven, all the ones Jaden knew and more besides, arrived in front of portal windows in the Portal building. Everybody watched their own home areas as the Gospel was spread in waves around the earth.

In his town, he saw Pascal talking to his teachers at school, asking them to let him speak to his class. Some listened and gave him time. Others did not.

In all classes, Pascal said the same thing, "It is time to read Bibles and pray. We hear things that are wrong. If you're a boy, when you grow up you marry a girl. A girl when she grows up marries a boy. People descended from people. Science shows that frogs have more chromosomes than people do. We are not descended from frogs or other animals. Read your Bible and pray. When you do that, you get happier, because you get to know God." Some of his teachers let him keep talking. Others threatened him with expulsion. But he was allowed to stay in the school.

People at other portals saw many other new preachers talk about the Bible at schools and work places. They had a hedge around them that no one could break through. As they watched, they saw angels with swords standing on top of buildings, fighting off dark beings, gagging their mouths and marching them off bound in chains to prisons. Reinforcements of dark beings were treated the same way. This was going on all over the earth.

Over the sound system in the Portal building, people heard, "This is not the end battle. You are watching a great revival of My Word. This revival must take place before the time of the Tribulation and before the time of the Millennium. Rejoice, for many are coming to know me." Again, he saw he was back in the throne room. He saw that there were more new people in the throne room. These also received the commission and went out.

The Father said to the children, "My children, it is time to rest. Take refreshments and go to your mansions." He went to the back of the throne room and filled a plate with almonds and a mango. Each almond had a different flavor, one like lamb, one like carrots and honey, and one like coconut and cinnamon. The other flavors he could not identify. The mango tasted like honey.

Chapter Twenty-Eight Recycling, Heaven-Style

Jaden woke up with a great big smile on his face, wider than usual. He felt ready for anything after watching Pascal. He wrote in his journal about some events of the previous day and how he felt about them, then put it aside and drew a picture of Hortense, the guinea pig. Not satisfied with how it turned out, he tried again, and liked the result.

He went down to breakfast, which smelled a lot like ham and eggs. He saw that the meal looked like it, too. "What's this made from? I know we don't really have meat, but it looks a lot like ham and eggs."

"How about that? Sometimes I can shape and color the vegetables to look like what I want to eat. Then the Father puts in the flavors that I'm thinking about. Today I missed Canadian bacon. So the Father gave me that flavor. Would you like some?"

"Sure. Yesterday I was thinking feta cheese and black olives. I found an olive tree. Even though the olives looked different from on Earth, they tasted just like the black olives. Then I found some vegetables that tasted like feta cheese. Tasty meal, if I do say so myself."

"So you're learning how to forage?"

"No, it was in my garden by the school."

As they finished eating, they heard a knock on the door. He went to answer it. "Good morning, child," Rosanna said. "I'm going to a warehouse-factory complex. Care to come?"

"Sure. What do they make or do there?" he asked as he hugged her and showed her both drawings of Hortense. "These are drawings of a guinea pig on Earth. See how much better the second try is?"

"Hey, you're getting really good. It's hard to describe what they do at the complex. It's better just to look and decide for yourself. It looks different each time I visit, and I've shown it to a lot of people. The Father wants some people to visit it at least once during their first few days in heaven. Others when they hear warehouse or factory remember those they saw on Earth and don't want to think about them. Take your notebook with you. Orpie, would you like to come along? I think you've gone, but not lately."

"I'd be glad to. It's something I wondered about on Earth, and saw here just that one time."

With that, they went down a path towards New Jerusalem, and then flew to the middle North Gate, on the far side of the city from their usual entrance. Inside the North Gate and perhaps about a mile west, they saw a number of buildings ornately decorated with gold, with diamond windows facing east, and numerous angels entering and leaving, carrying many objects. Most seemed to be from when Jaden was on Earth, with a few much older things, including rusty cars, broken lamps, guns, aquariums, jewelry, and many newer things.

Many things looked like they had never been used. Others, like the rusty cars, had been heavily used. There were several buildings for each type, with many floors in each. They seemed to stretch out for many miles close to the wall of North Jerusalem. The gap between the wall and the closest warehouse was no more than an acre.

"What do you think? Which would you like to visit?" Rosanna asked.

"I'm not sure," he answered, a little puzzled. "They all look so interesting. How about new toys? I've always wondered what happened when people made these."

Rosanna laughed. "Yes, toys are fun things, and grownups have their toys too. We'll go there."

So they followed an angel carrying some toys

into a building. Inside, they didn't see signs posting directions or hard hats. Instead, they saw more angels busy at work. Following their angel, they saw that it had seven cars, an airplane, and five motorcycles. Some were a size he had had, and others were like Pascal had.

The angel carried the toys into an office off to one side of the main entrance. There a receiving angel opened a register and noted each toy and the condition in columns. A messenger took them to the second floor. There were stations on the floor each with a different toy assigned to it. Dropping the toys off at stations, the messenger left. His family stayed to watch.

The cars and the motorcycles were each divided between two work stations. Battered toys were taken apart. Metal parts and plastic parts were separated into labeled boxes. Rubber parts were put into other boxes. Looking into one box, he saw it was almost full. While they watched, they saw an angel come and pick up the box. He followed the angel, the others joining them.

The angel went to a shredding machine. He took plastic parts from the box and guided them through a series of shredders, each smaller than the one before. Finally, the angel added a series of chemicals.

Strainers pulled out anything that floated to the top of the liquid. These were put into several buckets, each bucket with a different aroma, and a different color. When the last chemical was added and the last strainer had been used, the contents of each bucket were mixed together and formed into rocks. Some rocks had gemstones, had mica and other minerals. Finally, another angel picked up the buckets of rocks and left the building.

"So where are the new toys in this building?" he asked as a gentle looking man came up. "I know I asked to see the new toys."

"And so you shall, Jaden," the man said. "Many work stations on each floor are for recycling old parts into something the angels can take back to earth for people to find. But more are because the Father has made plans for some of these things. Remember the airplane, and the cars and motorcycles that were not recycled?"

"Yes. They're still here, but the angel seems to be working on them," he replied.

"When an angel brings things into these warehouses, there are usually one of two purposes: to recycle worn things that cannot be used as they are, or to correct problems and assign a personality to them."

"I get the recycling idea, but assigning a personality to them?" he asked.

"Did you ever hear your mom or dad talking to a car and calling it Bessie, or to a TV and calling it Roberto?"

"Come to think of it, that's what Dad called the car and Mom the TV. My bike was Old Sam, because that's what Bill called it. Jamal called one of his tools Jehoshaphat."

"See, there's a reason for it. The angels here assign personalities to everything people put special names to, even things you don't think of having a personality. They have a list of the things they get for their station, and a list of personalities to use that work day.

"While they are fixing what went wrong after these things were made, they call them the name assigned to it. The personality also gets woven into the parts of the object. After they are done fixing it and naming it, messenger angels assigned to that factory take it back to Earth. The whole process usually takes much less than a minute Earth time.

"Let's look at the new toy cars. This angel will

inspect and fix the cars you saw brought in and at least eighty others in an hour, if not more." They watched as the angel picked up one of the cars they had seen brought to the station. His hands seemed to fly as he moved a part of the toy just a fraction, then refitted another part, and added some glue to a third part. While he was working on it, they heard the name Angelica spoken several times. When he was finished, he put it into a box marked "Honduras." In much the same way he worked on the other two cars.

When the box was full, an angel took the box and flew out the building through a portal to that country. They watched the eyes of children light up as they received boxes with these cars and other things in them. Then they were back in the warehouse again.

"As you have seen, a few of the toys we get here go to poor countries. The angels assigned to give the toys pay for them at the factory, then follow through here with the angel assigned to fix the toys. When the toys are ready for those children, a messenger angel takes the toys to them.

"Some personalities you have seen have been reassigned many times to different things over centuries of Earth time. Those assigned to structures that have been around for centuries have their personalities changed when people around them change. Personalities are assigned based on the country and the person who will get it. So what would you like to see next?

Orpie said, "I would like to see how furniture is recycled."

He smiled. "I think we could arrange that. Let's follow one of the angels going past this building."

Leaving the building, they saw two angels, one carrying a beat-up oak dresser up and the other a bed in slightly better condition. They almost flew to keep up with the angels, and soon came to a huge building with two floors. As they entered the building, they were surprised by the number of offices they saw.

The first angel stopped at an office on the right. "Hello, good to see you again so soon," the clerk said to the angel. "We have a good spot for this dresser in someone's library. It needs just a little remodeling to get it looking good. Take the blueprint with you to the work station. Before you go, would you give these folks this paper? It has a history of the dresser on it."

The angel gave it to Orpie and they followed the dresser to a work station on the same floor as the office. While an angel was working on the dresser, she said, "Why I know these people! They were living down the street from me when I brought Joann to your town.

"It says here that they bought this dresser at a farmers' auction near Bredenton. Before they bought it, the farmer had it for thirty years. Then it lists three other owners before the farmer, and one after my friends owned it. So it must be very old. Oh, here's the date it was made. 1730. It got broken along the way, and the last owner didn't know how to fix it, so he threw it out."

"Yes, and the angel brought it so it could be fixed up for the library."

While they watched, they could see it being taken apart in some places, sawn in others, and then nailed and glued back together again. When it was ready for finishing, the carpenter angel added varnish and rubbed it to a brilliant shine.

The messenger angel picked up the dresser, now a sturdy bookcase, and went through the portal to another farmers' auction near Bredenton. The town librarian was at the auction, and the only person to bid on it. Later they saw the antique books that were stored in it in the library.

By now, Jaden was yawning. It was not that he was sleepy, but it was beginning to seem like he had already seen what they were looking at. He wondered if he should go to a park and play games, or find something else to do.

"I think it's time for us to relax and maybe have a picnic lunch. How's that sound?" Rosanna asked.

"Sounds great. Did you bring anything?"

"No, but there's a branch of the River of Life nearby, and lots of trees on either side of it. How about a swim in the River of Life first, then eating?"

"Yeah. I've done all this looking at things the past few days, and it feels a little like I saw a lot of the same things at that warehouse."

With that, she gently led him to the River. While the others swam, she encouraged him to sit and let it flow over him, sometimes splashing water on him. Soon he got up and joined others in their games.

While they were eating afterward, Jesus came up to them. "The children have decided it's time to take a couple days off from school. That way when they do get back to learning, they'll be enjoying it all the time. So for now they'll be doing only what they want to do, whether it's play, work, or relax."

"Good idea. We'll let him decide what to do," she said. "Jaden, we're going to the mansion for the afternoon, longer if you want. You can stay there as long as you want, go to the throne room when you want, and only visit where you want to visit."

"I'd like that. You mean it? No visiting places unless I want to? I can go to the throne room and stay there if I want to?"

"That's what your list said," Jesus said. "You wanted to be in the throne room every day. You've found out a lot about your new home. So have the other children at your school. You did your first assignment about the sashes very well, and the Father is pleased.

"You've studied very intensely. That's why you got so tired. This is time for refreshing and getting your pep back." With that, Jesus applied leaves from the Tree of Life to his body, especially his head. Jaden began to stretch out and run around after that and felt like he had slept overnight, which he may have done, in Earth time.

Orpie led him back to the mansion, where he rested and played quietly with some toys he had there. While in his room, he visited the throne room a number of times, going to the portal to go backwards to visit quieter times and forward to visit millennial times.

After a supper of yogurt, nuts, salad, honeyed carrots, and fruit, they watched a video before going to rest.

Chapter Twenty-Nine Rest, Throne Room, Play

He woke up feeling refreshed and ready for action of some sort, but he wasn't sure what. He could smell toast and eggs, so he knew it was breakfast time. He guessed that he'd slept a long time, and in Earth time it was the next day.

He went down to breakfast after spending some time talking with the Father. Sure enough, there were toast and eggs on the counter, along with some raspberries and cream. Helping himself to some of each, he found he was eating eggs flavored with nutmeg and cinnamon, and spreading the raspberries and cream on the toast, he had a dessert that tasted like raspberry pie, flavored with a sweet honey. Orpie was not there, but he was not concerned, because somehow it seemed later than usual.

He heard a knock on the door just as he finished some juice, and went to open it.

"Jaden, did you hear? We get to rest and visit the throne room and play today. I slept late but had a good breakfast. Want to go to the River of Life before we go to the throne room?" Chong was almost dancing in his excitement.

"Sure, but let's go to the branch nearby, and go slowly there today."

"Sounds good to me."

They went to a quiet area, much like the area Benjamin had taken him to, and waded into the stream, splashing each other leisurely. Gradually, as they spent more time in the River, Jaden felt his strength come back to him and even felt a little extra warmth for a time in certain areas of his body, especially where Jesus had touched him with the leaf.

When he felt fully recovered, he said, "Okay, let's go there now." As he said that, a chariot with two horses stopped in front of them. They got into it, joining all the other children in their Bible group. Some were chatting excitedly. Others were quiet, still resting.

Their ride to the throne room seemed long, but in Earth time it was less than a second. When they got to the building with the throne room, angels came to meet the children. Each was carried to a chair near Jesus. He was wearing his purple sash, but the children did not notice it. Instead, they saw His arms open wide to them, big enough to hold all of them at the same time.

But none noticed that, for each felt His arms around himself. Jaden took no notice of the others. While they sat on His lap, all talked about how they had spent their first days in heaven, how all their relatives showed them so many things they could do. They even talked about their visits to all the buildings.

When he was talking to Jesus, he said, "I saw so many buildings here, all of them so huge. But this place is the best of all. Grandma Orpie and Granny Rosanna took me lots of places and showed me many things to learn from, but this place is the best of all."

Jesus told him, "That's good. You must learn, for you have to grow in me, but you won't have to learn everything at once. You will learn much, but you won't have to learn it all at once. Let's make some plans after you've rested some more. Then you'll know more about how things work out. These first few days you've looked at a big picture, and that's sometimes hard to look at. Now I want you to get some food at the back of the throne room, then run and play."

Jaden joined Chong at the back of the throne room. The table had foods that each loved to eat, and they ate together, sharing from their plates, and talking excitedly about the things they had learned.

While the children were talking and eating, they

began to see that equipment for some games was being brought in. Then they noticed their surroundings were different. Somehow, they had been taken together to a baseball diamond. There was a team on the field, throwing practice balls, and some coaches. Instead of the throne room tables, they saw that they were now at picnic tables.

"You folks ready for a game? In this game today, all the coaches are going to do is walk up to you, help you swing, and then walk around the bases while you run. If the other team gets to play, they will have to walk, because the players played baseball a long time on earth and here, and you're just getting started. We won't keep score, except to tell you when there are three outs. If you want to keep your own score, that's fine. You choose who goes first."

One of the other boys went first on his team. They chose to alternate between boys and girls. It was a long ball game, because it took a while before someone had the first out. When the other team got to bat, the announcer pitched for his team. Their pitcher was the first to strike out. Later Hannah caught a fly ball, and the second player of that team to strike out closed the inning. When it looked like all were tired, the announcer called time. "Well, folks, we've all had a great day at the ball park. We'll play ball with you again. Meanwhile supper and snacks are being set at your tables. Those of you who are hungry, dig in."

Chong led the blessing at their table. All the other children, the other teams' pitcher and catcher, and a few onlookers joined them. "Hey, Jaden. We watched you play. Way to go."

"Jeb, I didn't know you were watching."

"We wouldn't want to miss our grandchild doing something like this," Rosanna said."

"You were here the whole time? That's great. It's a different kind of ball game, that's for sure. No winners, no losers, just a lot of fun. I wouldn't mind if all my baseball games were like that."

With that, Jaden followed Orpie, for she was there also, back to the mansion. When they got there, they just sat back and relaxed with a video, until Jaden fell asleep. She carried him to his room and rocked in the rocker for a while before going to sleep herself.

Chapter Thirty Graduation Ceremony

Jaden woke up feeling excited. Something was up. For one thing, he was no longer tired. Yesterday was a day of rest, for sure. But now, there seemed to be a new energy, a new readiness for something good to happen. What added to that was the fact that he smelled his favorite dinner—for breakfast.

He went down into the kitchen and saw Orpie and the rest of the family waiting for him, table all set for eight. "Hi, all. Who else is coming?"

"Surprise!" In popped Hannah. "Orpie asked me to come. After all, I see you so much and she helps with me till my parents come. There's something going on at school today I think you'll like."

"I thought I didn't have school today."

"You don't. You'll see. It's time to eat, now that you're up. We let you sleep in while everything was cooked and put together."

Jeb led the blessing for the food, and they all ate lamb-flavored vegetables, moussaka, feta cheese, black olives, and other festive foods they liked on Earth. After that, they got up and put all the dishes away, as they were already clean.

"Don't forget to pick some fruit," Hannah said. "Remember your special day?" They all nodded, except Jaden, who was still a little mystified. So each picked several apples from the tree in front, and put them in a bucket from the front steps of the mansion. Jeb carried it as he led the way to the school.

As they went to the school, they saw several other family groups carrying other foods with them as they went into the School of Orientation building. Jaden saw Chong, Jeff, and others from his Bible group. All of them looked as mystified as he felt.

Soon their faces cleared, though. At the center of the room was a sign that said, "Welcome to your graduation." As his family went to Jaden's chair, they saw a cap and gown waiting on the chair for him. His gown was a brilliant white, to match his robes of righteousness, and his cap was in the form of a crown. Rosanna helped him put on the robe, and Rosie helped him with the crown. Orpie stayed with Eddie, who just stood by and watched, a part of the family, but not really knowing him yet.

Hannah was jumping up and down with excitement. "He's my good friend. I met him when he first got to heaven, and he's so special." Others smiled as they looked at her. Some walked up, hugging her as she watched.

All around the room, family groups were talking excitedly with each other. In some of the groups, the graduate was a grown-up, for Orientation School was for all newcomers to heaven, not only those who came as children, but also those who came as adults, for there is much to learn during those first few days, as Jaden found out. Most of the graduates at his school this day were children, however.

While all were talking and milling around, a group of people wearing bright red and green sashes came in to the school. The leader called out, "Children of the Most High, welcome to this gathering. This is the conclusion of your orientation class. In honor of this occasion, we are holding a graduation ceremony for you. The people with me have asked me to allow them to give you your diplomas. After that, you will be free to celebrate in whatever manner that you and your family choose. Your Father will talk with you about your next school or your duties when you have rested or at a time of your choosing."

While he was speaking, all the graduates formed a line in front of their assigned chairs. Jaden stood in front of his chair, wondering what Pascal would have thought of graduating at the end of fourth grade, when there was still another grade before middle school. Then he remembered: this was only the first of several schools he would be going to, and the shortest at that. As their names were called, they left their places and walked to the center of the room, received their diplomas, and went back to stand with their families.

When Jaden went to the center of the room, he saw that the person handing him the diploma was none other than James Peterson, the man he had only talked with briefly on earth. "Jaden," he said, "I asked to give you this diploma because of the kindness you showed me in starting me on the road to Jesus. I would not be here if you had not obeyed the Lord on that day."

He hugged James, saying, "God is so faithful. I'm just happy you made it. Please stay with my family for dinner." Others in the room were saying much the same thing as they celebrated orientation graduation with the newest arrivals and their families.

After the graduation, and group hugs all around, all the graduates asked their families to bring the food into the school, saying that they wanted to celebrate together. And that's what they did, each in their family grouping, having a potluck with many different types of food. Again, Chong, Jaden, Hannah, and the others sampled each other's food as different languages blended in what seemed to be a chorus of worship to the Most High.

After what seemed a long day of celebration, those that wanted to, and it seemed like they all did, flew, rode, or walked to the throne room for worship, each in their own families. There was much dancing, many group hugs, and rejoicing as they noticed newcomers in the throne room. Some had a quiet time of talk with the Holy Spirit about future plans or sat in the Father's lap or talked with Jesus after their worship time.   Others worshiped for a long while before going to their mansions.   He did all of these, going from one to the next, making the rounds several times. After he fell asleep while worshiping after talking with the Father, Jeb carried him back to Orpie's mansion.

Bibliography

The author wishes to acknowledge the following books and Internet sources as being helpful in expanding her imagination about the scope of heaven.

Alcorn, Randy. Heaven. Carol Stream, IL: Tyndale House, 2008.

Burpo, Todd. Heaven is for Real: A Little Boy's Astounding Story of his Trip to Heaven and Back. Nashville, TN: Thomas Nelson, 2011.

Kerr, Kat & King, Patricia. Revealing Heaven and other videos on heaven. www.xpmedia.com

Malz, Betty. Heaven. Old Tappan, NJ: Chosen Books, 1989.

Piper, Don. 90 Minutes in Heaven: a True Story of Death and Life. Grand Rapids, MI: Revell, 2007.

Springer, Rebecca. Within Heaven's Gates. First published as Intra Muros, or, Within the Walls. A Dream of Heaven. Chicago: David C. Cook Pub., 1899

Thomas, Choo. Heaven is so Real. Lake Mary, FL: Charisma House, 2005.

Think Baby Names. http://www.thinkbabynames.com/meaning/1/Jaden

The initial article does not mention the meaning cited in the introduction, but the first comment does mention this meaning.

This list is by no means exhaustive. I have read many sources over the years, including numerous religious magazine articles, and some of these sources may seem to be included in some way. However, if they are included, it is as creative inspiration from the Holy Spirit.